ELVIS

and the
BLUE
MOON
CONSPIRACY

a novel by
Mark
McGinty

Enjoy!

Beaver's Pond Press, Inc.
Edina, Minnesota

ISBN 1-59298-030-9

Library of Congress Catalog Number: 2003111815

Typesetting and design by Mori Studio

Printed in the United States of America

First Printing: September 2003

07 06 05 04 03   5 4 3 2 1

Beaver's Pond Press, Inc.

7104 Ohms Lane, Suite 216
Edina, MN 55439
(952) 829-8818
www.beaverspondpress.com

to order, visit www.BookHouseFulfillment.com
or call 1-800-901-3480. Reseller discounts available.

For Loopy

I would like to thank the following people for their contributions.

Brandon Hall, for the right idea at the right time.
Mike Nelson, who was there from the beginning
Melody Jackson, for the cufflinks
Judd Spicer, for a point in the right direction
The Three Wise Men: Milt Adams, Doug Benson and Jack Caravela
Kim McGinty and Kate Heflin, who read this 'back in the day'
Nate McDonald, for a good eye at the last minute
Jay Monroe, for the dirty work and a great cover
Meridith Vollmar, for everything else

1999

Stagecoach, Nevada

*I*t was Elvis Presley's *Stuck On You*, and this guy was hitting every note. The a cappella voice rang from an opened second-floor apartment window above the town square. Yellow curtains, caught in the breeze, fluttered in rhythm with the singing. Dozens gathered below to hear the flawless voice, but the singing suddenly stopped.

The crowd watched and waited for him to appear on the balcony above them. For him to gaze down on his adherent fans and proclaim a triumphant return.

Finally, a figure appeared behind the blowing curtains. The people caught a glimpse of the man's dark hair and his bushy sideburns. They recognized his sunglasses and a hint of that unmistakable sneer. When the man winked at them, he flashed his trademark smile.

The crowd was agog. A man shouted, "He's back!"

Another yelled, "He was here all along!"

The people cheered and begged for more singing but a gust of wind flapped the curtains and when they settled, Elvis was gone. The people were stunned. They waited and waited for him to return but no one ever saw or heard that singing man again.

Knoxville, Tennessee

Old Ned Paris drove to the Pig Holler General Store and parked his Dodge pickup beside pump #2. It was a fine Saturday morning and Ned was out to do the weekend errands of a comfortable retired man. He didn't

need much. Gasoline, prunes, a dozen eggs and two car-
tons of menthol cigarettes for his wife Mable, who had
been smoking since the earth cooled.

Ned's beer belly hung over his boots like a parade
float as he filled his gas tank. He enjoyed the early
morning sun and watched the ticker pass three gallons.
Beside him, a beat-up blue Cadillac pulled in and
parked at the opposite pump. When the driver got out
to stretch, he grazed his hands over a plume of greasy,
obviously dyed, black hair. Bushy sideburns warmed his
chops, and a bald spot cast a divot along the back of his
outdated hairdo.

Ned swears to this day that the man was wearing a
soiled white jumpsuit with the initials E.P. stitched
across the chest in old, cloudy rhinestones. When EP
glanced across the pumps, he smiled and winked at Ned.
This EP had aged a perfect twenty-two years beyond
that of the EP everyone remembered.

Ned Paris couldn't believe his eyes. He stood in the
presence of a fallen king. It was like winning the lottery.
EP gave Ned a dispassionate nod, flipped on a pair of
oversized gold sunglasses and made his way into the
store. Five minutes later, Ned watched him leave with a
box of donuts and a six-pack of beer.

Cursing himself for not owning a camera, Ned paid
for his gas, jumped into his truck and raced home to tell
Mable, "Elvis Presley is alive and well and living here
in Knoxville!"

Peoria, Illinois

Debbie Denkins wore giant glasses with lenses as
thick as storm windows and frames like iron pipes. She
was driving her friends Diane and Amanda to the strip
mall when she looked in her rearview mirror and saw
the King. He drove a Cadillac and appeared to be wearing an old jumpsuit studded with rhinestones that had

since lost their luster. Debbie changed lanes and let Elvis get in front of her so she could follow, but her car ran out of gas before his did.

White Bear Lake, Minnesota

Valerie was watering the tulips that adorned her lavish lakefront property when she heard an awful, high-pitched scream and a bang and a clatter. She spun toward the sidewalk and was flabbergasted by what she saw. Elvis Presley was picking himself off the ground. He had just fallen off his bicycle.

He checked a tear in the elbow of his gritty white jumpsuit. Valerie noted his black hair had been shabbily dyed around the bald spot on top. What appeared to be an old rhinestone cape was tied around his waist like a sweatshirt.

The King brushed himself off, picked up his bicycle and smiled politely to Valerie. "Ma'am," he nodded. His breath offered the perfume of stale donuts and cheap beer. Seconds later Elvis was on his bike, pedaling away whistling *Amazing Grace*.

Valerie told everybody about the star-studded encounter but to her surprise, no one believed it happened.

"It couldn't have been him," they said.

And Valerie insisted it was.

They shrugged their shoulders and said, "But it couldn't have been Elvis Presley."

Daytona Beach, Florida

Bobby Roberts spat tobacco juice across his lawn and wiped his chin with his sleeve. The grass hadn't been mowed in months.

Detective Marks said, "Tell me again who you were living with?"

Bobby was already angry at the day's events, and this detective was making things worse. "I told you, I was splitting the rent with Elvis Presley and Jim Morrison and those two bastards moved out and took my grill!"

"Where did they go?"

"That doesn't matter! What I've been trying to tell you is that Elvis Presley *stole my grill!*"

"Uh-huh," Detective Marks nodded, registering a drowsy combination of interest and disbelief. After twelve years as a police officer, he had never encountered a case as futile as two dead celebrity fugitives with a stolen grill.

Bobby opened his tobacco tin and offered Marks a wad of black, wet chaw. "Care for a burger?"

Marks shook his head. "No," he said. "Tell me, when Mr. Presley left with your *grill*, where did he go?"

Bobby stuck a chew in place under his lower lip. "I have no idea. He could have gone to the moon for all I know."

Dallas, Texas

It was the VFW on a Saturday night. Lee Alton sat at the corner of the bar. His hands gripped the rail as he leaned close to read the blurry tabloid article. His brown tie floated on a puddle of beer on the bar.

"Ha!" He tapped at the magazine. "There's not a shred of truth to this."

Harvey groaned from the next corner. He was sick of Lee's theories. Lee was a know-it-all drunk who made VFW life the living hell that it was. Why couldn't Lee be more like the rest of the VFW's patrons: a bunch of apathetic drunks who managed to keep their faces in their bottles and mind their own business?

Lee got back to the article, ready for Harvey or Rich or Ted the bartender to jump in and ask what was so outrageous. When none of them spoke, Lee quoted the article. *"The U.S. flag appears to waver in the wind, an impossible phenomena since there is no air on the moon. It's obvious the waving flag is a result of the sound stage NASA used to film the phony Apollo missions."*

He tossed the paper aside. "Have you ever heard such a load of hooey?"

Harvey surrendered. "You mean, NASA *didn't* fake the moon landing, Lee?"

"They most certainly did!" Lee shouted. "But not the way this article would have you believe. This is based on the assumption that man never landed on the moon."

Ted poured a mug of beer and slid it across the bar to Lee. "One on the house if you can tell us just what the hell you are talking about."

Harvey interrupted. "Lee, weren't you in some kind of hospital?"

Lee looked into his beer. "Don't talk about that."

"Hospital? What happened, Lee?" Rich said from across the bar. "Appendix burst?" He cackled like a hyena and drained the rest of his beer.

"Why were you in the hospital, Lee?" Ted waited.

"Don't change the subject." Lee said. He didn't care to discuss his days at the institution. He wanted to talk about the moon missions. He wanted to tell the VFW crew how NASA had fooled the world.

"You know," said Harvey. "On their lunar hikes, the astronauts huffed and puffed like a couple flabby couch potatoes. Under one-sixth gravity, any lard-ass slacker would have had no trouble bounding along for a few minutes without breaking a sweat."

"That's true, isn't it, Lee?" Rich asked.

"Not really." Lee started to squirm. They had derailed his limelight.

Ted said, "Now the moon is a rather pleasant world, right? With vegetation and animal life and beautiful snowcapped mountains?"

"Yeah," Rich laughed. "With an anti-gravity monorail!"

"No," Lee said. "The moon has no vegetables. It has no animal life, no snowcapped peaks and no anti-gravity monorail."

"So tell us," Ted said. "What about the moon landing made it so phony?"

Before Lee could answer, Harvey slammed another beer and said, "I have a feeling he's going to tell us NASA murdered JFK and stashed his body on the moon!"

The others laughed. Only Lee shook his head, ashamed of people and their lack of common sense.

Chapter One

May 18th
Kennedy Space Center, Florida

*J*ack Monroe and Pete Dixon swirled scotch in the back of the NASA limousine after the Apollo 10 launch, and considered their options. Ever since JFK had made his immortal address to a joint session of Congress in 1961, where he had challenged the nation to put a man on the moon by the end of the decade, Dr. John Monroe had been living up to a promise he once made to the President. It was former JFK advisor Jack Monroe who thought the President should make the moon landing a priority. It was Jack Monroe who had written the speech.

"Great idea," Kennedy had said. "Now let's get right on that." The President saw to it that Dr. Monroe became the head of NASA and Monroe went right to work directing the pursuit of his own harebrained ploy.

The last time Jack Monroe saw the former president, Kennedy had said to him, "If that man-on-the-moon thing ever transpires, make it good. Show the Russkies what we're all about." Monroe had promised he wouldn't fail.

When Nixon arrived in the White House six years later, he met with Jack Monroe and told him, "It appears your NASA folks are going to make us all mighty proud. The moon landing is one of the most important events in the history of mankind. Make sure, Jack, that you give the human race a big, damn spectacle."

Jack was cutting it close, landing Apollo 11 with just six months to spare.

"Something troubles me," Monroe said to Dixon, his right hand man at NASA. Both men wore suits with loose ties and open collars. They balanced their scotch glasses on their knees as the limousine led them away from the Kennedy Space Center. The column of exhaust left in the wake of the Apollo 10 rocket had just now dissolved into the sky.

Dixon finished his cocktail in two sips and sat back with his eyes closed. "Let's just relax for a minute."

"Not yet," Monroe said. "Not time yet."

"Apollo 10 is up and away, Jack. It's out of our hands."

Jack glanced at Dixon's reflection in the chauffeur's window. He was shorter than Jack, and a shabbier dresser. Dixon was stocky, with fuzzy brown hair combed in uneven bunches, always scowling, lost in thought. A thinker, Jack's most trusted collaborator, and someone who knew how to get things done. Years of work together were finally about to climax with a political money shot scheduled for July 20th.

Eight weeks to go.

Jack looked at his own reflection. Age had discovered him and was attacking with wrinkles. His cheeks drooped and even his neck was starting to sag into little puffy folds. Jack compensated with a sharp appearance, the elegance of a politician. His tidy, shiny hair was jet black and perfect, as were his shoes and suit. When Jack was younger, he never looked like anything less than a million bucks; now he looked like a million bucks lost in the laundry. Despite his impressive demeanor, Jack could not hide that the pressures of NASA were taking their toll. It had been a long week.

A long decade.

He finished his scotch and reached for the bottle.

"What I'm getting at," Jack said as he filled their glasses. "Is that landing a man on the moon is a historic event. One of the greatest moments of all time."

"Sure," Dixon drained half his scotch and closed his eyes again. An arduous philosophical discussion with Jack Monroe was the last thing he wanted. He had no choice but to hold onto his cocktail, keep his eyes closed and listen to the man.

Jack said, "You know what I'm thinking, Peter?"

"What is it, Wise One?"

"Hyperbole aside, landing a man on the moon is nothing."

Dixon opened an eye. "What are you talking about?"

"They've asked us for a spectacle, Peter. Not just two presidents but an entire nation, an entire species. History demands an exhibition, Peter, and it's our job to deliver."

Dixon closed his eye. "That's too much to think about. Let's brainstorm when we get back to Houston."

"Wake up," Monroe elbowed him. Dixon's eyes snapped open. "Once that spacecraft touches the surface, safely or with a terrible crash, there will never be another first moon landing. This is our one chance in eternity, Peter. We need to guarantee that mankind is witness to the Super Bowl of historic moments."

"I liked your idea about the astronauts playing golf while they're up there."

"Maybe next mission. Not enough time to establish eighteen, even nine holes, much less play them."

"What are we supposed to do?"

They searched for answers in their cocktails.

Monroe said, "I mean what is all this?"

Dixon agreed. "What is this really?"

"The way Apollo 11 is now, it's just two guys walking around the moon, doing nothing."

Dixon sat up and got a closer look at his boss. He saw from Jack's commanding stare that the man was serious. "You really feel that way, Jack?"

"It's missing something. It's not what JFK wanted."

"Sure it is."

Jack shook his head. "You never knew him the way I did. He'd want us to hype it up with a big event, something to embarrass the Soviets for all the trouble they've caused, something that really packs a punch."

"Some kind of ceremony?"

"Something better than some phony ceremony. Something sensational!"

Dixon understood. "You want the moon landing to be about something more than two guys hopping around a giant sandbox with glass bubbles on their heads."

Monroe held up his hands in contempt. "This isn't about exploration. We're not Christopher Columbus."

"We're not Magellan."

"We know there's nothing on the moon that anyone needs. This is showmanship. Plain and simple. This is about who can look stronger and healthier and better. The moon landing is no longer a trial of discovery, it's a talent show. When Neil steps onto the moon, let's make sure Americans have something to cheer about."

Dixon knew what had to be done. The answer was easy, really. It was something Dixon had been secretly dreaming of the entire space race.

"Elvis."

"What about him?" asked Monroe.

"He's a cultural icon, the pinnacle of the American dream. The best we've got."

"You once said that without Elvis, America would be Canada."

Dixon nodded. "We would, it's true. We would definitely be Canada."

"And we can't have that."

"It's the last thing we want."

"Explain your plan."

Dixon licked his lips. "We put Elvis Presley on the moon."

Monroe paused. A smile started to break, then he shook his head, dismissing the idea. "Brilliant in theory, my clever friend, but technically impossible. Please, try not to clutter the mission with fan boy antics."

Like many, Dixon was a purebred Elvis fanatic. He collected Elvis memorabilia; his house was decorated with scores of Presley posters and records. Magazine covers, photographs and ticket stubs formed their own galaxy in his living room. The pride and joy of Dixon's Elvis collection sat atop his wooden brass-and-string symphonizer. It was a replica of the legendary Ivory Elvis, an ivory statuette of Elvis rescued from the jungles of Tanzania nearly a decade ago.

Dixon sold his proposal. "It's not the most outrageous idea you've ever heard."

"No," Monroe agreed. "But I don't see it working. What's Elvis supposed to do once he's on the moon?"

"He sings a song. A concert from the Sea of Tranquility."

"Technical issues," Monroe said. "Are you proposing we squeeze a fourth man onto the spacecraft? Or replace one of the astronauts with some untrained rock star?"

Dixon reasoned. "The technical mumbo-jumbo can be dealt with. Bottom line: landing a man on the moon is nothing without Elvis."

"It's a great passage for the history books, Peter, but unfortunately it's not exactly what JFK had in mind."

"Do you propose the astronauts play a JFK memorial lunar golf tournament instead?"

Monroe sighed.

Dixon said, "When you want spectacle, you call Elvis."

Monroe considered it over a swig of scotch. "The question is, 'how can we do it?'"

"I believe the question is, 'how can we *not* do it?'"

Monroe chuckled. "Why would anyone not send Elvis Presley to the moon?"

"We'd be fools to confine that man to Earth."

"An authentic Elvis moon rock would be a terrific addition to your collection of authentic Elvis paraphernalia."

The thought made Dixon salivate.

Then Monroe smiled. "Not only did we beat the Soviets to the moon, we brought Elvis Presley along for the ride."

Dixon smiled. "It makes perfect sense."

"It's brilliant." Monroe made the decision. "A terrific addition to the history books. I'll have it no other way. The mission is on! And you're a wonderful strategist."

They toasted their drinks.

"This means I'll finally get to meet the King!" Dixon said.

"He'll finally get to meet us." Monroe said, and became suddenly serious. "How do we know if Elvis will even want to do it? He's got tour dates, movies, family conflicts, haircuts and fittings."

Dixon wasn't concerned. "He was in the Army, Jack. He proved he's willing to serve his country. But this whole thing has to be a surprise. No one can know Elvis Presley is on Apollo 11 until they see him playing his song on the moon. We keep everything quiet, need-to-know, within the inner circle."

Monroe nodded. "Well, we can't squander the sensation on petty pre-launch activities. We save the boom-bah until show time and make a killing on T-shirts and autographs when they get back."

Dixon nodded his approval.

Monroe wondered, "What song should he sing up there?"

"I believe that's a decision for the King."

"How do we keep this from the public?"

"Easy," Dixon said. "We do what any true governmental PR wrangler would do. We manipulate the minds of the constituency with television."

Monroe liked the idea. "Convenient that our satellites control the broadcasts. We can edit and re-edit and show the world exactly what we want them to see with the flip of a switch. We give Americans exactly what they've always wanted: a moment they can cherish forever."

They finished their drinks and Jack reached for another. "And they said NASA was good for nothing."

Chapter Two

Back in 1960, an American physician arrived at Maasai Village in Tanzania. Sent by the Red Cross, the good doctor brought to the isolated villagers, medical supplies and a portable radio. Through atmospheric bounce, the radio picked up *Jailhouse Rock* from a station in New York.

The villagers gathered to hear the rhythmic tune and by the end of the song, the Maasai were clapping and dancing with delight. It wasn't long before they named *Jailhouse Rock* their village anthem.

The doctor produced a picture of Elvis Presley and told the villagers of the singer's popularity in America. That some regarded him as a king. The healthy villagers begged for more so the doctor returned with magazines and photographs.

A young tribesman named Moja studied the King's pictures and chiseled the tusk of a dead elephant into a glorious sculpture. It became the Ivory Elvis, a two-foot idol for the people of Maasai Village.

During the days of Elvis's rise to fame in Tanzania, the illegal ivory trade was becoming a big business. It wasn't that anyone particularly enjoyed killing elephants by the dozens and selling their tusks for black market cash, but elephant poachers needed to eat too. Most of them had fallen into their careers by accident. Kigoma, the modest tobacco farmer, was typical.

Every morning Kigoma tended his crops, but one afternoon he spotted a wild elephant wandering across his property, trampling his tobacco. Kigoma fired several shotgun blasts and brought the elephant down but it was too late. The tobacco crop was ruined and he needed to find—quickly—another way to feed his family.

Hoping to recoup his loss, Kigoma removed the elephant's tusks and showed them around. He soon got word of an underground ivory trade and sold his tusks to a pair of ivory runners who were on their way to Japan with a fresh shipment. They assured Kigoma they would return in six months and purchase more ivory from him, if he were still in business.

Six weeks later Kigoma was leading a small band of poachers through the Serengeti, killing entire herds of elephants and removing their tusks. No herd was too big, and soon Kigoma's men became rich and bought better weapons and supplies. Pickup trucks, automatic weapons, lanterns, and raincoats. The underground ivory trade grew and Kigoma became a sort of ivory kingpin. After three months, Kigoma and his gang were bigger than the futuristic activist group Americans for Cloning Elvis.

It all changed when *National Geographic* sent photographer Scott Richter to Tanzania to document the Serengeti. Richter was a pilot, and as he flew his small plane over the jungle, he could see the peak of Mt. Kilimanjaro rising above the scattered clouds. He circled and saw below him lions, giraffes and to his horror, a field of dead elephants.

Stomach churning, Richter turned his plane towards the carcasses and increased the throttle. Twenty seconds later, he soared above the massacre, and tried for a body count as he passed. There must have been fifty, he thought, as he turned the plane for another run. This time he observed the swamps of blood oozing from where the great animals' tusks should have been. With his heart beating furiously, Richter climbed higher, angrily scanning the ground for any sign of the perpetrators.

He flew circles for ten minutes, increasingly wider, until he spotted a convoy of pickup trucks fleeing the scene. Their beds were filled with bloody elephant tusks. Up ahead, Richter could see they were headed for a small village. People ran from their homes as the trucks arrived and their occupants began to raid the settlement.

Feeling powerless, Richter wished he had a fighter jet so he could fire his cannons and wipe out the poachers one by one. Just as they had done to those elephants. But his plane had no cannons, so Richter just kept circling and wondering what to do. Below him, the poachers ransacked the village.

What Richter didn't see was a lone Maasai fleeing the action with a two-foot object in a sack under his arm.

When the trucks finally left the village, they headed north towards Kilimanjaro. Richter flew ahead of them. He followed a road that curved around the jungle, and soon came across their destination. It was a small camp at the base of the mountain that appeared to have once been some type of farm. The camp was quiet, and Richter estimated he had thirty minutes before the poachers arrived.

He landed his plane in a nearby field, grabbed his knapsack and headed for the camp. He reached it quickly and didn't hesitate to set fire to the poachers' tents and sleeping bags. He torched their clothes, smashed their communications equipment and emptied their fuel and water supplies. Richter felt liberation and a sort of cosmic praise from the souls of the fallen elephants. He stood back and watched the poachers' camp burn and crumble to ashes.

A mile away, Kigoma and his men spotted the rising column of smoke at the base of Kilimanjaro. They knew instantly it was their camp that was burning.

"Hurry!" Kigoma ordered. "Salvage what you can!"

Richter knew he didn't have much time. He ran back to his plane and climbed into the cockpit just as a pair of pickup trucks appeared through the smoke. Richter had been spotted. He kicked the engine into full throttle and maneuvered his plane towards the field for takeoff.

The pickup trucks were catching up. Gunshots exploded behind him as Richter accelerated and started to outrun the poachers. Just as his plane reached the speed it needed to get off the ground, Richter felt a sudden jolt in his seat and then the plane dropped to the left and started to rumble. He had lost a tire. The plane bounced along the hard dirt and steered uncontrollably to the left. Richter hit the breaks but momentum and a blown tire were spinning the plane towards a patch of thick foliage.

The plane crashed into a tree, breaking Richter's left wrist on impact. He climbed out of the cockpit as the poachers' trucks arrived just yards away. One fired a shot but Richter had already disappeared into the jungle. He ran towards Kilimanjaro, clutching his broken wrist and dodging branches as he escaped the furious poachers.

"This way!" A voice called through the brush and Richter halted his jog, ready to defend himself from anyone who might attack. He saw a wiry villager crouching behind a tree. He seemed frightened and harmless, but the wary Richter kept his distance.

"I know the way out. Come!" The villager turned and disappeared into the jungle. Richter's instincts told him to follow.

When he reached a safe place, Moja stopped and waited for Richter to catch up. The two were soon sitting on a slab of rock beside Mt. Kilimanjaro. "I am Moja."

Richter nodded. "Scott," he said.

Moja inspected Richter's broken wrist. He used sticks and vines to concoct a splint, which he tied in place.

"They destroyed my village." Moja said as he worked. His eyes were red. Richter could see he had been crying. "I was on my way to a friendly settlement along the river when I heard gunshots."

"I couldn't let them get away with it. Your village, the elephants."

"And you destroyed their camp?"

Richter nodded and Moja smiled in appreciation. The two strangers had already developed a mutual respect for one another. Now they were stranded as the only survivors of the poachers' efforts.

"They wanted ivory," Moja said. "They wanted this."

Moja presented his sack and handed it to Richter. Richter reached inside and removed the white statuette. He regarded it with interest. "Is this Elvis?"

Moja nodded. "It is our idol. I carved it myself. *Jailhouse Rock.* No?"

Richter shrugged. "I guess not."

The ivory relic stood two feet tall. Elvis wore a suit and held a microphone at his mouth. The fires Kigoma's poachers had set at Maasai Village had charred the entire left side.

"This is the last relic of our people," Moja explained. "As long as it is in this jungle, it will not survive the ivory thieves. Take the Ivory Elvis to America, where it can safely reside forever. See to it that it stays in the right hands."

Richter cradled the figure. It was heavy and detailed. Even the folds of Presley's jacket had been meticulously carved into the ivory. Richter was impressed by Moja's craftsmanship. If it weren't for the blemish of heat across the left side, the Ivory Elvis would be pristine. But Richter felt the burn gave an earthy sense of character to the piece.

He humbly accepted his mission and promised Moja that in America his treasure would claim no price. Moja smiled. "Thank you, my American friend. Now I will take you to the river. You can catch a boat from there and find your way home."

"What about the poachers?"

Moja sadly hung his head. "You burned their camp so they will move elsewhere and find another herd."

Richter protested. "We've got to stop them."

"You tried and lost your plane."

Richter understood. The poachers would thrive and there was nothing he could do about it. Perhaps he could return one day with the resources to stop the poachers forever but now he had to leave. With the Ivory Elvis in his hand, Richter offered Moja the only thing he could, his camera.

But the modest villager only smiled. "Where would I develop the film?"

Richter was embarrassed that he had nothing else to trade.

"See the Ivory Elvis to safety," Moja told him. "That is your gift to me. Now you must hurry. They are approaching."

The sound of trucks rumbled in the distance.

"Come," Moja motioned for Richter to follow and the two men disappeared into the brush. They reached the river that night and two days later, Richter found himself in Istanbul, Turkey. With the Ivory Elvis tucked safely in a duffel bag, Richter wandered the town and found a hospital to treat his injured wrist. As soon as the cast was set, Richter was off to the airport. He passed customs when the agent regarded the ivory sculpture as a piece of worthless nostalgia, and hurried Richter through.

He flew to Madrid and sat beside an American on the airliner. The guy had a gray beard and a baseball hat and introduced himself as Deek Graceland. "But everybody calls me Tony," he told Richter with a heavy Southern twang.

Scott politely shook his hand and wondered if this was some strange coincidence.

"Say," Graceland jabbed Richter's cast. "I couldn't help but notice."

"What's that?" Richter asked.

Graceland pointed to Richter's duffle bag. "Elvis Presley."

Richter looked to the floor and saw the upper half of the Ivory Elvis was sticking out of his bag. He tried to push it back inside with his foot but Graceland asked, "Is that ivory?"

"It's nothing," Richter said and nudged the sculpture under the seat before him.

"If it's nothing then let's take a look." Graceland watched Richter, insistent on seeing the sculpture. Richter gave in. He reached into the bag and placed the Ivory Elvis on his tray table.

Graceland turned the statuette so Elvis was facing him. "Where did this come from?"

"Near Kilimanjaro." Richter didn't want to give away too much information.

Graceland inspected it with a curious eye. "The Kilimanjaro King, eh? Not bad. It has obvious East African influence. It looks tribal."

"It's one of a kind."

"How much you want for it?"

Richter was surprised. "It's not really for sale."

"What you have here is a rare ivory sculpture from an East African village and not only that, it's Elvis. This is like finding the lost ark, kid."

"You're not serious."

Graceland shrugged. "Millions of Elvis fans can't be wrong."

Richter nodded. In America, Moja's religious idol would become a decoration on some rich person's mantelpiece. Moja never wanted that for the Ivory Elvis. It was Richter's job to keep it from being misused.

"Sorry," Richter said. "It's not for sale."

"What are you going to do with it?"

It was clear that this man Graceland coveted the ivory idol, but Richter insisted on keeping his promise. He told Graceland the legend of the Ivory Elvis. Graceland was so amazed he offered to put the Ivory Elvis in the hands of the King himself.

"You can't do that," Richter challenged him.

"Can too," Graceland said. "I saved Elvis's life in Army basic. He doesn't call it Graceland for nothing."

Richter wanted to get this straight. "So Elvis Presley's house is named after you?"

"Damn right," Graceland nodded. He really seemed to believe what he was telling Richter, but Richter had obvious doubts.

Richter said, "Wasn't it called Graceland *before* he joined he Army?"

"Sure. We were friends then too."

"Uh-huh," nodded the photographer, not completely understanding the tale.

"I can walk up to Elvis Presley's front door and hand him that statue if you think it'll make your friend Moja happy. Just give the word and it will be so."

Which is exactly what they did. Upon returning to the states, they went directly to Tennessee and marched right up to the King's gates. To Richter's surprise, the guards recognized Graceland right away and let both men onto the property. Elvis greeted Graceland with a hug and told Richter how Graceland saved his life in Army basic.

"He told me to throw the live grenade I had forgotten about," Elvis grinned and lightly punched Graceland's shoulder. The relationship had been verified so Richter handed Elvis the ivory impersonation and told him the legend. Elvis agreed to keep the Maasai Village relic safe in his home, saying it would look great in the Graceland Jungle Room.

Elvis asked what Richter was going to do about the elephant poachers, and Richter told him he intended to return and stop them however he could. Elvis generally liked elephants so he offered his help. "How does a hundred thousand dollars sound?" he said as he crossed the room to a small writing desk, where he proceeded to make out a check.

Richter was amazed. "I couldn't accept that, Your Kingship."

"Take it," Elvis handed him the check. "Use it to fight those terrible poachers in Tanzania."

Gratefully, Richter accepted Elvis's money and used it to fund his own little Tanzanian war. He hired a group of mercenaries who patrolled the Serengeti and put an end to elephant poaching. The vigilante-style operation was illegal, of course, which is why *National Geographic* was never informed of Richter's experience.

The Ivory Elvis had found its home. It stayed safely in Presley's possession for nearly a decade, until 1969, when Elvis Presley met Peter Dixon and Jack Monroe.

Chapter Three

The sun had been shining on Dani Mitchell. Today the glow was especially bright. She'd been rewarded for nabbing an unexpected Dalai Lama interview for her magazine, *The Sensational Nation*. This very interview literally raised *TSN* to a new level in the world of journalism. Instead of sitting on the bottom rack with the tabloids, *TSN* now sat at eye level, side-by-side with *Time* and *Newsweek*.

Of course the rise of *The Sensational Nation* wasn't due entirely to Dani Mitchell's chance encounter with the Dalai Lama. Over the past several years, the magazine had strived for a reputation as one of the market's leading publishers of sensational journalism. The critically renowned Dalai Lama interview finally put *TSN* near the top.

Now Dani, just twenty-nine, was riding the success of *TSN*, hoping it would aid her ambitious journey into the publishing world. The Lama was her first major breakthrough. *TSN* Editor-in-Chief Richard Baker predicted Dani would one day take a serious shot at the coveted Pulitzer.

The cab ride with the Lama had been an accident. It was early morning and the Lama was in Midtown, killing time before he was to appear at the United Nations. After a visit to the Empire State Building, he moseyed along the sidewalk and found himself a pretzel vendor.

Dani spotted the Lama as he piled coils of mustard along the giant pretzel. Globs of it dripped off his napkin and onto his wrist. Dani caught up as the Lama hailed a cab, licking mustard off himself. He didn't notice that Dani pretended to hail the same cab and slipped conveniently beside in the backseat.

"I'm sorry," Dani said innocently when she was face-to-face with the Lama, "I didn't know this taxi was taken."

The Lama politely finished swallowing a bite of pretzel before he addressed the young lady with the auburn hair and guileless blue eyes. "Neither did I," he said.

Dani smiled as the Lama got a faint whiff of soap and water. This girl wore no perfume, an attribute the Lama had always appreciated. She dressed like the All-American businesswoman. A dark green suit jacket and matching skirt. Black shoes that were both stylish and adequate for walking from subway to subway, up and down stairs and all over Manhattan. Her hair was tied into a ponytail and she carried a leather briefcase. Her corporate appearance provided an unusual contrast to the Lama's flowing robes of red and yellow. But if the Lama weren't the Lama, he'd probably find Dani Mitchell quite attractive.

"Well, where are you headed?" she asked.

The Lama said, "I am on my way to the United Nations."

"Imagine that! So am I!"

The cab was already rolling east through Midtown. The Lama said, "Since we're on our way, I wonder if we should just split the fare and be happy?"

"Right on," Dani said. "I have no problem if you don't."

The Dalai Lama nodded and popped the last bite of pretzel into his mouth. A glob of mustard dripped to the seat, but the Lama wiped it away with his robe before the cabbie could notice the spill. Not that a tiny glob of mustard would matter in such a dirty taxi, but the Lama revered some level of cleanliness, even in things that weren't his.

Dani knew her time with the Lama was limited, so she started asking questions. Thirty minutes later, when they pulled up in front of the UN, Dani had a solid interview for the magazine. She was rewarded almost as soon as she'd turned it in. Baker promised her better assignments. He said she'd soon be wooing movie stars and dining with top athletes and politicians, and added that it wasn't too far-fetched to hope that one day she'd find herself in a face-to-face with Fidel Castro.

Both Mitchell and Baker knew that was just talk. But Dani had received her first tangible reward today, weeks after the interview had gone to print. Baker had called her into his office and handed her a plane ticket.

"Memphis," Dani said.

Baker sat at his desk beaming, his hands clasped behind a head of shaggy gray hair. When Dani had first met Richard Baker, his wrinkled clothes and his sloppy ways put her off. It was hard to believe he was the head of a national publication. But Baker had connections, a network that spanned the globe. This gave him the ability to track down almost any celebrity in the world—a must for *The Sensational Nation*. His long list of friends, acquaintances and business associates made Richard Baker the successful man he was.

Now Baker tossed a sheet of paper onto a desk cluttered by hundreds of other sheets of paper. It was the messiest office Dani had ever seen, with old magazines and newspapers stuffed into every nook and cranny as if they were trying to plug a leak.

Baker nodded at Dani's ticket. "I set you up for tomorrow afternoon."

Dani reached for the paper on the desk. It was her itinerary for a meeting in Memphis. When she saw the personality and the exact location, her heart fluttered and her jaw dropped to the floor.

"Is this for real?"

Baker nodded proudly. "You deserve it. Give him your best."

She tried not to feel overwhelmed. It was a one-on-one exclusive with Elvis Presley, presented to her on a silver platter. She planned to make the most of this opportunity, and then some.

"He knows I'm coming?"

Baker nodded again. "Absolutely."

"Great," Dani said. She noticed how much her hands were shaking when she slipped the itinerary and ticket into her briefcase. She closed the case and clicked the latch shut, then unlatched the case so she could latch it again and hear the click a second time.

"Why'd you do that?"

"Do what?"

He pointed at her briefcase. "You closed your case, opened it, and then closed it again."

"No, I didn't."

"You did."

"Oh," Dani shrugged, dismissing his observation. "I guess I didn't notice."

Baker watched curiously as she stood for the door. He wished her well and Dani Mitchell was on her way.

Dixon yawned and rubbed his eyes as the limo approached the White House. He only slept five hours the night before because Jack Monroe called and woke him at the crack of dawn. "Up and at em!" Jack had announced. "We've got an early flight."

"Where are we going?"

"Washington." Somehow Jack was wide-awake. "We're going to pitch your idea to the President. Pick you up in thirty."

Having just flown into Houston from Florida the night before, Dixon was not happy to have Jack summon him to duty so early in the morning. There was never a dull moment with Jack Monroe.

Dixon wearily rolled to his feet, unhappy to be 'up and at em' again. He showered quickly and as he dressed, he wondered about this idea to put Elvis Presley on the moon. They'd need to pull some strings to get Elvis to participate. They'd probably have to pay him a bundle as well. His manager, Tom Parker, had a reputation for being a shrewd businessman. Dixon wondered if anyone—let alone everyone—in the Elvis camp would be able to keep the secret.

Then Dixon considered NASA. It wouldn't be possible to hide Elvis from the astronauts, engineers and administration. They'd need to either convince everyone to go with the flow or limit knowledge of Elvis to a select few. Dixon could deal with that later. First and foremost were the dangers of the mission itself.

Aside from being the riskiest operation ever attempted, millions of fans would demand an explanation for why NASA put Presley's life on the line. And how the hell were they going to fit a fourth man into the spacecraft?

Dixon heard the car outside, so he fixed his tie and hurried out the door. He winked at his Ivory Elvis replica on the way out. The limousine waited. Dixon crawled into the backseat where Monroe greeted him with a cordial smile and a champagne cocktail. Dixon accepted the drink, hoping it might help him pick up some sleep on the flight to Washington.

Monroe got right down to business. "I talked to Kissinger last night. I told him your idea."

"My idea?" Dixon repeated, noticing how Monroe was already trying to shift the burden. "What did he say?"

"He loved it," Monroe said. "He got us thirty minutes with Nixon this afternoon."

"Only thirty?"

Monroe sipped his cocktail. "It's all you'll need. You're a wonderful strategist. Just tell them what you told me."

Dixon felt a slight cramp in his stomach and grimaced.

Noticing his friend's discomfort, Monroe said, "Relax, Peter. They're going to love it."

"But it's the most screwball idea ever conceived!"

Jack looked him in the eye. "Why are you always second guessing yourself? You're so doubtful. I wonder how you got so far when your head is constantly cluttered by negative thoughts."

Dixon tried not to sneer. "It must be nice to be so perfect."

"JFK told me in 1961 that if all day you're spinning your wheels, you have no time to enjoy the ride."

They were silent for a moment. Jack kept working on his cocktail as Dixon stared out the window and contemplated the words of the former president. Dixon wondered if they were taking on more than they could handle. If he was just using this mission to meet Elvis Presley. But Jack was confident—so confident that he had arranged a meeting with the president the day the mission had been altered.

"Tell me, Jack," Dixon said.

"What is it?"

"Why so motivated?"

Jack finished his drink. "I know a great plan when I hear it. We're not producing a once-in-a-lifetime moment. This is once in *eternity*. If we're going to make Elvis Presley the first man on the moon, we're going to do it in six weeks or never. No time to procrastinate. Like the old maxim says, 'don't talk about it, *do* it!'"

Dixon smiled. He could see right through Jack Monroe. "You're in it for the glory."

Monroe winked. "What glory? This is science."

The limousine parked outside the White House. Chief of Staff Bob Haldeman greeted Monroe and Dixon as they emerged from their limo, then led them through security and into the halls of the mansion. As they all walked to the West Wing, Haldeman told the NASA men, "The President is looking forward to the meeting." Then Haldeman spoke directly to Monroe. "We all know what a terrific job you did with JFK."

Monroe cleared his throat and nervously straightened his tie. Few knew the full extent of Jack Monroe's relationship with the former president, and it was those exact few that Monroe and Dixon were about to meet.

President Nixon came out of the Oval Office and met the two NASA officers in the secretary's anteroom. "A pleasure to see you again, Dr. Monroe. We were just discussing the exceptional work you did with JFK."

"Thank you, Mr. President."

Then the President turned to Dixon. "And you must be Peter Dixon."

"Yes, sir," Dixon replied.

Jack said, "I recruited Peter in 1964 out of the DoD. He's one of the best strategic thinkers you'll ever meet."

Nixon quickly sized up Dixon. Then he ushered everyone into his office. Dixon was surprised to see Secretary of State Henry Kissinger and FBI Director J. Edgar Hoover sitting on two couches, awaiting their arrival. President Nixon introduced everyone and the six conspirators got down to business.

As Jack Monroe took his seat beside the Secretary of State, Hoover inspected him from the opposite couch. The FBI had a thirty-one page file on Dr. John P. Monroe. Eighteen pages were classified. Hoover knew the contents of those classified pages and had nothing but the utmost respect for the doctor.

Now Nixon offered the floor to Peter Dixon, who started to outline the details of Operation Blue Moon. He told them how NASA would sneak Elvis Presley onto the Saturn V without word leaking to the public. How he would be trained in secrecy so that the public thought Neil Armstrong, Buzz Aldrin and Michael Collins constituted the entire Apollo 11 crew.

They'd keep Elvis silent and off-camera throughout the duration of the trip. Hoover assured the two NASA men that the FBI could plug any leak in a matter of hours. Just give the word and it would be so. Television broadcasts would run on a short delay and mission footage would be altered to suit the surprise concert before it was beamed to the masses via satellite.

"There is just one thing," Kissinger mentioned as he fiddled with his tie. "How do you expect Elvis Presley to play guitar while he's hunched inside that spacesuit?"

Dixon cursed himself. How did he forget about that?

Monroe covered wonderfully. He said, "Our engineers are highly competent. We're adjusting for every contingency." Nixon was close to believing Operation Blue Moon would be possible. The President glanced at Kissinger, who nodded his approval. J. Edgar Hoover also signaled his okay. Nixon saw that Bob Haldeman had already decided, as the Chief of Staff was perched on the edge of the couch, awaiting the President's decision.

"Elvis Presley," Nixon pondered. "The Concert in the Sea of Tranquility, 1969. It could go down in history as one of the most spectacular moments of all time."

Monroe nodded. "That was our assessment as well."

The President was still undecided. Dixon knew this was their only chance to receive a "Go" for the great mission, and now Nixon was on the fence. Dixon decided it was time to play the ace in the hole. He said, "Perhaps we could capitalize on merchandising." The others listened curiously as Dixon explained. "We can market T-shirts that say 'Concert from the Sea of Tranquility.' And we can sell Lunar Elvis action figures to kids."

Monroe winked at Dixon, urging him to continue with this fresh, brilliant idea.

Dixon said, "We can market a 'Greatest Moment of All Time' coffee mug. And the world will definitely need a 'Get Elvis to the Moon and Back' board game. It could generate millions in political capital."

The President's men drooled at the thought.

It was no longer a tough decision for the President. "It's a terrific idea," he smiled. "Elvis Presley is the first man to walk on the moon. Is there any better way to win the space race?"

Monroe and Dixon both said, "No, Mr. President."

President Nixon smiled at Jack Monroe. "I shall be the one to reveal Elvis to the world. To be Master of Ceremonies, so to speak. I will place a phone call to the moon and greet Neil and Buzz. Then on worldwide television, I will announce our very, very special guest star."

Monroe sincerely appreciated the President's gesture. "Yes, sir," he said. "It would be our pleasure."

"Then I wish you the best of luck. Operation Blue Moon is approved."

The meeting was adjourned. Nixon shook hands with Monroe, and then everyone shook hands with everyone else. The President walked Monroe and Dixon to the door and said, "I'll give Mr. Presley a call tonight. I'll remind him he once served his country and that we'd be honored if he'd serve it again."

"Perfect, Mr. President," Monroe agreed. "You soften him up so Peter and I can swoop in tomorrow with his paycheck and a contract."

Dixon felt a new weight on his shoulders and that cramp in his stomach again. Nixon said, "Keep me posted on all developments."

"Yes, sir, " they nodded.

Then the President leaned in close. "Gentlemen," he whispered.

They waited to hear his words.

"Excellent work."

Graceland was a castle that dominated the landscape along a stretch of US Highway 51. The white mansion sat on a hilltop, surrounded by oak trees and an endless green lawn. The driveway was guarded by a pair of steel gates decorated in a musical motif of notes and guitars. A wall of stone surrounded the 14-acre estate, and no one could get inside without permission.

This wall was covered with words written in chalk and crayon—"Praise to the King," and other proclamations of love and loyalty from his devoted subjects. Every word of graffiti along the "Wall of Love" was dedicated humbly to the owner of the mansion.

Dani Mitchell parked her rented Toyota at the corner of Winchester and US 51. Graceland was just ahead on her left. She was looking her best for this Presley interview. She wore a suit she thought he'd like, all white with gold trim. Her hair had been done that morning, and she was coming off eight hours of healthy sleep. An 8-track tape of *All Shook Up* played in her car, psyching her up for the encounter.

She checked herself in the rear-view mirror and saw she needed to freshen her layer of lipstick. When she finished she snapped the tube shut, opened it and touched up again (she didn't think her lipstick was perfect enough the first time), and snapped the tube shut a second time.

Then she checked her watch. Still thirteen minutes ahead of schedule. She'd wait another minute or so before rolling to the mansion and arriving roughly ten minutes early. Dani felt heart jitters, butterflies before the big game. She closed her eyes, took three deep breaths and clenched both fists as tight as she could. Then she relaxed and felt the tension drifting away. It came right back, as Dani expected it would. Who wouldn't be anxious about interviewing Elvis Presley? Dani was grateful that she never puked when she was nervous. The last thing she needed was vomit breath.

Another look at her watch and Dani decided it was time to go. She pulled onto the highway and approached the mansion. The gates were just ahead and Dani could see the long driveway running up to the house. Elvis's uncle, Vester Presley, sat outside guarding the gates, and Baker had said Vester would be expecting her arrival.

Just as Dani was about to turn in, a black limousine speeding from the opposite direction cut her off—nearly causing a crash—and beat her to the gates. Vester walked over to greet the limo as a frustrated Dani pulled in and stopped behind it.

"Who the hell are these idiots?" Dani cursed and punched the steering wheel. This limousine mucked up her plans. It broke her groove. Now she needed to get psyched up all over again.

Dani waited as Vester talked to the chauffeur. He kept nodding okay as the chauffeur apparently explained something Dani could not hear. She tapped her right foot impatiently on the gas pedal while holding down the brake with her left. Then she realized, that might be Elvis inside that limousine. Dani suddenly wasn't so frustrated.

The gates opened and the limousine drove through leaving Dani behind. The gates slammed shut in front of her and Vester motioned for her to remain halted as he walked over. She rolled down her window and was face to face with Uncle Presley.

"Was that Elvis?" Dani nodded towards the limousine that approached the house.

"No," Vester said plainly and waited.

Dani gave him a nervous smile. "I'm Dani Mitchell from *The Sensational Nation*. I'm scheduled for an interview this afternoon."

Vester gave her a blank look. "They should have called your office."

"Why would they call my office?"

"Elvis had a commitment and had to cancel."

Dani sat up. "You can't be serious."

"I'm afraid so. I'm sorry."

"Should I come back later?"

Vester shook his head. "Not today. He's all booked up."

She noticed Vester failed to show any compassion for squashing her dreams. Denial turned to rage. "Who's in that limousine?"

Vester shrugged. "Don't know."

Dani was insulted. "You can't just cancel!" she cried, her raised voice shaking with anger. Dani felt like she was in high school, when her date stood her up for homecoming sophomore year.

"Sorry, lady. I don't make the rules." Vester turned and walked away. Elvis had cancelled because he had a commitment. Imagine the nerve of him. She suddenly hated every little aspect of Elvis Presley's glitzy little life. How could he just cancel? What could be more important than an interview with *The Sensational Nation*?

Before Dani backed away she tried to get a look at exactly who Elvis had to see instead of her. Way up at the house she could see the limousine had parked, and two men in suits hopped out. One was tall, the other short and stocky. The tall man shined with elegance, the other was a bit stumpy. Whoever those men were, they had blocked her bid for a Pulitzer. She wasn't about to head home just yet.

Dixon was so star-struck, he was on the verge of hyperventilating.

Jack Monroe was completely relaxed. "Control your breathing, will you? And calm down. You sound like you're giving birth."

"Huh?" Dixon managed to say as they walked to the front steps of Graceland.

"Stop huffing and puffing," Jack ordered as he knocked on the mansion's front door. They stood on the porch in the middle of four white columns. It was peaceful here even though the busy city of Memphis surrounded the property on every side.

Dixon relaxed a bit. He swiveled his neck and rotated his shoulders to remove the kinks. "Just psyching myself up, Jack. I brought this for him to sign." Dixon reached into the folder he carried and showed Jack Monroe the jacket of a 45 rpm record of *Return to Sender*.

Jack frowned. "Put that away. No wait, give it to me." Monroe grabbed for the record but Dixon held it out of reach.

"You're not worthy," he proclaimed. Monroe rolled his eyes.

The door opened and Vernon Presley greeted them with a cordial smile. This was Elvis Presley's father. He invited the two men inside and told them Elvis was just finishing his lunch and would be with them shortly. Then Vernon disappeared down a hallway beside the grand staircase that ascended upward from a space beyond the foyer.

Monroe had entered first and casually began to look around. If he was impressed, he didn't show it. When Dixon crossed the threshold, it was like stepping onto sacred ground. He wondered if he should genuflect or make the sign of the cross.

To his right was a glorious white living room that continued into a smaller music room with a grand piano. Dixon wondered if Elvis ever sat there and plunked out songs in his leisure time. He felt Monroe's elbow jab him in the ribs.

"Snap out of it, will you? You look like you're on mushrooms."

"Jack, this is where he sleeps."

"It's business, Peter."

Dixon agreed and brought himself back to reality. They wandered further into the house. There was a dining room with a chandelier to their left, and the staircase in front of them. Monroe peered down the hallway where Vernon had disappeared. Dixon cautiously stayed behind until Jack motioned for him to follow. They could hear a TV around the corner, and the sound of someone crumpling a paper bag and throwing it into the trash.

Monroe waited, wondering if he should follow Vernon or at least peer around the corner. He looked back to Dixon who was still cautiously waiting, wondering where Vernon had gone and if they were supposed to follow or wait.

Monroe decided to be casual about the whole thing. "Let's go," he said to Dixon. When he turned to round the corner he bumped into someone. Dixon was shocked to see that person was Elvis Presley. He was buttoning a blue denim shirt and had half a McDonald's burger in his mouth.

Dixon had never been this close to the King. He'd seen him in Kansas City in 1956 and again in Mississippi that same year. Then there was Dallas in '57 and Pittsburgh, 1960. Not to mention countless TV appearances, movies and photographs. But Dixon had never experienced such an intimate encounter with his greatness. He was surprised at how sloppy greatness could be. Dixon noticed a glob of ketchup on Presley's cheek. The King's shirt was wrinkled and his hair was in slight disarray.

"Excuse me," Elvis apologized to Monroe. "I'm sorry about that, I didn't mean to bump into you. Just finishing my lunch and noticed I'm running a little late. You the guys from NASA?"

"That's us," Monroe said. "I'm Jack Monroe." He offered his hand and Presley shook it.

"Nice to meet you, sir," Elvis said.

Then Presley nodded to Dixon and extended his hand but Dixon was awestruck and frozen in place. Elvis reached out and grasped Dixon's hand. "Nice to meet you."

Dixon stared wide-eyed at the King. "Peter Dixon, Mr. Presley. The pleasure is all mine." He longed to ask Elvis about the synchronizer upstairs, and tell him about the copy he had at his home in Houston, on top of which, stood his replica Ivory Elvis.

The three men were quiet for a moment, uncomfortably looking at each other, waiting for someone to speak. Jack finally said, "I understand you spoke to the President last night."

"Yes, sir," Elvis nodded and suddenly became very serious, shifting his stance so he was almost standing at attention. "President Nixon told me everything and I told him I'd be happy to help."

Dixon was still awestruck. Even Monroe felt humbled. Elvis noticed how they politely kept their distance. To break the tension, Elvis offered to lead them on a quick tour of the mansion. Monroe and Dixon happily accepted.

They followed Elvis through the kitchen and into the Jungle Room. This was Elvis's favorite room. Brick walls were covered in vines and surrounded by foliage. The green shag carpet provided underbrush for chairs and couches covered with leopard print upholstery. There was a dark wood rocking chair whose seat and back were covered with maroon vinyl, and whose arms were carved into open-mouthed dragons. This chair, Elvis told them, was his favorite place to sit and relax. On the table in the center of the room was the original Ivory Elvis.

Dixon only saw it for a moment. It looked just like his replica, but the char marks were real and not a graphite imitation. He yearned to study the idol up close and quiz Elvis about the legend, but the King of Rock and Roll ushered them outside to show them the property.

The backyard was the size of a football field. A white house sat in a cluster of trees on the far side. This was where Vernon lived with his wife Dee and Dee's three children. A covered walkway ran the length of the lawn to the right and ended at the indoor racquetball court, which also contained a living room with a piano and a bar.

Adjacent to the mansion, was the trophy room. This was filled with gold records, guns, plaques and awards of every shape and size. Outside the trophy room was the pool, shaped like a kidney and shaded on one side. Beside it on a lawn chair lay Colonel Tom Parker, sunning his plump belly. His eyes were closed and he seemed to be napping. Elvis called to the Colonel and informed him that the NASA men were here. Parker awoke and began to dress. Dixon felt he looked more like a bum than the business mastermind he was made out to be.

Beyond the pool was Elvis's meditation garden. It was circular, with a fountain in the middle and a brick wall wrapping around the back end. Plants and flowers were everywhere, and made it a place to sit quietly and enjoy the peace.

Now it was time to get back to business. Elvis suggested that everyone return to the Jungle Room, where they could sit comfortably and discuss the proposal. Elvis, Monroe and Dixon walked back to the house as Parker excused himself, saying he needed to clean up and would join them shortly.

The NASA men were impressed by Elvis's polite charm, the modest way he showed them the wealth he had amassed. It was as if Elvis were humbled by his own success. An admirable quality, Monroe thought, that would define the mission and its place in history.

Once they made it back to the Jungle Room, Dixon felt he had the King right where he wanted him. With Parker still missing and a few minutes to kill, Dixon finally asked about the Ivory Elvis.

"This?" Elvis smiled and walked to the table where the statuette stood in all its glory. It was the centerpiece and Dixon hunched down to take a closer look. He saw how the microphone was carved with meticulous precision. The artist had even carved the hinges and screws that attached it to the stand.

"This was a gift," Elvis said. "A gift from a Maasai man named Moja."

Dixon nodded and stared at the piece. "Rescued and hand delivered by *National Geographic* photographer Scott Richter."

Elvis grinned. "You know the legend."

"I've read stories."

Monroe rolled his eyes while he watched this exchange. He took a seat on the couch and opened his briefcase beside him. He pulled out his files and got organized for the meeting, which he thought Dixon should do instead of chatting with Elvis about some worthless statue.

But Dixon was forming a healthy little bond with the King. He said, "I have a replica at my place. But the char marks look completely fake."

Parker entered the room with his shirt half-tucked and a slobbery cigar in his mouth. Monroe thought Parker looked terrible, ashamed that Parker looked this bad after supposedly having just cleaned up. The NASA chief would never appear so scruffy at such an important meeting.

Parker's first concern was the money.

"The President has put one million dollars into Mr. Presley's retainer."

Parker and Elvis shared raised eyebrows. His normal fee was twenty thousand.

Monroe said, "There is to be no contact with the media. The mission is strictly confidential. It's a *surprise* concert from the moon."

The truth was Elvis had already decided to say yes hours before Monroe and Dixon arrived. He had made a verbal pact with President Nixon, this meeting was only a formality.

While Jack outlined the mission parameters, Dixon's eyes began soaking up the sights of the jungle motif. The plants and shag carpet gave him the feeling he was in the jungle, hiding from the poachers with Moja. The carpet had the effect of appearing like jungle foliage, thought Dixon, as he rubbed his loafer along the top of the carpet.

Then he spotted something in the shag. There was a sliver of fingernail sitting on the carpet a few inches from his left shoe. Dixon knew it had to be Elvis's fingernail. It just had to be. The King had said this was his favorite place to sit and relax. And sitting relaxed is usually the ideal time to trim one's fingernails.

Dixon glanced at the others and saw Presley and Parker had all their attention on Jack, who was explaining how Elvis would be trained. Dixon leaned forward a bit and rested an elbow on his left knee. He shifted a bit in his seat so that if he dropped his arm to the floor, he'd be close enough to snatch the lone fingernail.

Brilliant.

As Monroe moved onto the more technical aspects of the mission, Dixon let himself slouch further. He let his arm hang loosely above the fingernail. Just when he was sure no one would notice, Dixon dropped his arm and gave his ankle a quick scratch. He glanced down to the fingernail and was about to pick it up when he became aware that Monroe was addressing him. First softly, then louder.

"Peter!" Monroe clenched his teeth.

Dixon snapped to attention. "Sir!"

For the second time Monroe said, "Explain how we'll modify the spacecraft."

"Of course," Dixon said and cleared his throat. He was already planning another shot at the fingernail. "The Apollo 11 Command Module is called the *Columbia*. In the past, the Command Module, or CM, has had enough room for three astronauts. They sit on a couch side-by-side-by-side in a cramped space surrounded by windows and instrument panels. Behind them, a tunnel leads into the Lunar Excursion Module, or LEM. This is the *Eagle*, which will detach from *Columbia* and land on the surface.

"It's a tight space in both but we're going to modify the CM to fit Mr. Presley. Under the astronauts' couch there is a row of equipment lockers. They run the length of the floor, below the astronauts' feet. We're going to remove these lockers and install a long seat on the floor, sort of like a stretcher, where Elvis will be strapped. Like I said, Mr. Presley, it's going to be a very tight fit."

"Okay," Elvis said, sensing Dixon was about to deliver the bad news.

"We're going to need you to go on a diet."

"A diet?" Elvis couldn't believe it. He was supposed to take a journey to the moon but he wasn't supposed to eat?

"A strict water diet. For the next few weeks," Dixon said.

"Until you slim down a bit," Monroe finished, rather rudely in Dixon's opinion.

Elvis sat back and glanced at the Colonel. It was obvious Parker liked NASA's proposal. If Elvis needed to drop a few pounds for a chance to walk on the moon, he would comply with NASA's requirements. And one million dollars was a healthy paycheck. Parker was waiting for Elvis, who nodded that it was okay for the Colonel to speak for him.

Parker looked at Monroe. "We want life insurance."

"You got it," Monroe said.

"A three million dollar policy."

"Done."

Parker was satisfied. Dixon smiled. It appeared Operation Blue Moon would be executed. All four men were noticeably excited by the scope of the mission. There was suddenly a lot of energy in the room. Elvis actually laughed.

"Heck," he smiled with a little bit of sneer. "I think it's a great idea!"

"Good," Monroe smiled warmly. He handed a file to Parker. "Here's the paperwork. Contracts, agreements…money."

Parker eagerly accepted the file and began to page through as Elvis looked on and Monroe explained. While those three were busy shuffling papers and signing their names, Dixon took a chance and reached down to the carpet. He knew exactly where the fingernail was so he didn't have to look down. It took only a second before Dixon had the fingernail in his hand. He sat up, slipped the hand into the pocket of his suit coat and dropped the fingernail inside with a devilish smile.

It had been a perfect day. Elvis was officially part of the mission and Pete Dixon had a great new addition to his collection of King memorabilia.

Elvis saw them to the door and Monroe promised they'd send their own private jet to Memphis in a week. The transition to Houston would be secret just as everything would be until Elvis was standing on the moon.

He walked onto the front porch with them and shook their hands one last time.

"See you in a week then," Elvis said as Monroe and Dixon climbed into the waiting limousine. They waved goodbye and pulled away from the mansion. Both breathed sighs of relief in the back of the limo as they loosened their ties and reached to the bar for cocktails. Jack poured two glasses of scotch and handed one to Dixon. Then he sat back in his seat and shut his eyes.

"That went well," Monroe said.

Dixon sipped his drink and silently agreed. Then he reached into his pocket to get a closer look at the fingernail. There was a good chance it really did belong to Elvis. There was no nail polish so it couldn't belong to Priscilla or Dee. Yes, Dixon decided. This fingernail was once that of the King.

He nudged Monroe. "Check this out."

"What is it?" Jack squinted to get a better look at what Dixon was holding. "It's a fingernail. Throw it away, it's gross."

"It's not just a fingernail—"

Monroe interrupted, "It's disgusting, Peter! Throw it away!"

Dixon was defensive. "I found it in the Jungle Room."

"And you kept it?"

"It was right next to his chair, Jack. It's Elvis Presley's fingernail."

Monroe leaned back and closed his eyes. "You're an idiot."

Dani watched the limousine leave the property and then handed the binoculars back to the fan girl she'd borrowed them from. Several dozen fans were grouped along the Wall of Love, pointing binoculars and cameras at the distant mansion.

Today the fans had been lucky enough to enjoy a short Elvis sighting. He stepped onto his porch for a few seconds to bid farewell to two visitors, and the fans got frantic, snapping pictures and scurrying along the property to get a better look.

The fan girl who owned the binoculars tried to get them back from Dani, but Dani held them out of reach. "Uh-uh," Dani shook her head. "I'm using them."

"But they're *my* binoculars!" The girl frantically pleaded as her eyes kept shooting back and forth between Dani and Graceland. Everyone wanted to see Elvis.

Only Dani had her eyes on the two men from the limousine. Those two men who crashed her interview and ruined her chance to meet the King. She pushed the fan girl away and got a good look through the binoculars. One was tall and lanky, fifty, with perfectly tapered hair that glistened and a suit that had probably never been wrinkled. He seemed like he was the boss. Dani called him Mr. Shiny Hair.

The other guy was half a foot shorter, stocky and roughly forty, forty-five years old. He looked like some kind of yes-man. A sidekick. Dani named him Stumpy.

Stumpy and Mr. Shiny Hair, whoever they were, were responsible for destroying Dani's opportunity that day. Sure, they had no idea she was there, and sure they were just doing their job, but nobody could halt Dani Mitchell's shot at the Pulitzer and expect to get away clean.

She handed the binoculars back to the owner, who snatched them from Dani and pointed them at the mansion, too little too late. Dani headed back to her car and swore that if she ever saw those two men again, there would be retribution.

Chapter Four

Dixon created a list of code words to maintain the secrecy of Operation Blue Moon. Elvis Presley would now be referred to as The Bacon, and the astronauts would be The Eggs. The *Columbia* Command Module would be The Frying Pan, and the *Eagle* would be The Platter. The Sea of Tranquility on the surface of the moon would be The Kitchen Table. Dixon felt it appropriate to refer to the entire Apollo 11 mission simply as Breakfast.

Monroe looked over this list, approved it with a curt nod and suggested that the Pacific Ocean—where The Frying Pan would splash down to complete the mission—be called The Sink. Dixon agreed and they progressed to their next task: announcing the new Apollo 11 mission parameters to key NASA personnel.

A small selection of the space agency's top executives gathered in a conference room and awaited Jack Monroe's emergency meeting. Aside from Peter Dixon, there was Gene Kranz, NASA's Mission Control Director, Deke Slayton, the Director of Flight Crew Operations, and Television Officer Aggie Gallagher.

There was a lot of chatter among the men who all wondered what the meeting could be about. The Television Officer thought it concerned the return of Apollo 10, which had completed its simulated lunar landing earlier that day and was just beginning its long journey back to Earth.

Kranz said the Apollo 10 mission was running smoothly and didn't need to be discussed in an emergency meeting. The astronauts would be home in a few days, end of story. Something else was going on today.

Monroe entered the room carrying a manila folder, looking sharp as always. Navy blue suit, navy blue silk tie. His hair was tapered neatly above his ears and collar. His black leather shoes reflected the overhead lights with gleaming perfection. The inner circle of NASA executives became quiet as the meeting was called to order.

"Our mission objectives have changed," Monroe announced. "What was 'perform a manned lunar landing and return safely' is now 'perform a live Elvis Presley concert from the lunar surface and return safely.'"

The room was overcome with a lot of head-turning and murmuring. They wanted to know what Monroe meant and when he told them about Breakfast, the chatter was replaced by a stunned silence.

Making Elvis Presley the first man on the moon had to be the craziest idea ever conceived. Monroe said, "Operation Blue Moon is no joke. It has been approved by the President of the United States. I need to remind you that the next launch window is July 16th and that there is no excuse for missing this opportunity. This is serious business, not open to debate, and it's time to get to work."

As the reality of the new mission began to sink in, a torrent of questions burst forth.

"How will we fit a fourth man onto that tiny little spacecraft?"

"Is it possible to stash Elvis in the LEM?"

"Do we really need Buzz Aldrin?"

"Where do we put his guitar?"

"Where will he sleep?"

"With no air on the moon, how will his guitar make a sound?"

But Pete Dixon had an answer for everything. He shot down every question with thoughtful ingenuity and soon NASA's top brass agreed that Operation Blue Moon would be difficult but certainly not impossible. The time frame was short, but the mission would be accomplished. Some of them even laughed when they realized the exhilaration the world would know once they saw Elvis Presley performing on lunar soil.

"I love Elvis," Slayton said. "I can hardly wait to meet the son of a gun!"

It was unanimous: NASA would use everything in its power to make Elvis Presley the first man on the moon. Monroe passed out confidentiality agreements and told everyone, "In exchange for your silence, NASA is prepared to compensate each of you with a hefty bonus upon completion of the mission. If a word of this were to leak, and we all know it won't, J. Edgar Hoover has assured me he will use all his power to prevent the leak from surfacing. Everybody understand?"

They nodded, pledged their silence and became accessories to the stunt.

"Cancelled!"

"What do you mean 'cancelled?'"

"I mean what I said," Dani was upset. "Elvis cancelled."

Baker became silent on the other end of the phone. Then, "What did they say?"

"That he had another commitment and wasn't able to reschedule."

More silence as Baker considered the options. He said, "Sit tight. You at the hotel?"

"Yeah."

"What's the number there?"

She gave it and Baker said he'd call back in a couple minutes after making a few calls. She hung up and waited for Baker to come up with something brilliant to replace the career-making interview she wasn't going to have.

Dani chewed a fingernail and spit it across the hotel room like a sunflower seed. She paced for five minutes and then opened the room's small refrigerator. Inside were dozens of miniature liquor bottles. She thought about slamming a few and putting them on her *TSN* expense account, but the magazine wasn't responsible for her misery. It wouldn't be fair to make them pay.

She shut the refrigerator door, opened it, arranged the miniature liquor bottles alphabetically by name, then rearranged them numerically by alcohol content, and then shut the door again.

Five more minutes passed and the phone rang.

Baker. "Yep, you're definitely cancelled."

No shit, Dani thought. "I need to hear some good news, Richard."

"Here's what I've got," he said. Dani could hear him shuffling papers. She imagined his desk cluttered with piles of memos and articles and printouts. Baker found the paper he wanted and announced, "Bobby Neal Newman."

"Who the hell is Bobby Neal Newman?"

"Half-brother of actor Paul Newman. Self-proclaimed."

"Paul Newman?" Dani melted. "The man with the most fabulous blue eyes in Hollywood?"

"No," Baker said. "His brother Bobby Neal. He's a country blues singer living in Memphis. They say he's coming up in the world, and I've set you up with him for next week."

Dani made no effort to mask her disappointment. "Who wants to interview some two-bit Hollywood half-brother?"

"Dani," Baker sounded stern, like her father. "This is your assignment."

Dani closed her eyes. A sigh. "Is that the best we can do?"

"For now."

"It's just so lackluster. He goes against everything we stand for."

Baker was disappointed. "It's your job, Dani, to make it sensational."

The call ended and Dani immediately went to the refrigerator. She cracked open a shot of bourbon and drained it in one gulp. *The Sensational Nation* could pick up the tab for one drink.

Possibly a second...

It took a third shot of bourbon for Dani to come to terms with her ill-fated attempt to follow that wonderful Dalai Lama interview with another blockbuster. Then she evened things out with a fourth shot.

She thought back to Graceland and how those two suits ruined her chance to meet the King. Stumpy and Mr. Shiny Hair were to blame. She would never, ever forget those faces.

Monroe had given Dixon the job of telling the astronauts how the mission had been drastically modified, but Dixon wasn't concerned. He knew the astronauts wouldn't protest or shun the plan for its technological impracticalities. They were professionals and would do whatever was in the best interests of NASA.

He started with Neil Armstrong, the Apollo 11 mission commander, a civilian, former naval aviator, veteran of the Korean War and one of the nicest guys Dixon had ever met. He invited the astronaut into his office, sat him down and gently delivered the difficult news. Dixon was pleased when Armstrong smiled and said, "No, Mr. Dixon, I don't mind if Elvis Presley is the first man on the moon instead of me. I think it's a great idea!"

Buzz Aldrin also reacted warmly to the announcement of Operation Blue Moon. He said, "It would be an honor to fly with the King."

Dixon agreed with a grin and shook hands with Aldrin to end the meeting.

Michael Collins was the last Apollo 11 astronaut to be notified. He scowled when Dixon broke the news and said, "Let me get this straight. You are going to send me all the way to the moon, where I have to sit in an orbiting coffee can and listen while three men hop around like a bunch of children, and I don't even get to see the show? All the way there and you're not going to let me watch Elvis play?"

Collins stood and started for the door. "I'm a chaperone. No, I'm a chauffeur. The first person to drive a cosmic concert tour bus."

Dani Mitchell needed to get the hell out of Memphis. Sitting around a hotel room wasn't going to hack it in the big leagues, which is where Dani Mitchell knew she belonged. She had a Dalai Lama interview under her belt! She shouldn't be sitting around waiting to meet some country blues nobody who claimed to be kin to a five-time Academy Award nominee. She needed to be out and about, interviewing celebrities and winning awards.

She figured she had two choices: hang around Memphis as Richard Baker's yes-man, or get off her butt and make things happen. If she was a reporter of sensational news, then she needed to find something better than Elvis Presley.

Two months from now man would walk on the moon for the first time. She needed to build on her Dalai Lama interview by interviewing an astronaut. She wanted Neil Armstrong. In two months, who would be bigger than him? She picked up the phone and, out of her own pocket, booked a flight to Houston.

Above and beyond all things Apollo, Jack Monroe's chief concern was winning the space race. Whether it was Armstrong or Elvis who took those first steps, the race was approaching a most difficult moment that would justify all the years of effort and hope.

Monroe knew NASA had a lock on the finish line. Moscow was too far behind to mount any kind of comeback. They were sending an unmanned probe called Luna 15 to orbit the moon the same week Apollo 11 would land. He laughed at the Soviet's feeble attempt to stay in the race and their dismissal of manned space flight as an unnecessary risk of human life.

Anything Moscow could do at this point was rubbish, in Monroe's not-so-humble opinion. The Soviets knew they were beaten, as did the rest of the world. Now America's victory was only a matter of time.

Monroe thought back to his days with President Kennedy. Jack Monroe had been the one to suggest that the United States put a man on the moon by the end of the decade. That idea had won Jack Monroe his appointment to NASA during the final days of the Kennedy presidency. How proud JFK would be to know about Operation Blue Moon!

Jack gave a wink to the former president, wherever he was, and got back to work. The next item on his desk was a list of lunar experiments to be conducted by Armstrong and Aldrin. Now that Elvis was along for the ride, all the scientific mumbo-jumbo would take a backseat to the musical aspects of the mission.

Monroe read over the list of experiments and decided, "There's no time for any of this bullshit." He began crossing them off one-by-one.

The Soil Mechanics Investigation: scrubbed!

The Solar Wind Composition Experiment: junk!

The Passive Seismic Activity Experiment: a useless waste of time!

The Laser Ranging Retroflector: garbage!

The Lunar Dust Detector: Ha! Who were they kidding?!?

Monroe scratched them all away until the entire time spent on the lunar surface was dedicated to one task: Elvis and nothing but Elvis.

He checked his calendar. Elvis was scheduled to arrive at the space center on May 29th for six weeks of crash training. Everything had been perfect up to this point. Monroe could only pray for the same when it came down to show time.

Dani used her *TSN* press pass to get into the space center. Here she was nothing more than another hunk of media cattle, another face in the herd. The Apollo 11 frenzy was the biggest media event of all time. Still six weeks until the launch and already the excitement was growing beyond that of any Super Bowl or Hollywood trial. And it would only get worse.

Dani didn't plan on being here any longer than necessary. She did intend to meet Bobby Neal Newman as she had been instructed, but first she wanted an exclusive one-on-one with Neil Armstrong.

The drawback for Dani was that she was cold-calling—attempting an unscheduled walkup and competing with hundreds of reporters. The important thing was she was here, ringside, ready to rock and roll.

Once Dani was on site, she and several other reporters were given a tour of the space center. It was fascinating. The complexity of the manpower, technology and science that went into the Apollo program was beyond Dani's wildest expectations. For a few short moments, she wished she were an astronaut, and the first American woman to fly into space. It would be a sensational accomplishment that Dani could only dream about.

After the tour the reporters were dropped off in a cafeteria used by the general public, tourists and the media. The astronauts' and technicians' cafeteria was located elsewhere and was not open to visitors. Now Dani wandered out of the café and through the gift shop. She was starting to feel that the trip was a bust, that she should be ashamed of this useless waste of money.

She wondered if she should pay a visit to El Lago, a community of NASA employees who lived in an enclave in the suburbs of Houston. But again she would be cold-calling, and she wasn't exactly Walter Cronkite. She decided to call Richard Baker for advice.

"Hey, Dani, what's up?" Baker was chewing something, eating lunch at his desk again.

"I'm in Houston."

The chewing stopped. "Why are you in Houston?"

"Trying something new," Dani said. "Can you hook me up with Neil Armstrong?"

A curious chuckle and Baker said, "He doesn't do private interviews." He was amused that she didn't know this.

"What about Buzz Aldrin?"

"Cold walk ups? Why aren't you in Memphis, Dani?"

"I need something good, Richard. And this moon landing is the top draw. Can you set me up with someone here? Who do you know?"

Baker set his sandwich on his desk and scratched the back of his head. "I think my sister-in-law went to school with John Glenn."

"I'll take it."

"You sound desperate, Dani. I hope you're not planning to miss the Bobby Neal engagement."

"Not yet," she sulked.

"Not ever, Dani. Reputation. You don't want to be known as the reporter who ditches her interviews."

"I won't," she promised, knowing her editor was right. "But I need something to hold me over. A better Lama follow-up than Bobby Neal."

"Okay," Baker said and picked up his sandwich. "I'll see what I can do."

"Thanks, Richard. I'll call you back."

They hung up and Dani went to get herself some lunch. She ate alone and watched the cafeteria fill with reporters and tourists and random NASA personnel. After a few minutes Dani wondered if she'd ever even see an astronaut while she was here. They seemed to be hidden away, sequestered from the very media they were designed to impress. With her appetite nearly spent, she sighed and wearily poked at her lasagna. Depression had that effect on the young reporter.

"Care for some company?"

Dani looked up from her tray and saw the voice belonged to a lanky fellow about her age. He was clean cut with a nice smile, tall, dark, handsome, and totally not Dani's type. But he appeared harmless, so Dani invited him to sit. He slid his lunch tray onto the table across from her. She saw a press pass hanging from his pocket as he took his seat.

He introduced himself. "Tony Silverman, *New York Newsday*."

"I'm Dani Mitchell," she smiled politely.

Tony knew the name. "From *The Sensational Nation*." She nodded.

"Great Dalai Lama interview."

"Thank you," she tried to sound pleased but was hardly in the mood to talk about her achievements.

"So," Tony smiled as he unfolded a napkin across his lap. "You're probably here to interview Neil Armstrong or something."

A modest smile. "If only he'd do an exclusive."

"It's tough, isn't it? Six dozen reporters all chasing the same astronaut. I think we're lucky to be playing *some* part in this extravaganza."

The conversation made Dani feel emptier. At least Tony had a reason to be in Houston. Dani could only think of her failed attempt to meet Elvis Presley— which now felt like the beginning of an early decline into a canyon of obscurity.

Tony said, "There's a press conference after lunch. Probably the only chance to see these guys up close and personal before it gets too hectic."

"I have to go to that," Dani said.

So after lunch, they went. They found standing room at the back of the packed auditorium. Hundreds of reporters were audience to Armstrong, Aldrin and Collins, who wore suits and sat at a table covered with a blue cloth bearing the NASA emblem.

Dani faded into the crowd and barely listened to the astronauts. This was not what she had expected, nor did she think she could spin it into anything worthwhile. Perhaps it was time to go back to New York.

Across the room, two men caught her attention. One Dani did not recognize, but the other had a face and a build that had been branded into Dani's memory for the past three days. It was that short, stocky character from Graceland who had put the big kibosh on her day with Elvis. He was standing right there in the same room, watching the press conference.

A one hundred percent positive identification of Stumpy in the flesh. Stumpy caught a few words from Neil Armstrong and then nudged his counterpart and together they left the room. Dani followed as quietly as she could.

"Well, The Salt doesn't need to go anywhere we don't want it to go," Dixon told the Television Officer, using the code created for the mission, as they paused outside the cafeteria. "And it definitely won't touch The Bacon until The Platter's on The Kitchen Table."

"As long as we maintain control over The Jelly Rolls, we won't have to worry about The Salt."

"To what degree can we control The Jelly Rolls?"

"There are still a few kinks to be worked out," said Television Officer Aggie Gallagher, "but there shouldn't be too much of a problem."

Gallagher had come up with the new code words. His concern was the TV signal (The Salt) and a method of encryption to prevent it from being intercepted by anyone outside of NASA. The Jelly Rolls were the television satellites controlled by NASA. The Television Officer was in charge of the broadcast and making sure it ran on a short delay so that The Bacon (Elvis) would be the perfect surprise it was intended to be. There were still a few bugs in the technology so he needed to meet with Dixon to discuss the problems.

"Great," Dixon said. "Let's get together later. We can discuss Breakfast over dinner. Meet at Joe's?"

"Around seven?"

"You know where it is, right?"

"Yeah, on 44th. Will Jack be there?"

Dixon laughed. "Yeah, right. Monroe won't hang out with anyone after work. He's too good for us."

Gallagher chuckled, knowing Dixon was serious. "See you at seven, Pete."

"Right," Dixon said, and they went their separate ways.

Dani lurked behind in the corridor, sorting out the information she'd just overheard. All this talk about bacon and jellyrolls and breakfast sounded like some sort of NASA code. She wondered who Stumpy was and what he was doing in the space center. It seemed like a huge coincidence that he worked here, but Dani just figured she had been blessed by sensational luck.

She had him pegged. His name was Pete and tonight he'd be at Joe's on 44th. Seven o'clock. Dani didn't know if this omen was good or bad or if fate had brought her to Stumpy Pete, but this opportunity could not be missed. Stumpy was an asset and Dani intended to exploit him to the fullest.

Joe's was your typical sports bar in the suburbs of Houston. There was a rectangular bar in the center surrounded by tables on all sides with a giant TV against the wall opposite the front entrance.

Dani was already camped in a dark corner of the bar when Dixon and Gallagher arrived with Gene Kranz. She hunched down in her seat incognito and watched them take their seats near the TV on the other side of the bar.

Dixon ordered a vodka rocks for himself, the others ordered light beer, and they got down to business.

"Monroe wants some in-flight footage of The Bacon but nothing to be released until after they're in The

Sink. Sort of an archived look at Breakfast, to be released after we've put all the dishes away."

The others nodded. NASA wanted to document the mission in its entirety, but wanted to save Elvis for the landing. The Television Officer said, "We encrypt the signal from The Eggs to The Jelly Rolls and hold it until we know it's Bacon-free and safe to beam to the rest of the world."

Dixon agreed. Gallagher was saying the signal from the astronauts' TV camera could be picked up by anyone who had the means, so it was important to encrypt the signal, review it and edit the footage before they beamed it to the rest of the world.

Kranz said, "The risk of interception is low and no one but the Russians has the technology to break the code."

"Still," Dixon said, "We should hide The Bacon as much as possible, save it for show time."

Once Elvis was on the moon singing whatever song he chose to sing, NASA would record the concert and delay the broadcast until everything was completed without a hitch. Only after the astronauts were safely back inside the Lunar Excursion Module would NASA show the moon landing to the rest of the world.

That knot in his stomach was back. Dixon tried to soothe it with a gulp of ice-cold vodka but it hardly helped.

"Feeling okay, Pete?" Kranz asked.

"Fine," Dixon said. "Just a stomach bug or something."

Kranz and Gallagher began working out the details of the broadcast while Dixon started thinking about Elvis Presley. The man was an idol to millions of people all over the world. The Apollo program had already claimed the lives of three astronauts when a cockpit fire killed the crew of Apollo 1 on the launch pad. With Apollo 11 being the riskiest mission of all, Dixon wondered if he needed to devise a backup plan. A method of cover, should anything happen during the crucial flight.

They talked more technology and Dixon ordered another vodka. Dani observed the meeting while pretending to watch the Houston Astros baseball game on TV. Dixon and his gang were right in her line of sight. She couldn't hear a word of their conversation, but they looked serious. Stumpy Pete seemed especially concerned about something—his eyes kept wandering across the bar, lost in thought.

She decided the double Stumpy encounters were more than dumb luck. This meant something. She wasn't sure what it was, but it was her job to find out.

"Turn on channel six! The Dodgers are on channel six!" A drunk at the bar was shouting to the bartender. On TV the Astros game had ended and this guy wanted to watch something else.

The bartender sneered back. "Turn to six yourself, Donny. I ain't your gopher."

Donny finished his beer and walked to the big-screen TV. He flipped through a few commercials and paused when he landed on a channel that was playing a movie called *The Parent Trap*.

"My daughter loves this movie!" Donny announced proudly before he flipped two more channels and found the Dodgers game. Dixon watched him take his seat as *The Parent Trap* stayed in his mind. He knew the movie fairly well. Early sixties, Haley Mills played two parts— two sisters, twins, who are able to fool their divorced parents into thinking one was the other.

Their plan worked out perfectly. The sisters were able to switch places and recover lost time with parents they'd otherwise never see. Two people who looked exactly alike were able to fool even the people closest to them.

Dixon suddenly had an idea. He realized there was a way to deal with a major mission concern with a little sleight of hand. He finished his drink and excused himself from the table. When his companions asked where he was headed, Dixon casually said, "I need to take care of something." Then he paid his share of the tab and left to track down Jimmy Orr, the only person who could help him with this aspect of Operation Blue Moon.

Dani saw Stumpy Pete pay his check and leave the bar. She waited a moment, then paid hers and followed him out.

Chapter Five

Dani followed Dixon's Buick in her rented Dodge. She stayed far enough behind to remain inconspicuous as she followed him onto the highway. They drove for a few miles before Dixon exited in a different part of town. This area was glitzier and the numerous bars and nightclubs along the main drag spoke more of play than work.

He chose a bar called Spicer's Slop Ranch, parked and went inside. Dani stayed behind to strategize. She was still a stranger to Stumpy Pete, who had never seen her face. She needed to approach him, to talk with him and find out why a NASA worker was causing Elvis Presley to cancel interviews at Graceland.

She fixed her hair and her lipstick. A shower would have been nice, but she had to settle for a drop of perfume, which she rarely used but kept in her purse for special occasions such as this.

Stumpy Pete was sitting at a bar that ran the length of the club. The floor to the left was spread with tables and packed with people who were watching an empty stage in the far corner. There was a drum set and stacks and stacks of speakers and amplifiers, but the show had yet to start. Dani could feel the anticipation. The band would be out any minute.

Dani sat next to Dixon and read a sign taped to the mirror behind the bar that said *"Apollo 11—I'll Drink to That!"* She ordered scotch and soda. Dixon had his back to her; his attention was focused on the stage across the room. He was drinking a beer and seemed to be preoccupied with something.

"What are you drinking?"

Dixon looked beside him and was pleased to see an attractive brunette ten years younger than he. She had cloudy blue eyes that were watching him intently. "Beer," he said. "You?"

"Just a little teaser," she smiled and nodded towards the stage. "When's the show start?"

"Soon," Dixon glanced to the empty stage then back to Dani. "You a fan?"

She shrugged playfully. "Who isn't?"

He smiled. This girl was cute and he liked her perfume. He asked her name.

"Kim. Yours?" She smiled and toasted her scotch glass against his beer with two strokes, *clink-clank*.

"Pete Dixon," he said.

"What kind of work do you do, Pete Dixon? Or what line of work are you in?"

He looked into his beer for a moment and then eyed Dani. "I work on the Apollo program at NASA."

"Wow!" Dani made her eyes big. "Are you an astronaut?"

"No," Dixon laughed. "No, I'm the operations officer. I make sure everything works the way it should."

"Wow," she said again, eyes still big. "Everything?"

"Yep," Dixon nodded through a gulp of beer.

"Then you must be close friends with Neil Armstrong."

Dixon had never considered himself to be anything more than Armstrong's coworker. "Not really. It's not like I see him all the time. We're both pretty busy, as you can imagine."

"But you still see him."

"We run into each other from time to time."

"Neat," Dani sipped her drink and wondered how to proceed. She wanted Dixon in her pocket, but didn't want to scare him away. "Is there a Mrs. Dixon?"

"There was," Dixon smiled nervously.

Dani sensed tension. "I'm sorry. Did I...?"

"It's nothing," Dixon casually waved it off. "We divorced years ago. Is there a Mr...?"

"Clark," Dani finished. "Last name's Clark. And no, there is no Mr."

Dixon smiled towards the Apollo sign on the mirror. "I'll drink to that," he grinned and again they toasted. They had been so involved for the last few minutes that they didn't notice the band had taken the stage until they started playing. It was the opening *clang-clang* of *Jailhouse Rock* that snapped Dixon's attention to the back of the bar and away from Dani Mitchell.

Dani followed his eyes to the stage when the music started. The packed house was applauding the band, which was fronted by…Elvis Presley?

"Oh my God," Dani muttered and squinted for a better look. The King was wildly pumping his hips to the opening bars of the song. Elvis closed his eyes and belted out the first line of lyrics about the warden's party in the county jail. Dani felt her heart quicken as Elvis swaggered through the intro and broke into the chorus. The rest of the bar rocked along with him.

But Elvis would never play a venue this small and this far from home. This wasn't Elvis Presley, it was an amazing lookalike. He had the hair, the sideburns and even that unmistakable smile. His voice was dead-on and the hip gyrations were second to none. From where she sat, it was like Dani was watching the real thing.

She peered at Dixon. He was rocking and shaking to the music like everyone else, but he seemed to be studying the singer. Plotting some sort of seduction.

The whole situation was getting very weird.

A NASA bigwig was scouting an Elvis impersonator three days after meeting the real thing in Memphis. Dani didn't know if he was some rabid Presley fanatic or if this encounter was in any way related to the Apollo 11 moon landing, but the whole idea of a NASA-Elvis connection was irresistible given the timing. She slid her stool closer to Dixon and shouted above the music, "You like Elvis, huh?"

Dixon turned and nodded. He looked serious, as if it was about more than just *liking* Elvis Presley. Dixon appeared to be obsessed. She asked, "Ever seen him in person?"

Now Dixon smiled and raised his voice above the music. "Sure! Kansas City, 1956! He was fantastic!" And he turned his attention back to the stage.

"No," Dani patted him on the back and spoke into his ear, "Have you ever met him *up close?*"

This girl was asking too many questions. "No," he said. "We've never met."

Now Dani knew she was on to something. Why else would he lie about meeting the King? She persisted. "Ever been to Graceland?"

Dixon wasn't giving her any more information. He had sworn his secrecy to the President of the United States, so he turned the conversation back to Kim. "Have you ever been to Graceland?"

"Yes," she said. "I wrote my name on the wall." Now Dani gave him a coy smile and set her empty cocktail glass on the bar. Dixon liked the way she did that. A quiet voice told him he was on his third drink and he should avoid Kim Clark, but a louder voice reminded him how long it had been, and that this girl looked like she needed another drink.

He smiled back. "May I buy you another?"

"Yes, you have to buy me another," Dani made her eyes shine. She hoped Dixon would get drunk enough to tell all, or at least some of his story. He bought another round.

"Who are we watching?" Dani shouted as the singer broke into *Heartbreak Hotel.*

Dixon watched her curiously. The girl was too cute to resist. "His name's Jimmy Orr," Dixon shouted proudly and distributed the drinks the bartender had replenished. "He does the best Elvis in the land!"

"He's great!" Dani agreed. "If you can tell him apart from the real thing you must be a *really* big Elvis fan!"

Dixon played it off. "I guess I am. I collect some of his stuff." Dixon immediately wished he could swallow those words. The alcohol caused him to let down his guard. Luckily he caught himself before he told Kim about the fingernail he'd retrieved from Graceland, which now sat in a miniature jar amid the shrine on his mantle.

"I'm an Elvis collector too," Dani played along.

Dixon was drunk enough to believe her. "What's your best piece?"

"What's yours?"

Dixon chose something safe. "A gift coupon he used at McDonald's. Signed his name on it and everything."

Dani tried to top it with a tidbit she remembered from an old *TSN* article on celebrity memorabilia. "I have a cancelled check he wrote to the Sahara Hotel in 1961."

That was pretty good, but how dare this woman challenge his devotion to the King! Dixon was ready to go head-to-head on this, and the alcohol made him even more aggressive. "I have his expired *health insurance* card from Blue Cross. Late fifties. Paid twenty-six hundred for it two years ago. Probably worth four g's today. Will be worth ten, twenty thousand in fifteen years."

Dixon shut up. He remembered the alcohol he'd consumed and half-expected Kim to throw her share in his face. Instead she laughed as if Dixon's proclamation had been some big joke. He appreciated her sense of humor and laughed with her.

Dani knew she had this guy. He looked kind of desperate, but Dani felt she should end this now and keep him wondering. Better to do that than to stay here and wear out her welcome.

The band finished *Heartbreak Hotel* and while the crowd cheered, Jimmy Orr sneered like Elvis and said, "Thank you very much."

She said to Dixon, "Listen, I'd love to stay and chat but I've got to get going. You have a number where I can reach you, Pete?"

He scribbled his home phone on a cocktail napkin. Dani took it and slipped it into her purse. "It was nice meeting you. Thanks for the drink." She gulped down her last drops of scotch and stood.

Dixon was enjoying her company yet he was also relieved that she was leaving. It would be better if his new friend didn't know he was meeting with Jimmy Orr.

"Let's get together next week," she said as the band broke into *Don't Be Cruel*. Dixon invited Dani to give him a call. She jabbed him lightly on the shoulder and bid farewell.

Dixon watched her go, checking her out as she made for the door. An attractive girl, Dixon thought, but dealing with women had never been his strong point. Even though this one seemed to like him, he decided it was best to not get his hopes up. There were bigger fish to fry.

After Elvis Presley agreed to perform live from the surface of the moon, he locked himself inside the walls of Graceland and spent the next week exploring his mortality. This amounted to horseback riding with Priscilla and swimming with Lisa Marie during the day, and hosting wild parties all night.

The King's whole entourage was at Graceland for these parties, and the Presleys invited nearly everyone else they knew too. The crowds swam and watched movies and danced until dawn and Elvis never once mentioned his planned trip to the moon. He claimed these parties were merely for fun. A token of his appre-

ciation for his family and friends. Only Priscilla and
Tom Parker were in on Operation Blue Moon.

Elvis would have hardly any time off until the end
of the summer. The next six weeks would be filled with
tedious mission training. He had a gig July 31ˢᵗ when he
was scheduled to make his triumphant return to Las
Vegas. It would be just a week after the moon mission
had ended, and only two days after Elvis was scheduled
to leave post-mission quarantine. He intended to enjoy
these next few days at home as a lazy, casual earthling
and no one could stop him.

Sometimes Elvis would steal away from the parties
and all-night movie marathons and make his way to
Graceland's Meditation Garden. There he would sit and
watch the moon shine overhead. He thought about Jack
Monroe and the phone call from the President.

It was no surprise Elvis would jump at the chance to
walk on the moon. He had been chosen to represent
mankind's greatest achievement, and there was no way
he'd have hesitated to sign the NASA contract. It just
wasn't the kind of offer a person should turn down.

On May 28ᵗʰ, Elvis arrived at the space center one day
ahead of schedule. The Memphis Mafia stayed behind.
They were not a crime organization, but rather Elvis
Presley's personal army of bodyguards, gophers and yes-
men. They stayed at Graceland and hosted parties during
Elvis's absence, all under the guise of Elvis being at home,
enjoying his private life. Elvis had paid them off, so that
if anyone asked where he was, they said, "He's around
here somewhere. Have you checked the kitchen?"

Elvis traveled alone, under the security of J. Edgar
Hoover's best agents. Like the chauffeur who drove Elvis
from Graceland to a military airfield outside Memphis.

And the pilots who flew his private jet non-stop to Houston. They landed under fighter escort in the middle of the night.

Dixon waited on the runway, leaning against a limousine with his arms crossed, wondering if Kim was ever going to call. It had been four days. He planned to abandon hope after a week.

Now the jet carrying Elvis taxied to the limo and halted in front of Dixon. The engines shut down and a stairway was wheeled to the door. Moments later the door opened. Two FBI agents burst out with Elvis between them and hustled him down the stairs and into the back of the limo. Dixon jumped in after him, and they were whisked away to a garage where Elvis was safely behind closed doors.

Looking through the limousine's window, Elvis saw that the garage held a small welcoming party—tables with food and drink and an impressive NASA welcoming committee: Neil Armstrong, Buzz Aldrin, Michael Collins and Jack Monroe. They wore suits and ties and looked their best, making Elvis feel underdressed in his leather jacket and blue jeans.

"I hope you're ready for this," Dixon said with his hand on the door handle, before they stepped out.

Elvis nodded to Dixon. "Let's do it, baby."

Dixon stepped out of the limo. "Gentlemen," he announced to the crew of Apollo 11. "Meet Elvis Presley!"

Elvis emerged slowly and Neil Armstrong came forward to shake his hand. "It's an honor to meet you, Mr. Presley."

Elvis smiled his unmistakable smile. "The honor's all mine."

Buzz Aldrin gyrated his hips mimicking Elvis, much to the pleasure of the group. Elvis shook hands with everyone and after the introductions, the astronauts enjoyed cocktails and finger food. Because of his new diet, Elvis's portions were limited to water and health food. Celery sticks and cucumber sandwiches. He felt it a slight gyp, but knew his duties and let it slide.

After the gathering, Monroe and Dixon showed Elvis to his room. Tomorrow morning he'd tour the space facility and begin training for the historic journey. Monroe didn't leave Elvis before telling him, "You know, King, you can back out of this deal at any time."

Elvis winked. "Forget it, Jack. There's no way I'm missing this gig."

They wished him goodnight, and flipped off his lights. Elvis laid awake. He knew it would be another hour before he would fall asleep. The anxiety of the mission, and the uncertainty of his new room, combined with hunger to give him an unpleasant case of insomnia. He was rescued late in the night by Peter Dixon, who smuggled a McDonald's hamburger into Elvis's quarters and slipped it to the King.

"Thank God for you, baby," Elvis said and he devoured the burger.

"I've got to get out of here," Dixon whispered. "Monroe will kill me if he finds out."

Elvis nodded as he chewed.

Dixon held out his hand. "Wrapper?"

Elvis crumpled the hamburger wrapper and handed it over. He smiled as he swallowed and prepared for a good night's sleep. Elvis winked at Dixon. "We've got to do this again."

"Gotta go," whispered Dixon. "See you tomorrow." And he hurried away.

May 29th

Dani was back in Memphis for her meeting with Bobby Neal Newman. The last three days had been uneventful. Baker had been unable to set her up with an exclusive astronaut interview. The only other thing he had was a sit-down with some new British rock band called Led Zeppelin on May 31st. They'd be at the Filmore East in New York City for two nights and Baker insisted that they were the kind of people who don't usually grant interviews.

"And they're going to be the next big British new wave band!"

"I'm sick of British bands," Dani groaned. "Beetles, Rolling Stones, The Who. They all sound the same after a few beers." Baker told her Zeppelin wasn't playing for another two days, so she should do her job with Bobby Neal in Memphis and consider Zeppelin as a follow up.

It sounded like a dismal solution but Dani met Bobby Neal at his house, a modest bungalow on the opposite side of Memphis from Graceland. Bobby Neal sat on a wooden chair on his porch, strumming a beat-up acoustic guitar. When Dani stepped out of her car and greeted him, they sized each other up and neither liked what they saw.

Bobby Neal looked nothing like Paul Newman. He had the same build but his hair was too dark, his features too rounded, and he had dreary brown eyes, instead of shiny blue ones like his half-brother. He wore a denim jacket and cowboy boots, and hadn't half the charm of Paul Newman. He looked, at most, like he could *maybe* be a distant cousin.

"You the girl from the magazine?" He called from the porch as Dani walked to the steps. He didn't like the way she carried herself. The reporter looked like a goody-goody, someone who would nag him endlessly.

"I'm Dani Mitchell," she called back. "You Bobby Neal?"

He waved her to a wooden chair beside his. "Have yourself some lemonade." A stool between the chairs held a pitcher of lemonade and a stack of paper cups. It was a hot and fairly humid summer day, so Dani welcomed the offer.

"Thanks," she said as she poured herself a cup and took a seat beside Bobby Neal. He quietly strummed a blues lick on his guitar and watched Dani take a sip. She puckered at the sour taste.

"I'm Bobby Neal Newman," he proclaimed and handed Dani a 45 record. She read the title: *Stuffed Best Friend*, by Bobby Neal Newman. "It's my newest single," he said. "Keep it or something."

Dani set the record aside, already positive this inter-view would be a waste of time. "Your newest single implies you have another *older* single, does it not?"

Bobby glared at her. "What are you saying?"

"Just that I haven't heard of you, really. I mean, I wasn't aware Paul Newman had any half-brothers."

Bobby Neal looked like he was ready to argue. "You here to promote my stuff or what?"

She corrected him, "I'm here to find out who you are. Why don't you tell me about *Stuffed Best Friend*."

"It's an ode to my dog, Buck," Bobby Neal said sadly. "He's inside. Want to see him?"

"Not just yet," she said and took out her notepad. "How is he stuffed? Did he eat too much? Or is it some-thing else?"

"How about I sing you the song or something?"

"Sure," Dani reluctantly obliged.

Bobby Neal cleared his throat. "This one will make me famous." He strummed a rolling blues rhythm that sounded like it came from a Johnny Cash song. His voice was scratchy from too many cigarettes, and barely on key as he sang the crudely written lyrics:

My dog named Buck is dead and stuffed
Cuz I done run him over with my pickup truck
I leaned out the window and I told him to duck
But it came too late cuz his head'd been struck

Up on the mantle in his permanent seat
He's stuffed and sittin' there looking sweet
He's got little coasters restin' under his feet
But he don't have to eat and he don't need sleep

Lookin' mighty pretty with hound dog taste
One eye fell out but I popped it back in place
He's angled so to hide from the rest of the place
Those nasty Chevy grill marks that done slapped
him in the face

When he finished he looked at Dani as if fully expecting her to gush with praise. Instead she stared lifelessly at the singer and hoped the rest of her career wouldn't be as hopeless as today. She wondered about that British band in New York.

"That's your new single?" Dani said. "The song that will make you famous?"

He rolled his eyes. "Well, yeah."

Dani asked. "How is that song supposed to make you famous?"

"Because Paul Newman is my half-brother!"

Dani gave him a blank look. "Uh-huh."

"We grew up together. It was 1949–"

"Stop," Dani interrupted and held up her hand.

"What?" Bobby waited. "You need your tape recorder or something?"

"No." She shook her head. "Just stop. I'm not going to finish the interview."

With that Dani picked up her things and walked to her car, leaving an angry Bobby Neal glaring after her. He was a stupid waste of time, the type you'd be reluctant to interview even for your high school paper. He had nowhere near the prestige to justify the expense of *The Sensational Nation*. Dani felt no guilt ditching the interview.

Richard Baker was to blame for this shitty assignment, and it was his fault she had no article. When she went back to her hotel, there was a message to call him at the office. There was no reason to call back. She could only tell Baker she had nothing for the next issue of *The Sensational Nation*.

She envisioned her slow decline into an undeserved obscurity. There was always Led Zeppelin on the 31st, but Dani had no idea who they were. Probably some cheap Rolling Stones knockoff assembled to sell records instead of music. And she hated British rock.

She thought of Stumpy Pete and his strange connections. They were vague, yet intriguing. A NASA guy meets Elvis in person and then goes to watch an Elvis impersonator a few days later. More legwork was required before Dani could gauge where Dixon's path would take her. And she couldn't investigate him from Memphis.

She was hesitant, so she decided to go for a drive. She did her best thinking in the car.

They toured the space facilities and showed Elvis where he'd spend most of his time. Then he sat with Dixon and the astronauts and received his first mission briefing from Jack Monroe.

"Our next launch window is the morning of July 16th, six weeks away, and we are prepared to take full advantage of that opportunity." Monroe pointed to a diagram on the wall that mapped the entire mission. He started with Earth. "You blast off at 9:30 in the morning. Fifteen minutes later, after three stages have been fired one after the other, you will enter low earth orbit. You'll circle once around, and halfway through your second orbit, the third stage will fire again and propel you out of the earth's gravity and onto your lunar trajectory."

Elvis raised his hand. "What do I do during all this?"

Monroe winked. "You just sit tight, Big E. Once the lunar trajectory is underway, the *Eagle* lander will be unpacked from its compartment and joined head-to-head with the *Columbia* command module. Then you will separate from the rocket and continue towards the moon. For the next eight hours the crew will proceed with routine housekeeping until bedtime, somewhere around 9:00 p.m., Houston time. At this point, Apollo 11 will be approximately 63,000 miles from home."

The astronauts were nodding. They could recite this in their sleep. It was Elvis who was overwhelmed with the complexity of the mission. He watched intently as Monroe continued to explain the flight plan.

"Now, Elvis, you're silent and off-camera during all this. Even into day two, which will begin around 8:30 a.m. We'll call you up and start the day with a news update, including sports. We figure you guys will want to know what you're missing.

"If any course corrections are needed, they will be made at this point. You will also conduct an engine test for lunar orbit insertion and departure. Elvis, you are still off-radio into day two. After lunch the crew will continue housekeeping and system monitoring until that evening, when Apollo will broadcast its first live television transmission. Now this is very important. Peter?" Monroe nodded to Dixon, who took the floor.

"We want to document the mission in its entirety," Dixon said. "Without losing the element of surprise. No one outside of NASA's Mission Control will know Elvis is part of the mission until he's on the surface, playing his song. We all know Elvis stays off camera until show time, but we still plan to get a few shots of the King en route, purely for the NASA archives. Footage that won't be released to the public until after the mission. Remember, we determine what the public sees. The purpose of these live telecasts are to make the world think only three men are on the spacecraft."

Monroe said, "Because no matter how hungry or sick or poor you are, if you are an American, your television will be on and you will believe every word."

Dixon agreed. "It's going to be quite a moment when Elvis steps out of the spacecraft and plants his foot on the surface."

"There will be several great moments during the mission," Monroe said. "But next is day three."

Everyone settled and returned their attention to Monroe's briefing. "In the morning you'll charge the batteries and conduct additional course corrections if they are needed. Apollo 11 will be about 175,000 miles from the earth and 48,000 miles from the moon. We'll have our second Elvis-free television broadcast that afternoon."

Dixon said, "All Elvis content will be edited out before the 'live' broadcast."

"We'll keep any Elvis footage in the archives and release it as a documentary after the mission is complete. Elvis Presley and the True Story of Apollo 11."

"Sounds terrific," Elvis said, and the astronauts agreed.

Monroe said, "After the television broadcast, you'll open the hatch to the Lunar Excursion Module for the first time and power up the *Eagle*. By ten or eleven that night, you will be within the moon's sphere of influence, about 33,000 miles away. It will be the evening of July 18th.

"On day four you will enter lunar orbit and circle approximately 60 miles above the surface. If all systems are go—and we know they will be—Neil, Buzz and Elvis will begin relocating to the LEM. You'll pack your gear and get everything in place for the events of day five.

"This is the big one. Mike stays behind in *Columbia* and orbits the moon while you three separate for *Eagle's* descent. This is an extremely dangerous time, Elvis, so you need to make sure you are virtually motionless for the entire journey to the surface. There will not be very much room on the LEM; you guys will be crammed in there pretty tight. Any unnecessary movement, Mr. Presley, and you could jeopardize the mission."

Elvis nodded. "I understand, Dr. Monroe."

"Good. You'll land, you'll put your spacesuits on, and then you'll open the hatch. Now Elvis takes the first steps, but there is no live television broadcast. We are on a two-hour delay, recording everything. President Nixon will tape an introduction and then Elvis will sing his song. When he's finished, we check the sound and edit for content. Then from the top, we put the broadcast on the air. While the world is watching you guys walk on the moon, you'll actually be packing into the LEM and preparing for your return home."

Here Monroe smiled. "It's going to be sensational."

After the briefing, Dixon and Monroe took Elvis to a fitting room and presented the King with his spacesuit. "E. PRESLEY" was stenciled onto its front in black letters. Elvis stepped into the suit and two NASA engineers pulled it to his waist.

"How's it fit?" Dixon asked.

"It's roomy," Elvis nodded, looking for the armholes. He found them and the engineers helped pull the heavy suit over his shoulders. It was a significant weight on his back, and Monroe assured him it wouldn't feel as heavy under the one-sixth gravity of the moon. They zipped the suit and let him walk around.

The King of Rock and Roll took two steps and fell over, much to the delight of Neil Armstrong and Buzz Aldrin, who watched from the sidelines. They rushed over to help Elvis to his feet, to give him words of encouragement and slaps on the back.

"Thanks," Elvis smiled innocently. "This suit ain't nothin' like any of my regular getups." He moved his arms around and took a few careful steps. It wasn't easy to move under the bulk and weight of the suit. He had to concentrate on every step.

It would be nearly impossible to gyrate his hips.

Then Elvis looked at his space gloves. "What should we do about these? I'm not sure I can strum guitar with these things on."

"Well, King." Monroe said slowly, "we were kind of hoping you might have some ideas. We're pretty stumped on this one."

Elvis thought it over. "We can cover the pinky finger of my left glove with a metal slide, and the thumb of my right glove with a giant guitar pick. I can use an open tuning here, on this here guitar, and strum it bottleneck style."

Dixon agreed and Monroe said it was brilliant.

Elvis explained. "With an open tuning you get more of that bluesy feel."

"We love it," Dixon assured him and smiled at Monroe.

The King said, "If I could make just one last suggestion."

Dixon answered, "Anything, Elvis."

"Well, this mission is all about sensationalism, is it not?"

Dixon nodded thoughtfully. "An impossible task of epic proportions. Everything and more standing in our way. Pulling it off with fanfare and ceremony for a television audience of a billion people. Sounds sensational to me."

Elvis said, "There is one way to make it better."

"Tell us how," Monroe demanded.

"There is a key element you must include."

"What?" Dixon wanted to know. "What is it, Big E?"

Elvis pulled them aside and told them his idea for the spacesuit.

After two hours of driving around Memphis, Dani Mitchell still had no idea what to do. It was either those British guys in New York tomorrow night or back to Houston to follow the Peter Dixon lead. She still hadn't contacted Baker to tell him about her walkout on the Bobby Neal affair. She needed to come up with a plan before she reported back to *The Sensational Nation*.

She decided to drive past Graceland one last time. It was an impressive structure that she couldn't resist. A crowd was gathered on either side of the front gates but the guards were letting no one through. Apparently the partying still happened within. Dani should have been there days ago, touring the mansion room by room with Elvis at her side. But that annoying Peter Dixon and Mr. Shiny Hair were more important. She wondered if old Stumpy would open up and tell her what he knew. Maybe he knew why Elvis was throwing a seemingly endless party. She needed to give Dixon another try.

And to hell with Led Zeppelin. They wouldn't amount to smack. Just another bunch of longhairs trying to imitate The Who. A waste of time, Dani decided. The story was in Houston.

She turned the car back to her hotel. As she pulled into traffic, a white limousine squealed towards her from the oncoming lane and sideswiped her front fender. Glass shattered, walls shook and Dani was disoriented for a moment. She wondered if she had been knocked out and why she hadn't seen that car coming.

She sat in shock for a moment before she noticed her car was angled across two lanes and blocking traffic. Her car horn was blaring uncontrollably and the limousine chauffeur was trying frantically to open her door.

"Are you okay, Miss?" he anxiously called to her as he fumbled with her door handle. Dani came to her senses and saw the front of her rented car had been smashed on the driver's side. The chauffeur knocked again and Dani nodded to assure him she was okay.

He stepped back cautiously as Dani tried to back her car out of traffic and back into the gas station parking lot. She could barely turn the wheel; the alignment was ruined. Dani cursed and beat the steering wheel with a fist. It was dark out and her horn was still blaring.

"Try to open your door!" the chauffeur called as impatient drivers in the backed-up traffic began to honk their horns as well. It was a mass of noise and confusion and Dani was stuck in the middle. She shoved her damaged door open with a shoulder and stepped out, trying her hardest to hold back mounting tears.

The chauffeur was genuinely concerned. "Anything broken?"

"No," Dani shook her head and glanced around her. Cars were slowly beginning to make their way around the accident scene, which was a sea of broken glass and pieces of metal, most of which seemed to be from the rented Dodge. The chauffeur fixed her blaring horn, and the two gathered to exchange information. Dani didn't know who was at fault, but she wondered who was inside that limousine.

"I'll need a tow truck," she said to the chauffeur.

"I could possibly drive you to wherever you're going if my passenger gives the okay."

Dani looked at the idling limousine which had suffered relatively little damage from the collision. "Who's your passenger?"

The back door opened almost on cue, and onto the street stepped Liberace, dressed in his finest white suit. His fingers were covered with rings and a giant necklace was wrapped around his throat like a jeweled neck brace.

All noise, traffic and confusion seemed to stop as Liberace strolled calmly to where the two cars were merged to survey the wreckage. Dani and the chauffeur were silent, waiting for him to speak. Liberace looked over the damage and then at Dani. He seemed pleased, despite the unfortunate event, and politely smiled at Dani. "Need a ride?"

One of the world's most sensational celebrities had fallen mysteriously into her lap. Dani couldn't believe her luck. She took the opportunity by the throat. "You bet I would," she replied and waited for Liberace to invite her into his limo.

Instead he pointed to her wrecked Dodge. "First you'd better move the car. We can call a tow truck from the limo." He said with a cordial smile. "We have a car phone."

Dani nodded and steered the car while three helpful motorists from the traffic jam helped push her car to a nearby gas station. She left it in a parking spot, informed the attendant that a tow-truck would be by to pick it up shortly, and hurried to the limo.

The chauffeur held the back door for her and she practically dove into the backseat. "It's an honor to meet you, Mr. Liberace," Dani grinned as she slid in place beside the pianist/actor/legend/seducer. Liberace was already on the phone, calling the car's location to a tow-truck dispatcher who assured him the Dodge would be retrieved within forty-five minutes.

He hung up the phone and turned to Dani. His jewelry glittered in the streetlights. "I'm sorry that we won't be spending much time together tonight. I'm expected at a gathering and will be dropped off shortly."

She needed to take advantage of her time with Liberace. Dani asked, "Mr. Liberace, if you don't mind my asking where you're headed tonight?"

"Up the street," he said. "To a party."

Dani's eyes widened playfully. "What's the occasion? I'll be damned if I missed your birthday, Mr. Liberace."

He smiled as he looked to the chauffeur. "Just going to a friend's house." Then, "Antonius, it's just to your right."

"Yes, sir," said Antonius. "I know, sir." And Antonius slowed the car as Graceland approached just ahead. Dani couldn't believe her luck.

Then Liberace looked her way. "Now regarding this accident. I'm terribly sorry about your car."

Dani smiled her way onto his good side. "It wasn't my car."

"I'm sorry," Liberace squinted. "A friend's?"

"A rental."

"Ah!" he said. "Perhaps I should reimburse you for the damage?"

Dani was impressed by Liberace's gracious reaction to the accident. She looked over the gigantic rings on his fingers and the shine of his white suit. Dani looked him in the eye. "You could do me a favor?"

"Yes?" Liberace waited as Antonius rolled down the window and stopped the limousine outside the gates of Graceland.

Dani licked her lips. "Take me to the party."

Liberace's expression didn't change. He sat looking at her as he considered her suggestion. She wondered if he'd kick her out and withdraw his offer to pay for the Dodge. Instead he nodded. "It would be my honor."

She relaxed and sat back in her seat with a happy grin.

Liberace said, "I don't believe I got your name."

"Clark." Dani smiled as the limo went up the driveway towards the marvelous Presley mansion. "The name's Kim Clark."

Chapter Six

Liberace offered his arm to Dani for their entrance into the mansion. On Graceland's front steps, Dani saw Chuck Berry having a cigarette with Zsa Zsa Gabor and Stones drummer Charlie Watts. Already Dani was immersed in fame and she knew it would only get better once she was inside. This party would be a cornucopia of sensational celebrity tidbits, but her number one concern was the King. His friends were good fodder for her next *TSN* article, but without Elvis she had nothing.

Joe Esposito, or "Diamond Joe," Elvis Presley's top aide, was outside the front door drinking a bottle of Coke. He nodded politely to Liberace, eyed Dani curiously and then stepped aside, holding the front door open for both of them. Dani took a breath and stepped into the mansion.

Graceland was a palace. A grand staircase opened before her. She wondered who, if anyone, was upstairs. A commotion turned her attention to the living room on her right. The couches and chairs of the majestic white room had been pushed to the walls and a Twister mat had been arranged in the middle of the floor. On the mat Dani was shocked to see Jim Morrison, Charro and 280-pound Presley bodyguard Charlie Sutton tangled in an intense match.

Sutton was on all fours and laughing as Charro struggled unsuccessfully to place her left foot on a yellow dot far under Sutton's gut. Her arms were wrapped around Morrison, who was holding himself up like a crab beneath her.

Morrison saw Liberace enter the mansion and he lifted his hand to wave. Without Morrison's arm there to hold up himself and Charro, they both collapsed on the mat as Sutton held his place and laughed at their fall.

"That's another game for the big man!" Sutton gladly announced and crawled to the white loveseat, where he recorded another tally on their scorecard.

Liberace said to Dani, "Pay no attention to them. Let's see who's in the kitchen."

Dani agreed and they walked around the staircase and down the hall that led them deeper into the mansion. A closet door to Dani's right suddenly popped open and Ann-Margret stumbled out and fell to the floor. A midget with gray hair and a squeaky voice pranced out after her crossly and shouted, "That's the last time I play 'five minutes in the closet' with her!"

The angry midget stormed into the kitchen and left Ann-Margret behind to pick herself up from the floor. Liberace helped her to her feet and introduced his companion.

"My friend, Kim," he said. A flustered Ann-Margret looked her over as she adjusted her skintight pants and blouse. Her red hair twinkled and her rounded cheeks seemed to smile, although the actress frowned. She seemed disinterested in Dani, which told the reporter she still had a long way to climb from the pits of obscurity. Dani was just a year older than Ann-Margret, and infinitely jealous of her success.

"Nice to meet you," Ann-Margret said. Dani wanted to tell the actress how beautiful she looked, even in the wake of an angry midget who'd rejected her love. She had a million questions for her, but Liberace pulled Dani into the kitchen where she was suddenly face to face with Priscilla Presley.

In her flowery pink dress, the wife of Elvis Presley was more stunning than Ann-Margret. She was only twenty-four, with sparkling eyes that made Dani's blood boil with envy. Priscilla could sit and talk to Elvis whenever she wanted. Now the King's wife smiled when she saw Elvis's old pal Liberace.

"So good to see you!" she said as she offered a snack tray.

Dani politely took a cracker spread with little slices of smoked salmon. Liberace introduced the two young women but Priscilla barely paid attention. Not that she was rude, just that she was so busy hosting the party, she couldn't give Dani more than a smile and a nod. Liberace asked about Elvis and Priscilla said, "He's around here somewhere. Have you checked the pool?"

"Not yet," Liberace said and made more small talk with Priscilla. Deeper into the kitchen Dani could see several members of the Memphis Mafia at the table talking over hamburgers and hot dogs. She recognized Billy and Gene Smith, two of Elvis Presley's cousins and bodyguards, but longed to head out to the pool to try and locate Elvis.

In walked Liza—just twenty-three and coming off her role as Pookie Adams in *The Sterile Cuckoo*—carrying a metal cocktail shaker and a bottle of piña colada mix. She wore a purple dress that almost had a tie-dye pattern. She set her bottle and shaker on the counter next to Dani and pointed at the refrigerator. "Get me another tray of ice, would you dear?" Dani looked behind her, wondering if Liza was talking to someone else. She was not, and it became apparent to Dani that Liza Minnelli thought she was some kind of waitress.

But it was Liza, so Dani obliged and handed her a tray of ice from the freezer. Liberace and Priscilla continued their friendly chat as Liza mixed a tropical drink in her shaker. It was a virgin cocktail, as alcohol wasn't served at Graceland. Dani watched and thought of Liza's parents. Judy Garland and Vincente Minnelli, both Oscar-winning celebrities. One day, Liza herself could be legend. Dani decided to try her luck.

She said to the actress, "Word on the street is that your portrayal of Pookie is already in the running for an Academy Award."

"I don't know about that." Liza said, "The key is a thorough shake." And Liza shook the mixture so wildly, that she bonked herself in the head with the shaker and fell unconscious. Her cocktail spilled across the floor.

Priscilla turned to the Memphis Mafia members at the table and shouted, "Somebody get her out of here!"

Dani had seen enough. She slipped around the corner and found herself in the Jungle Room, where she saw Audrey Hepburn and Keith Richards at the stereo arguing. An Elvis statuette stood on the center table.

"Turn it back," Audrey said. "I want to hear *Moon River* by Sinatra."

"He's not a bad bloke," Keith said. "But I was hoping for *Ride of the Valkyries* by Wagner. It's quite an inspiring tune."

Dani waved as she passed through, and made her way to the back door where she was finally alone and able to gather her thoughts. This was incredible. This party had more talent than the Academy Awards, which said a lot and nothing at the same time. Still Dani needed to find the man. What good was a story about Graceland without a few words from Big E?

She headed for the pool, where the smell of a barbecue still lingered. On the patio were the remnants of a pig roast, with half a cooked boar on a skewer above the fire pit. Buffet tables were arranged along one side of the patio with coolers of juice and soda on the ends.

Marlon Brando and Raymond Burr were circling over the leftovers. Burr was at the buffet helping himself to another serving of potatoes and gravy while Brando stood at the skewer, picking strips of meat off the remains of the pig.

Several other people relaxed and talked on lawn chairs surrounding the pool but Dani only recognized the two actors. She approached Brando. She asked, "Have you seen Elvis?"

"Sure," Brando mumbled without taking his concentration off the barbecued pig. "Vegas, 1956. He was terrific."

"I mean, I wonder if he could be upstairs? Or maybe we should check the basement?"

Brando shrugged and snatched a chunk of pork off the pig's gut. He threw it down his gullet and spoke while he chewed, and Dani couldn't understand a word of the bulky actor's mumbling. She gave up on him and made for the Trophy Room. Nobody at this party recognized her, and Brando had failed even to make eye contact. This party could change everything, could be the springboard that would propel her into journalistic greatness. If only she could locate the King.

The Trophy Room was filled with a group that gathered on the couches beside a piano, drinking and singing while Little Richard's hand danced across the keys. He sang Long Tall Sally for several Memphis Mafia bodyguards and baby Lisa Marie, who sat clapping on her grandfather Vernon's lap. The crowd was into the song and didn't notice Dani as she peered into the room and observed the celebration as she searched the faces for Elvis.

He wasn't here either. That left the Meditation Garden, and Dani wondered what Elvis would do if he was disturbed there. Probably kick her out and promise he'd never speak to her again. Dani decided she couldn't just give up and left the Trophy Room for the sacred garden.

The only thing she found in the Meditation Garden was a couple she didn't recognize who were busy making out near the far wall. It was a disgrace to the King's good name, Dani thought. If Elvis saw this he'd throw a fit!

She headed back to the house to see if old Liberace had had any luck finding the big man. On her way across the pool deck she saw Jerry Lewis was filling a plate at the buffet table. Priscilla walked out to refill a cooler with juice and soda and Lewis asked her about Elvis.

"He's around here somewhere," Priscilla said. "Have you checked the kitchen?"

It sounded like a cover to Dani. Priscilla had said a similar thing to Liberace when they were in the kitchen. Perhaps Priscilla could explain her husband's convenient absence from the party. Before Dani could confront the King's wife, Marlon Brando poked her on the shoulder.

He mumbled something Dani couldn't understand.

"He said 'you're that reporter.'"

Dani turned to see a young man in a suit standing next to Brando. He looked like Brando's assistant. "Mike Nelson," he introduced himself. "I'm Marlon Brando's interpreter."

"You're kidding," Dani eyed the actor, who was pointing a finger and mumbling at her. She couldn't tell what he was saying but it sounded like an accusation.

"I'm Kim," she said quickly. "I'm nobody."

Nelson listened until Brando finished mumbling, then translated, "You did that Dalai Lama article. You're from *The Sensational Nation*."

"Excuse me?" Priscilla was suddenly beside them, having overheard their conversation. "But did you say *The Sensational Nation*?"

"No," Dani said, but Brando and Nelson both said yes.

"I'm sorry," Priscilla smiled politely. "But I'm afraid I'm going to have to ask you to leave the party."

"Please," Dani shook her head in protest as Presley bodyguard Dick Grob made his way over and placed his hand gently on Dani's back.

"Don't make a scene," Priscilla warned, sensing a rise from Dani. "But no reporters allowed."

"No, I have to meet Elvis. I'm a guest of Liberace!"

Brando pointed at her again and Nelson translated, "I've seen your picture in the magazine. Of that girl. You."

But Dani was already on her way out. "You don't understand," Dani pleaded as Dick walked her back to the house. "I'm not a reporter. I'm not with *The Sensational Nation.* I'm not with any nation! I'm here with Liberace!"

No one listened.

Two minutes later Dani was unceremoniously pushed out the front door by Dick Grob and Diamond Joe. She stumbled on the top step and lost her footing, falling the rest of the way and landing on her back with a thud. She looked up and saw Chuck Berry looking down at her. He flicked his cigarette butt onto the lawn.

"Gotta learn how to communicate better," he said. "Gotta respect the little people. You never know when you'll be one yourself."

She replied sarcastically, "Yeah, I've heard that one before." She sat up and Berry took a seat on a bench, sat back and closed his eyes.

She smirked, "Liberace's never around when you need him."

Dani looked at the mansion, then back at Chuck. He was her last chance to save the day from being a complete bust. "So, Mr. Berry," she said as she got to her knees and wiped dirt off her blouse. "You are the real King of Rock and Roll, are you not?"

Nobody would ever know why Chuck Berry was in such a bad mood that night. He stood and walked to the front door. "Kissing butt won't get you nowhere," he said and went inside.

Dani didn't dare follow. She could already feel the bruises from her fall down the stairs and she didn't care to see those bodyguards again. And she knew Chuck Berry was right. Hard work was the only thing that would put her over the top. She had to give up on this Elvis vendetta. There were possibilities elsewhere.

She could book an early flight to Houston and hopefully see Dixon tomorrow night. He was a goofy character but his connections to Elvis made this whole Graceland ordeal seem like a bad dream. She needed to give Stumpy Pete another shot.

She stopped back at the hotel and was given a message at the front desk. It was from Baker, who wanted her to call. It was just after 10:00 p.m. in New York so she tried him at home.

"Why didn't you call me sooner?" Baker sounded bored.

Dani felt edginess in his voice, so she lied. "I didn't get your message until now."

"Well, I wanted to tell you to skip the Bobby Neal interview."

Dani masked her surprise. "I should have skipped it, he's junk."

"He's a fake."

"A fake?"

"A fake," Baker said. "He's not Paul Newman's half-brother. He's nobody. So whatever you've got, throw it in the trash. And come on back to New York tonight if you can. I want you to meet with that British rock band who're in town tomorrow."

"You mean the next product of the British Invasion? Those bands are all the same. Don't make me waste time on some carbon copy quartet."

"Have you heard their first album, Dani? They're pretty good."

"I don't care to," she said.

"Well, they're here for two nights."

"Not interested."

Baker was blunt. "I hear depression talking." Then, "What do you plan to do instead?"

She considered telling him of her visit to Graceland but decided to keep it to herself. It had been an interesting night, but there was no story. "I have something cooking at NASA."

"You found something at NASA?" Baker sounded interested. "What's the scoop?"

"I'll know in a couple days," she said. "It could be good. Pulitzer caliber."

"Don't start saying that," Baker advised. "You could jinx the whole thing."

Dani knew he was right. She said, "I have a good feeling about this one, Richard. Like it could put me over the top."

"You'll be there one day, Dani," he smiled. "Don't give up."

They said goodbye, and when she hung up the hotel phone, the bells inside made a ding. She picked up the phone and hung up again so she could hear the ding a second time. Then she searched her purse for Peter Dixon's phone number.

Jimmy Orr stood before the full-length mirror in his apartment doing his daily hip gyration exercises. He had his Elvis impression down to a science, perfect in every way except for two things: Jimmy was half an inch taller than the King, and he could not make it through *Love Me Tender* without cracking his voice. The song was just too emotional for the Elvis lover and look-alike. It brought him back to the days of lost love and forgotten promise.

Jimmy compensated for the height issue simply by styling his hair with a little less poof. As for *Love Me Tender*, it was a song Jimmy Orr refused to sing. He had too much talent to let one little hit single stand in the way of his success.

Instead, Jimmy concentrated on the real rocking tunes, much to the approval of his band Small Potatoes. He'd been with these guys since high school, when they played nothing but Chuck Berry hits, and Jimmy duck-walked across the stage during their gig at the homecoming dance.

Back then nobody had ever heard of Elvis Presley. When the King broke onto the scene and suddenly swept the world off its feet, Jimmy Orr became a sort of local icon. People would always mistake him for Elvis in bars and nightclubs. They'd say he looked exactly like the King and ask if he was related. Even the members of Small Potatoes suggested Jimmy try his luck at imitating the King on stage.

Guitarist Johnny Wichita said, "You look just like Presley, and I love *Baby Let's Play House*. Think you can sing it like he does?"

Jimmy quickly learned that he could. Bass player Petie Podobinski—or Petie Podo—told Jimmy, "It's not just your looks either, man." Podo's long, stringy blonde hair wavered like a curtain as he talked. "But the way you move. The way you sound. I swear to God, man, you are the lost twin brother of Elvis Presley."

Small Potatoes drummer Tom Washburn agreed. "Jimmy, you do such a striking Elvis impression, I wouldn't mind concentrating full time on the entire Presley catalogue."

Which is what they did. Jimmy Orr became Elvis, and Small Potatoes became the premiere tribute band of the 50's and 60's—though it didn't happen overnight. Jimmy spent years studying every aspect of Presley's life. He analyzed the voice, the swagger, the clothes and the smile. He learned Elvis's favorite foods, his pet peeves. Everything that was available to know, he knew. He learned it down to the most minute detail. He could imitate it all.

He took karate on weeknights so even his kicks and chops were accurate.

All except for that awful ballad *Love Me Tender*.

Small Potatoes soon took their act on the road and dazzled audiences with the flawless look-alike front man. They traveled the south and east, west to Vegas, and as far north as Chicago and Montreal. They relished the glamour and excitement but loved nothing more than Spicer's Slop Ranch, their old hometown venue where the faces were as familiar as the restroom graffiti.

They played Spicer's fifty times a year, usually more if they didn't feel like traveling. Now Jimmy Orr was thinking about their latest show from the Slop Ranch. It was just a few nights ago they'd played Spicer's when a man named Peter Dixon had approached Jimmy with a proposition.

"You do a great Elvis," Dixon had said once they were backstage and alone.

"Best Elvis in the state," Jimmy replied with a perfect Elvis drawl as he toweled sweat off his forehead with a hanky. "Maybe even the whole country; what do you think?"

Dixon was all business. "I'd like to discuss something with you, Mr. Orr. A proposition, if you will."

Jimmy set his hanky aside and looked upon this stumpy little man. "You some kind of talent agent? I've already got a manager if you are."

"I'm a federal official, Jimmy." Dixon flashed his NASA ID badge so fast Jimmy couldn't make out a word. "I'm about to reveal Top Secret information. Revelation of which will land you in huge trouble with federal government. The IRS, the FBI, the works. On top of which, I will deny everything."

Jimmy swallowed, not wanting to hear any more, but knowing he had no other choice. "So why you telling me? Did I win some kind of contest?"

Dixon smiled warmly. "No, Jimmy. This is science." He slipped his business card into Jimmy's hand. Orr read the name and the logo and glanced carefully at Dixon. "What's this all about?"

Dixon put his arm around Orr and invited him outside for a stroll. When Dixon finished making his proposition, Orr went home with a strange weight on his shoulders, vaguely suspecting he had better polish his hip gyrations and karate chops.

The Elvis Presley merchandise had arrived at a secret NASA warehouse in Houston. Pete Dixon was there to sign the invoice while a fleet of forklifts unloaded truckloads of cardboard boxes. The boxes were piled on wooden skids, which were stacked anonymously in a giant storage room. Dixon waited until all the workers had gone home, then he went for the boxes.

He tore one open, threw the packaging paper aside and pulled out a coffee mug. An Apollo 11 banner wrapped around the rim and there was a picture of Elvis Presley on either side of the handle. A caption read "I Witnessed The Greatest Moment of All Time."

Dixon grinned and set the mug aside.

The shipment came from a manufacturing company that specialized in providing supplies for all manner of covert operations. Top Secret goods and services from a corporation you could trust.

Using the serial numbers off his invoice, Dixon was able to locate the rest of the Elvis lot. Dixon found the T-shirts first. He yanked one out and held it up to see Elvis Presley in a spacesuit, posing on the moon with his guitar. Glittering words across the top said "Lunar Elvis LIVE!"

Dixon folded the T-shirt and stuffed it into his pocket. It was another great addition to his Elvis shrine. Since Dixon met Elvis at Graceland, his collection was getting better and better. First the fingernail, now all this.

He looked on the invoice and saw there was a shipment of board games sitting in the warehouse. "Get Elvis to the Moon and Back" they had been titled, and Dixon couldn't wait to play. The next entry on his invoice read "action figures." This was the one he had been waiting for. Little Elvis Presley dolls, clad in NASA spacesuits.

Dixon couldn't find them. He examined every crate, looked at every box and still could not match a serial number to the sequence on his invoice.

"Where the hell are my action figures?"

He called the manufacturer and told them, "There was supposed to be a truckload of action figures, like those little G.I. Joes for kids. Where are they?"

The manufacturer said, "They must be en route. Call us when they arrive," and then hung up.

Dixon glanced around the warehouse. He had his coffee mugs, his T-shirts and his board game. But those damn action figures were still in transit. He would have to wait at least another day. Frustrated by his bad luck, Dixon kicked a cardboard box, muttered a few curse words, and shuffled back to his office.

That night he gazed upon his Elvis shrine and decided it needed a slight rearranging. There was another, smaller shrine in the kitchen, but tonight Dixon was concerned with the living room, the main attraction, the shrine that was home to all the best Elvis artifacts.

The Ivory Elvis replica was still the focal point of the room, standing atop Dixon's symphonizer, illuminated by a spotlight overhead. What a treat it had been to see the real thing!

Above the fireplace was an oil painting of the King's likeness, and along the mantle were Dixon's favorite trinkets. The pair of Elvis collector's dinner plates served as end pieces on either side. There was Elvis Presley's expired Blue Cross health insurance card, a McDonald's coupon signed by the King, and the fingernail Dixon had retrieved from Graceland—which was now in a glass jar on a small pedestal in the center of the mantle.

To the right of that were ticket stubs to the world premiere of Presley's *Blue Hawaii*, an 8x10 of Elvis Presley with Bobby Darin, autographed by both, and then the second Elvis collector's plate.

Between the ticket stubs and the fingernail Dixon cleared a small opening. There he placed a small cardboard placard where he had written the words "future home of the authentic Elvis moon rock." Beside the placard, Dixon set the Apollo 11 Elvis mug in place. He was wearing NASA's Elvis T-shirt. He took a step back and admired his collection.

Suddenly Dixon felt a sharp pain in his abdomen. He sat on the keyboard bench because it hurt too much to stand. This brutal stomach cramp had been plaguing him for several days, and he wondered if it could be an ulcer. Dixon realized he'd been thinking about Jimmy Orr. It was too early to tell Monroe of the backup plan. He would dismiss it as a ridiculous waste of time. Dixon needed to keep Jimmy Orr in his pocket for now.

As his stomach pain began to subside, the phone rang. "Hi, Pete," said Kim Clark. Dixon perked to attention.

"Hey," he answered. The pain in his stomach disappeared.

She sounded happy to hear his voice. Her tone conveyed a smile. "It's Kim from the other night. You busy this weekend?"

Chapter Seven

Saturday night. Peter Dixon and Dani Mitchell had agreed to meet for a drink at Galati's, a local steakhouse with a great bar and the best prime rib in town. A movie theater across the street was showing Marilyn Monroe in *Some Like It Hot*, which they had decided to see.

Dixon arrived first, and took a spot at the bar below a television that was showing a rodeo. He ordered gin and tonic and checked himself in the mirror. Dixon thought he looked pretty good for a man beyond his physical prime. He didn't think he was meeting the girl of his dreams, but something told him Kim was worth the effort. Yet Dixon was wary. His last relationship had been with his wife, a marriage that had quietly ended nearly four years ago. Dixon wasn't sure if he was ready for something new, but he was curious enough to see where this would go.

His drink arrived and he kept it before him. He wondered about Kim, as he had wondered since she called the night before. It was unusual for a girl to call a guy for a first date. Especially for an attractive, single girl in her twenties to be chasing a divorced shortie pushing fifty. Kim Clark was a mystery woman. Dixon had no idea where she was from or what she wanted, but he could not stop thinking about her.

Now she was suddenly standing beside him. He caught her figure in the corner of his eye and a sweet sting of that perfume. She smiled and said, "Howdy. Been waiting long?"

"Not enough to start on my drink." smiled Dixon. "Have a seat."

She seated herself beside him at the bar, turning her chair to face his. Kim looked twice as good as he'd remembered. A black dress revealed curves Dixon hadn't noticed the first time they met. Her hair and eyes shined around a smile Dixon had not known in years. The last woman to look at him like that was his wife, Maggie, back when they had been a somewhat happy couple. He was love-starved, indeed.

Dani ordered a glass of chardonnay. "Well," she said. Dani normally wasn't attracted to older guys but Stumpy cleaned up pretty well. "We meet again. How have you been?"

"Extremely busy," he replied. "Apollo 10 returned last week. We've been debriefing the crew as well as starting the final push for the next mission, the big one." Dixon expected her to be bored by his science talk but was surprised to see her hanging on his words.

She said, "That's amazing—you get to work with all that groovy space stuff. You said the other night, that you're the operations chief. Does that make you the boss?"

Dixon chuckled modestly. "One of them I suppose. The *boss* is Jack Monroe."

Dani wondered if Jack Monroe was Mr. Shiny Hair. "Is he a nice guy?"

"Sometimes. He used to be a Navy pilot. He fought in the Korean War, where he met Neil Armstrong. But Jack was shot down and wounded in combat. So badly he was grounded. He never flew again."

"Wounded how?"

Dixon's eyes fell to his drink. "I'll tell you some other time. Tell me," he stirred his drink with a cocktail straw. "What's a pretty girl like you doing at a bar with a dirty old man like me?"

Dani covered with an embarrassed smile. "We like the same music."

Dixon thought of Elvis hidden safely in the space center, preparing a surprise Dani couldn't possibly expect. "Okay, mystery woman, what's your claim to fame?"

"Mystery woman?" She grinned.

"I know hardly a thing about you. What do you do for a living? What's going to make you famous?"

"Nothing, really," she scratched her head as if she had no idea. "I'm just getting started. I work out of New York for CBS. I'm the liaison for the local television network here. Plenty of travel, lots of contacts."

"I'm sure. Do you live in New York or Houston?"

"Both," she replied. The questions were making her more nervous than she expected. She started tapping the side of her wine glass with her fingernail.

Tap, tap. Tap, tap.

"My home is New York," she continued. "But I spend a lot of my time here. In fact, I'll be in Houston most of the summer, what with the moon landing and everything."

Tap, tap. Tap, tap.

Dixon noticed her tapping and ignored it. "It's a media circus around here." he said and glanced around nervously, fearing he was coming across a loss for words. "So long as they stay out of *my* way, I'm happy. I don't mean you, of course."

"Of course," Dani smiled, accepting the implied apology. She decided the ice had been broken and it was time to dig deeper. "Being such an Elvis fan," she leaned a bit closer, "you must usually know where he is. Where he's going to appear next."

Tap, tap. Tap, tap.

Dixon observed her tapping and began to count along in rhythm. One, two. Three, four. Tap, tap. Tap, tap. Oddly, her statement was true but Dixon shook his head and lied. "I have no idea where he is. I'm a fan, but I'm not obsessed."

"You must be," she poked his hand with a cocky smile. "You have his expired health insurance card." Her voice stressed the lunacy of the nostalgia. Both she and Dixon burst into laughter.

When he calmed himself, Dixon admitted, "I'm a collector; it's been a hobby of mine for quite some time. My house is full of Presley artifacts and folklore. Top of the line merchandise, top of the line trivia too. How many of us can claim we know the legend of the Ivory Elvis?"

"I won't ask what that is," Dani laughed, amused by his playful sarcasm. "How did you get so into him?"

Dixon shrugged. "Don't know. I played piano and guitar in my younger years, long before rock and roll was ever invented. I lost interested when I started college but then Chuck Berry and Elvis Presley burst onto the scene, and immediately I wished I was fifteen again."

"I *was* fifteen!" Dani announced, elated with nostalgia. "And they were great, weren't they?"

Dixon smiled. "They were great!"

Dani decided to try the question Dixon had evaded when they first met. "Ever been to Graceland?"

It caught him off guard, but he still smiled. "No," he said. "I've never been to Graceland." Immediately he wondered if he had been spotted there, but the odds of her seeing him in Memphis and then running into him in Houston were impossible. Weren't they?

Liar! Thought Dani.

She acted surprised. "Don't you ever travel?"

"Sure, I travel. Not nearly as much as I used to, but I get around."

"You've been to Memphis?"

Dixon started growing uncomfortable. "Sure, I've been there."

"What kind of an Elvis Presley fan *doesn't* stop by Graceland when he's in Memphis?"

Dixon needed to change the subject. He suspected the girl was up to something and figured he was about to get burned. A voice told him to get up, and walk away. Say goodnight. Bid farewell. But instead, he said, "You a Marilyn Monroe fan?"

Dani shrugged and filed her Graceland tidbits away for later. "I think her life was interesting"

Few celebrities were more sensational than Marilyn Monroe. Dani had been in college when she saw the news report of Marilyn's death. She was one of the reasons Dani had decided to become a journalist. It had always been a dream of Dani's to sit back and schmooze with such a cultural goddess.

But now Elvis Presley had replaced her at the top of Dani's list. And this guy, Peter Dixon, held the key to the gates. Even if Dixon wouldn't admit it, he knew the way to Elvis.

And if he couldn't get her to Elvis, he could lead her to Neil Armstrong, the next best thing. Dixon had the in. Everything around him was the story. Dani was starting to like this guy, as sneaky as he was. He was definitely a good man to know.

"I liked *Some Like It Hot*," Dixon said. "I love the banter between Jack Lemmon and Tony Curtis."

"I love their woman costumes," Dani giggled. "Jack Lemmon is so prissy. Curtis is just a brute."

Dixon laughed. "What could they do? They're hiding from the Mafia. And when Tony Curtis becomes Junior from Shell Oil, he's able to fool Marilyn Monroe with *two* false identities."

Dani agreed. "They have no choice but to pretend they're someone else."

Dixon thought of *The Parent Trap* and his ensuing discussion with Jimmy Orr. "Everyone's got a secret identity," he said.

There followed an uncomfortable silence.

Dani looked at her watch. "It's about that time. Movie starts in ten minutes." She slammed the rest of her wine. "Shall we?"

Dixon nodded and reached for his wallet.

"Allow me," Dani stopped him. She reached into her pocketbook and laid a handful of bills on the bar.

"I'll pick up the movie," Dixon offered in return.

"Fair enough," Dani nodded as she snapped her pocketbook shut. Then she unsnapped it, and snapped it again.

"What was that?"

She saw Dixon was pointing at her pocketbook. "What was what?"

"You closed your pocketbook, then opened it and closed it again." Dixon thought of her tapping her wine glass in rhythm. One, two. Three, four. "Why'd you do it twice?"

"It's nothing," Dani played it off. "I just wanted to make sure my car keys were inside. It's nothing. Let's enjoy the movie."

They did. They laughed in all the same places, Dani even reached over and grabbed his hand as they chuckled. After the movie they took a walk around the block, through the neighborhood, and finally back to Dani's car. There they parted with a hug and with Dani handing Dixon her number at the hotel.

"You give me a tour of that space center one day," she said as she climbed into her car. Dixon closed the door behind her and stood watching as she drove away.

The evening had been a success. He liked Kim and she seemed to enjoy his company, although Dixon had no idea he was being used for her own personal benefit. He figured he'd try to keep it together for at least a few months. Cautious as he was about Kim, her company was good therapy, relief from the stress of NASA.

At her hotel Dani tried sorting her facts into a story. Peter Dixon had met Elvis Presley at Graceland and Dixon had later claimed that he never met Elvis and had never been to Graceland. Then there was Jimmy Orr. He probably fit into this puzzle, but Dani needed more information before she could guess how.

She could always make her way back to the Slop Ranch and talk to Jimmy herself, but at the risk of being encountered by Dixon. She would decide on that later. The next step was to solidify her bond with Stumpy Pete, to get into his house and look through his stuff. That little trickster was hiding something. Something better than two guys hopping around a giant sandbox with glass bubbles on their heads.

Before she could go after Dixon, there was something Dani needed to take care of. She waited until morning and called Baker at home. He was still in bed and the phone rang several times before he picked it up groggily and answered, "Hullo?"

"Richard, it's almost noon. Are you still asleep?"

"Had a late night," he sounded hung over. "Saw Led Zeppelin at the Filmore. You should have been there, they were fantastic!"

"I'm not into acid rock. Say, Richard, I'm going to be here for a few weeks."

"You got a scoop?"

"I've got something."

Baker was slowly waking up. Now he turned and sat up on the edge of his bed, rubbing his eyes. His young wife was still sleeping behind him. "What are you working on?"

"I'm not sure yet," Dani admitted.

"Then why do you need me on a Sunday morning?"

"I need to extend my stay in Houston, and I'm running out of money. Have to renew the rental car, the hotel, my appetite."

Baker sighed. "Sure," he said. He didn't like floating her bill, but he trusted her. If she said she needed to stay and follow a lead, then it had to be something good. "I'll wire your paycheck."

"Great," Dani said. "Thanks, Richard. I owe you one."

The next morning Dixon awoke early and went for a jog, but ended up at McDonald's instead. Seeing Kim motivated him to trim down and get back into shape, but it had been only his second session of exercise that calendar year. He did more walking than running and after panting for four blocks, he gave up and carried his side-ache to McDonald's for pancakes, and a copy of the Sunday paper.

Monday he arrived at the space center with new life. There was a bounce in his step that annoyed Jack Monroe to high heaven. "Why so upbeat?" he scowled when he saw Dixon with a rare Monday morning smile.

"Had a good weekend."

Monroe frowned. "What's this blasé attitude? Get laid or something?"

"No," Dixon said carelessly. "Just had a nice date."

Monroe rolled his eyes. "Dating is for high school kids."

Now Dixon frowned. Only Jack Monroe could take the wind so effortlessly out of his sails. Dixon poured himself some coffee and followed Jack to the NASA soundstage.

Today NASA was conducting a full dress rehearsal for the Concert from the Sea of Tranquility. A gigantic soundstage had been decorated into an impressive moonscape. An *Eagle* lander mockup rested in a sea of gray sand and rocks. The walls were painted with three-dimensional scenery, so the lunar horizon appeared to be miles and miles away. A half-Earth was painted in the darkness above the surface. The vast room made the cast and crew feel isolated, as if they were actually standing, and working on the moon. Monroe wanted the astronauts to practice in the most authentic environment NASA could muster.

They wore their spacesuits and practiced their exit from the *Eagle* one at a time. Elvis went first, then Neil, then Buzz. NASA cameras filmed the rehearsal for later analysis and critique, as the astronauts prepared the concert stage and Elvis sat down to sing his song. It was still a mystery as to what he'd sing, and the eager NASA bunch was already starting to place bets on what song he would choose. Elvis still didn't want to give away the surprise, so he sang *Twinkle, Twinkle Little Star* instead, and still sounded terrific.

After rehearsal, a worried Jack Monroe approached the King. "Sounded great, Elvis, but I had just one question."

"Sure. Lay it on me, baby."

"I know this is only rehearsal, and I know you're not going to reveal your choice for the moon-song until show time, but I was just hoping..."

Elvis waited as Jack struggled with the words.

Finally, the NASA Administrator said, "You're not going to sing *Twinkle, Twinkle Little Star* up there, are you?"

"Heck no!" said Elvis. "This is just practice. I've got something special lined up instead."

"Good," Monroe exhaled. "I wouldn't want you to embarrass anyone with kid stuff like that. We're hoping for something that really packs a punch."

Elvis understood. "No need to worry about me, baby!"

Chapter Eight

I was back to business as usual. The crew became acquainted with the new mission parameters as Elvis Presley's flight training continued. The chief concern was the lack of space within the capsules. The tight fit meant there could be hardly any movement without someone bumping into someone or something else. Elvis was two weeks into his water diet, and had lost only two pounds. Hardly enough.

Monroe wondered, "Does this guy have the metabolism of a can of syrup, or is someone sneaking him hamburgers in the middle of the night?"

Dixon ignored Monroe's defeatist comments and concentrated on choreographing the astronauts' every movement. Their on-board actions would be as scripted and rehearsed as the actual flight operations. Dixon was so busy he barely had time to think about Kim Clark and their date the weekend before. He never even got to check and see if the Lunar Elvis action figures had arrived.

Thursday he called her just to say hello. They decided to meet Saturday for lunch and a tour of the space center. Dixon had the rest of the week to make sure Elvis was locked away and all evidence of Operation Blue Moon was hidden for Kim's visit.

Dani spent that week learning the layout of Houston. She tried writing an article detailing her experience at Graceland, but a few paragraphs in she realized there was no story without Elvis. Peter Dixon was more interesting. It seemed her relationship with the NASA man was going to last, and she needed to cover the details of her concocted life.

Her story of being a network liaison for CBS would be credible only if she showed competent knowledge of the city. She drove all over town, she navigated the 610 beltway, and north on Interstate 45, then east to Houston Intercontinental Airport, which would open next Sunday, and replace Hobby Airport. Further south on 45 was Ellington Field, where the astronauts flew flight ops, and then the Manned Spacecraft Center, where Dixon worked.

Off 610 in the southwest corner of the city, Dani found the Houston Astrodome. Downtown at 7000 Regency Square Boulevard was her "office" at CBS Houston. She learned it all, from Galveston Bay to Cullen Baker Park.

More important than all the great landmarks of the city, however, was the inside of Peter Dixon's home. There had to be more useful information in his house than anywhere in the city. She needed to find a way to infiltrate it as she had done at Graceland.

There were five Peter Dixons in the Houston phone book. Two lived in apartments between Texas Southern and the University of Houston. Most likely college students. The other three lived in houses. The first house she drove by was in the slums, and she quickly crossed it off the list. The next was in North Houston, the opposite side of town from the space center, at least an hour drive for Dixon. The last Peter Dixon lived in Pasadena, roughly ten miles from the space complex.

When Dani drove past this house she knew it had to be the one. It was modest in size and showed no signs of children or a family. No toys in the yard, no life in the plants. It almost looked like the house had been abandoned. Not run down or shabby, but like the lonely dwelling of a hermit.

Soon Dani would find her way inside.

Saturday afternoon they met at a hole-in-the-wall burger joint outside Pasadena. Even on Saturday Dixon wore a tie and a jacket. He looked tired.

"Been busy?"

He nodded as he stabbed a handful of fries into a puddle of ketchup. "I was in early this morning, after staying late last night. It's hectic, long hours. What have you been up to?"

"Just working."

"When do you head back to New York?"

She concentrated on her burger. "I don't know. Probably not for a while. I want to try to get down to Florida for the launch."

Dixon sighed. "The launch. Less than six weeks until the launch."

"You look worn."

"Been having these cramps. I don't know. Probably just need more exercise." He hadn't had the time to do any running since his marathon last Sunday, and the stomach pains had returned with the long hours at work.

Dani watched him. He looked beat, but he managed to smile and hold a pleasant conversation throughout their lunch. It was mostly small talk; they both knew there'd be a lot to say once they were in the space center.

Dixon still debated whether or not he should bring her on the tour. Monroe might be there and he'd surely frown on Dixon bringing an unnecessary set of eyes into the building, even if all Elvis-related operations were confined to the most secure locations. But Monroe mentioned he was meeting the governor for tennis later that afternoon, so most likely he'd be gone.

Dani didn't expect to see much at the space center in the way of *TSN* material. It would be nice to meet

Neil Armstrong, but how could she organize an exclusive interview with Dixon at her side?

She'd keep her eyes open for any clue of a connection to Elvis, but her plan was to get back to Dixon's house. She intended to look through his stuff, even if it meant spending the night. If she expected to rummage through Dixon's belongings for clues, there was no avoiding at least some intimacy.

It wouldn't be too bad, she decided as Dixon showed her around the space center. He was a lonely man, but he was fairly attractive. Dani enjoyed his company enough to get a little closer. As long as she didn't get *too* close—her plan was to take the story and run.

She was blown away when Dixon led her into the Apollo Mission control room in Building 40. It was a technological wonder, filled with computer consoles and giant television screens. The room was idle as no spacecraft was in flight, but Dani was amazed at Dixon's explanation of each computer console. She had no idea it was this complicated.

"But when it's all working together it's pretty smooth," he said. "You should see this place during a mission. You've never experienced anxiety like that." He smiled when he said it, as if he wanted Dani to know—despite the headaches—how much he enjoyed his work and that he lived for the challenge.

He took her to his office. She peeked inside for a moment but there was really nothing to see. It was much cleaner than Richard Baker's, and more spacious but, no clue of Elvis was anywhere to be found.

Down the hall Dixon could see Monroe's office door was still open. A light was on inside. Dixon hurried to direct her around a corner so they could miss Monroe, but it was too late. The light in Jack's office went out as he appeared in the doorway with a pile of folders under his arm. He closed the door, locked it behind him, and turned to see Dixon before he was out of sight.

"Pete." Monroe was surprised to see him and even more surprised to see the girl. He approached them calmly, waiting for Dixon's explanation.

"Jack," Dixon said nonchalantly. "My friend, Kim Clark. Kim, Jack Monroe."

She smiled and shook hands with Mr. Shiny Hair. Mr. Slick, Peter Dixon's cohort at the mansion in Memphis. Although she took a liking to Peter Dixon, seeing Mr. Shiny Hair reminded her of the failure at Graceland. These men were responsible for that, and for pushing her into what seemed to be turning into a wild-goose chase. She was still seething inwardly about the opportunity they had cost her.

"Nice to meet you," she smiled at Jack who seemed to sneer at her.

Monroe looked to Dixon. "What's going on?"

"Just giving her a little tour," Dixon said, wanting to wink at Jack and assure him everything was okay. The boss wasn't happy, just as Dixon had predicted.

Monroe perceived Kim as a threat. If Dixon let her get too close, she could learn of the surprise concert from the Sea of Tranquility and ruin it for everybody. No, Monroe decided. He didn't like Kim Clark one bit. He said to her without smiling, "I hope you enjoy what you see here."

Dixon didn't like the growing tension. He reminded Monroe about his tennis date with the governor.

"He can wait a few more minutes," Monroe said and shot a quick glare of disapproval at Dixon before he marched off and disappeared into a stairwell.

"What a jerk," Dani grunted after he'd gone.

Dixon agreed. "Yeah, he gets like that."

Then Monroe's voice echoed from the stairwell, "I can still hear you!"

And Dani and Peter scurried away laughing.

After they finished the tour, Dixon drove Dani back

to the burger joint where her car was parked. Once they arrived, they were confronted with what they should do next. It was late afternoon on Saturday, and Dani saw this as the perfect opportunity to find her way inside Dixon's home.

Before she stepped out of his car she smiled at him. "What are you doing later?"

Dixon didn't want to see her go just yet. This evening had potential. "What do you have in mind?"

A bashful smile, a gentle shrug. "What do you say we go back to your place and whatever happens, happens?"

She took her car and they sped to Dixon's house. He led her in through the kitchen door on the side of the house. The front door opened into the living room where Dixon's Elvis shrine still housed the Elvis moon rock placard. If Kim saw that, the cover was blown and Dixon could be out of a job.

He seated her at the kitchen table and offered her a drink. Dani chose beer and looked over Dixon's kitchen Elvis shrine as he excused himself, telling her he needed to use the bathroom. On the way, he snatched the Elvis moon rock placard, the mug and the fingernail and stashed them away in his bedroom closet.

Dani waited in the kitchen. This shrine was light on trinkets and heavy on pictures. There were several photos of the young 50's Elvis taped to the refrigerator. Two magazine covers hung on the wall. One was *Movie Land* from 1956, with a headline, "Elvis Presley Fights His Critics" and the other was *Movie Life* with a headline, "Why Elvis Can't Sleep Nights." Below the magazine covers was an 8x10 of a young Elvis Presley wearing a shiny gold suit, and on the counter beside the telephone was a 1968 Comeback Cookie Jar, sculpted to Elvis Presley's likeness.

Dixon returned shortly and Dani said, "I can't believe with all this Elvis stuff you've never met the guy."

He was tempted to tell her not only of Operation Blue Moon, but also of how he had bonded with the King and was becoming friends with His Greatness. But those were stories for another day. He only needed to hold off for another six weeks.

Now Dixon led her into the living room so she could see the main Elvis shrine. She was drawn to the room's centerpiece, the statuette atop Dixon's symphonizer.

"The Ivory Elvis," he announced proudly. "This is a replica. The real one Elvis keeps in the Jungle Room at Graceland."

Dani thought back to her visit to Graceland. She had only walked through the famous Jungle Room but she did remember seeing a similar figurine. Dani asked, "How do you know the real Ivory Elvis is in Graceland?"

Dixon smiled, invited her to sit on the couch, and told the legend. She was angered by the malicious elephant poachers and touched by Scott Richter's compassion. When she asked about the whereabouts of Moja, Dixon raised his hands and told her nobody knew what had happened to him. He had disappeared into the jungle after giving the sculpture to Richter and was never heard from again.

Dani couldn't help but be touched by Dixon's love of the story and how Elvis helped Richter destroy the elephant poachers in Tanzania. She moved close to Dixon, so that her knee touched his. He noticed this and turned to look at her. Moments later they were kissing, then groping, then Dixon led her into his bedroom.

They stayed there for the rest of the night, rolling between the sheets like college kids discovering sex for the first time. Though Dani felt a twinge of uneasiness about using sex to get into Dixon's head, she climaxed twice before Dixon had finished his first.

As they fell exhausted beside each other, gazing at the ceiling shoulder-to-shoulder, Dixon said, "This is nice...Let's try to keep this going, for at least a couple months."

Dani snuggled close to him, saying yes without saying a word. They were silent for a long while, savoring the moment. Dixon even considered telling Kim about the all-new Apollo 11 but decided against it once again.

Then Dani said, "I came twice."

"Yeah," Dixon hummed.

"How about you?"

"Once," Dixon said. "I'm still trying to catch my breath."

"That's three orgasms," Dani noted. "You need to have another."

Dixon glanced her direction. "Say *what?*"

"You need to come again. That way we both did twice."

Dixon didn't understand her reasoning, but it was logic no man could protest. They did it again and Dixon was spent for the rest of the evening. As they held each other close, Dani asked about Jack Monroe, wondering if Mr. Slick would be any help to her mission. It was awkward to ask from a post-coital embrace, but Dani did it anyway.

Dixon was slightly jealous that Kim was thinking about Dr. Monroe at this moment, but the feeling passed as quickly as it came. He told her, "Jack's dealt with some serious shit in his life. He used to work for President Kennedy."

"What about his Korean War injury?"

Dixon couldn't help but laugh at how he was about to abase his boss. Thinking back to their uncomfortable encounter with Jack's attitude earlier that day, Dixon decided he would tell Kim the story. "Jack flew an F-4. He was flying a mission above the Yalu River. Anti-aircraft fire was pretty heavy that day. His jet took a few rounds, one of which penetrated the cockpit from below. A bullet came through the floor and hit him right in the balls. I'm dead serious when I say that. The shell brushed his thigh, hit a testicle, kept going, deflected off his facemask and fell dead.

"Jack lost control, took another blaze of gunfire across the wings and his jet went down. Jack ejected, bleeding and nearly unconscious, he parachuted into the sea where a rescue chopper met him and brought him back to the carrier. Jack survived, but his left testicle did not."

Dani had been suppressing laughter this whole time, and when Dixon finished she let it out. "My God," she exclaimed. "Mr. Shiny Hair only has one ball!"

"Mr. Shiny Hair?" Dixon squinted. "Yeah, he has only one. Can you image the damage to the psyche? It's part of why his wife left him."

"It also explains why he's such a jerk."

Dixon felt he needed to defend his boss after revealing so personal a tale. "He's not always a jerk, he's just a little egotistical. Went to work for Kennedy after he was grounded. Jack actually wrote JFK's famous man-on-the-moon speech."

"I didn't know that," Dani said, genuinely impressed.

"Nobody does," Dixon said. "Jack did all kinds of things for JFK, marvelous work. A lot of things he won't talk about, no matter how drunk he gets."

"Is he related to Marilyn Monroe?"

"Don't ask," Dixon said.

"Why not?"

"Because Jack hates it when people ask him that."

Dani laughed. There were so many secrets, so much mystery, so much to hide. Those brains held more bullshit than a convention of used car salesmen. These were absolutely the right men to know. She snuggled closer to Dixon, and threw him a curveball. "Tell me about your wife."

Dixon sighed and became quiet for a long while.

"I'm sorry," she said. "Should I not have asked?"

"We didn't have much of a marriage," he started. "I used to work for the military as a civilian. I traveled constantly, all over the world. I was never, ever, ever there for her." Dixon paused a moment to think about Maggie. "We thought getting married would make us happy. For a short while, it made us happier but it didn't make us happy. I was a workaholic. She left; I was recruited by Dr. Monroe."

Dani tried to comfort him. "There's nothing wrong with being a workaholic."

"I have no social life," he said. "Just a job and a hobby, this fascination with Elvis Presley."

Dani laughed. She longed to confront him about his trip to Graceland. To tell him flat out that she had seen him at the mansion. She said, "I still can't believe you've never met the King."

"Believe it," he said with conviction, and kissed her on the forehead. She hid her frown by snuggling closer. If Dixon wasn't going to talk, Dani needed to proceed with her plan. She intended to wait until he was asleep so she could snoop around and see what he had to hide. In the meantime she rested her head on his chest and relaxed.

With his arm still around her they lay still. Dixon's breathing started to slow and soon it became a quiet snore. She waited another twenty minutes and when she was certain Dixon had fallen into a deep sleep, Dani slipped out of bed.

Besides the bed, his bedroom had only a dresser, a nightstand, and an old recliner. She needed to explore the house. She tiptoed through the darkness and made her way down the hall to Dixon's study.

As dark as it was, Dani could see a couch on one side of the study and a desk on the other. Behind the desk was a wall of bookshelves and a stack of file cabinets. The walls were covered with framed photographs but none of them had anything to do with Elvis. This was Dixon's NASA shrine. Each picture was Dixon with a different astronaut. Dixon with John Glenn. Dixon with Alan Shepard. Dixon with Deke Slayton. Dixon with Neil Armstrong. There was a picture of Dixon and Jack Monroe fishing with Buzz Aldrin and a photograph of planet earth taken from outer space. There were plaques and diplomas above the bookshelf. Dixon had a degree in economic theory and a Masters in physics. Dani's eye fell to the file cabinets. She longed for a copy machine and hours of time, but with only a few minutes available, she had to work quickly.

She started with the papers on the desk, but they contained nothing but NASA gibberish that Dani did not understand. She moved to the desk drawers. The long drawer on top held nothing but pens, paper clips and scraps of paper. The first side drawer was filled with folders and notepads. She pulled them out and started paging through. More NASA documents, but nothing that caught her eye.

On a yellow legal pad, Dani came across a strange list of breakfast foods. The Eggs, The Bacon, The Jellyrolls and more. She had heard Dixon using these words once before, but she had no idea what they meant. Probably code words for some Top Secret NASA operation. Dani put the list away and shuffled through more folders. At the very bottom of the drawer, she came across a photograph. It was Dixon, slightly younger, with his arm around a pretty brunette. They were sitting at a restaurant table, both smiling. Maggie, Dani thought. Dixon's ex-wife. They looked very happy that day. It was a shame things hadn't worked out.

Despite his lying about the Graceland encounter, Dixon was a sweet man. A nice guy, a good listener, and judging by his lifestyle, he brought home a pretty decent paycheck. If he hadn't ruined her shot at Elvis, she mused, Peter Dixon may have been a good match.

A toilet suddenly flushed. Dani froze in place and strained to listen for footsteps. The bathroom was just down the hall, but the house was dead silent. She inched around the desk towards the hall and stopped at the doorway. Quickly she peered around the corner and saw the bathroom door was closed; a sliver of light crept out from underneath it.

Dani slipped into the hallway and hurried in the opposite direction to the living room, then to the kitchen. There she felt safe and more able to explain her absence from the bedroom. She opened the refrigerator and retrieved a gallon jug of water just as Dixon shuffled around the corner wearing boxers and a T-shirt. His eyes were half-closed.

"Thirsty?" Dani asked.

He shook his head. "Stomach pain woke me up."

She handed him the water jug, and Dixon took a hearty gulp. He handed it back to her and turned to leave. Dani watched him disappear into the living room. He had been unaware of her unproductive visit to the study. He still had no idea why she was in this relationship. And with no story for *The Sensational Nation*, Dani wondered if she had been wasting her time on Peter Dixon.

Chapter Nine

June 9th

"**W**here have you been?"

"Following leads," she told Baker. It was her Monday morning call to *TSN* headquarters.

"That NASA angle," he said. "What's the deal?"

"I skipped the rank and file and went right to top brass. There's a story here, Richard, but it's not quite finished."

"Apollo 11 is *the story* of the summer. You're talking to Neil Armstrong, are you not?"

"No," Dani said and nibbled a fingernail. She feared Baker would not let her off easy.

"Buzz Aldrin then?"

"No." She wanted to tell him about her encounters with Pete Dixon, and the connections between Graceland and NASA, but Baker would never publish speculation. She needed to stall. "I met the Administrator," she said. "He's helping me out."

Baker jogged his memory. "Ah, yes, Jack Monroe!"

"You know him?"

"Of him," Baker said. "He was a name during the Kennedy presidency. Apparently he played a part in ending the Cuban Missile Crisis."

"Well, I need a few more days, Richard."

A warning. "You're running out of time. If you want your contribution in the July issue, we need something by the end of next week."

"Next week?" It was time to gamble with her Graceland card. "I found my way into Graceland, Richard. I met Priscilla, Liberace, Brando, Berry...I met *Liza*."

"When was this?"

She told him of her accident with Liberace and the ensuing visit to the Presley mansion.

"That's incredible," Richard remarked once she finished. "You've got a knack for tracking down the big names. But we can't use any of this in the magazine. Without Elvis, a party at Graceland is just tabloid garbage. You can do better than that, Dani. And you've got two weeks to make it happen."

She agreed, and her next call was to Peter Dixon. "What are you doing this week?"

He was pouring his morning coffee. "Working. What's up?"

"I wanted to check in to see if maybe we can get together later."

Dixon thought it was a bit strange that Kim was calling first thing Monday morning to set up a date, but that thought was banished by his sudden realization that she was becoming irresistible. "Sure, I want to get together. I think Jack's having some kind of party this Friday. A small thing at his house. Interested?"

"Sure!"

Pleased, Dixon told Dani he'd pick her up early Friday evening for the coat-and-tie affair. He looked forward to another chance to get close to Kim. Dani, on the other hand, was after gossip from NASA brass.

Friday arrived quickly. Dixon met Dani in the lobby of her hotel and drove her to Jack Monroe's. They dressed as if they were to dine in a five star restaurant: Dixon in a suit, and Dani in a cocktail dress.

Monroe lived in El Lago, the NASA enclave outside Houston, in a house he'd purchased after the divorce. His house stood taller than Dixon's, more elegant. More arrogant, Dani thought as they parked on the street near a handful of luxury sedans. As they approached the house, they could see through the large front window that several astronauts and NASA brass were already inside, schmoozing and clinking glasses with the head of NASA.

Dani was nervous about entering the home of Jack Monroe. He was the boss of NASA but he was also one of the most arrogant people Dani had ever met and she knew he didn't want her around. Thankfully, Dixon would be there to watch her back and ward off Monroe's dirty looks.

The lawn and hedges around the house were neatly trimmed, probably by landscapers. Monroe wouldn't have time to do it himself. The driveway was freshly paved and the house looked to have a new paintjob. Monroe took pride in his property and kept it as clean and shiny as his hair.

Dani giggled and Dixon asked why. "No reason," she said, and wrapped her arm in his. Dixon knocked on the front door, and it opened to a smiling Jack Monroe.

"Hey," he shook hands with Dixon. "Come on in."

Dani stepped into an elegant foyer that opened into a wide living room filled with white couches and white carpet. Hallways extended from either side of the foyer. To the right was the kitchen; to the left, a bedroom and part of an office. A half dozen guests mingled in the living room, two astronauts stood at a bar to the right. Pop Art decorated the living room, a wall of photographs stood behind the bar along with a reprint of Warhol's Marilyn Monroe silkscreen. Again, Dani wondered about Jack's relationship with the platinum blonde star.

"Kim, right?" Jack was smiling at her.

"Yes," she nodded. "Kim Clark."

Jack pointed to the bar. "Pour you guys a drink?"

They agreed. Dani was surprised that Mr. Shiny Hair could be so cordial. Then she decided that anyone would be more relaxed at a social setting in his own home.

Monroe led them to a bar where the two astronauts stood admiring Jack's photographs. As Jack mixed gin and tonics, Dani and Dixon looked over the pictures. There was one of Jack shaking hands with President Kennedy in the Oval Office, and another of Dr. Monroe with Lyndon Johnson. Next to that was Monroe with RFK. They wore T-shirts and sunglasses and were toasting bottles of beer beside someone's swimming pool.

There was another picture of a younger Jack Monroe in a U.S. Navy flight suit with his arm around a young Neil Armstrong. Dani smiled and remembered the old war story about the bullet and Jack's testicle.

The last picture was Jack fishing in the tropics with two men Dani did not recognize. One of the astronauts at the bar turned to her. He had dark hair that was straight and short, and the cocky smile of a fighter jock. He pointed at the picture of Jack fishing. "Richard Feynman and J. Robert Oppenheimer."

Dani raised an eyebrow. "The atomic bomb guys?"

Monroe handed her a gin and tonic. "The original A-bomb guys. I knew them back in the 50's."

Dani smiled. "Sensational."

Dixon asked Dani, "Have you met Al?"

"No," she looked back to the fighter pilot, who smiled pleasantly.

"Alan Shepard." He introduced himself and they shook hands.

Dixon said, "The first American in space."

"Cool," Dani grinned as a *TSN* article started budding in her mind. Dixon introduced her as Kim and then she met the other man at the bar, a more serious man with a crew cut, named Deke Slayton, NASA's Director of Flight Crew Operations—a member of

Operation Blue Moon's inner circle.

"Tell us, Kim," Jack said. "What line of work are you in?"

She nervously cleared her throat. "I work for CBS. I'm a network liaison for here...and New York...for television, here in Houston." A curt nod and Dani waited for Monroe's response.

He only smiled, looking deeper. Inspecting her.

Dixon nudged Dani and pointed towards the couch. "Over there is John Glenn, Kim, the first American to orbit the earth." Dani looked to the couches where John Glenn was talking to the wives of Shepard and Slayton as well as his own spouse, Anna.

Monroe tapped Dixon on the elbow. "Help me in the kitchen, will you?"

Dixon followed his boss. Once they were alone, Monroe glared at him. "CBS?"

"She's just a messenger, Jack. A liaison. She's not a reporter."

"I don't like it." Jack handed Dixon two bottles of wine. "Bring these to the bar. And keep your girlfriend out of our business."

"Yes, sir," Dixon said and brought more wine out to the party.

The evening moved along pleasantly. Dani and Dixon talked with John Glenn and his wife and learned that Glenn had become a business executive after leaving the astronaut corps. He was in town on a visit. Deke Slayton told Dani that he had been grounded in 1959 because of a heart condition, but that he hoped to fly again one day.

Monroe gave her a guided tour of his art collection and she really dug his Warhol. She discovered Jack Monroe wasn't such a bad guy, and she admired his taste.

But the person whom Dani enjoyed the most was Alan Shepard. She was fascinated that he had blazed

America's trail into space. He told her how the space race between the United States and the Soviets had once been neck-and-neck, tooth-and-nail, but was now a turkey shoot, with the U.S. running away with the grand prize.

Dani learned Shepard had been restored to active flight status just weeks earlier after corrective surgery for an inner-ear disorder. He told her the talk was that he'd be going to the moon on Apollo 14 as long as everything went as planned.

She was amazed by the people she met, with their knowledge and their experience. She wondered, maybe this could be her chance to get dirt on Elvis Presley's connection to NASA.

She steered the conversation to music and then asked Shepard what he thought about Elvis, but he was either clueless or playing dumb. He said he liked the King's music, but that's about all he would say. She wondered if there was any connection at all, if she should conclude Dixon was nothing more than an Elvis fanatic.

But there was that secret. That trip to Graceland Dixon had denied.

Her eyes fell upon Jack Monroe. He had been at Graceland too, and judging by the decorations in his home, he wasn't a tenth the fan Dixon was. She moseyed over to the NASA Administrator as he mixed another round of drinks at the bar.

"So what kind of music are you into, Jack?"

He shrugged. "Blues, mostly. I like Robert Johnson and Willie Dixon and Buddy Guy. Eddie Cochran was fun when I was twenty-something, trying to get laid."

They both laughed and Dani slid her empty cocktail glass across the bar. Jack took it and poured another gin and tonic. "What about Elvis?"

Monroe sensed an ulterior motive right away. "What about him?"

"Ever seen him?"

"Sure. Dallas, 1958. He was fantastic."

Dani smiled at Jack. She was onto something and they both knew it. She decided to end the conversation and make her way back to Dixon. Monroe watched her walk away and wondered if Dixon had leaked their plan to his new girlfriend, if Operation Blue Moon had been revealed to non-NASA ears.

Monroe hoped—Monroe *prayed*—that his lieutenant had the fortitude to keep his mouth shut about Elvis. If Monroe's instincts were correct, this Kim Clark babe was bad news, and she needed to be dealt with immediately.

But what could he do about her? He could only trust Dixon's judgment and pour himself another drink. Which is exactly what he did.

Dani spent the next day writing an article about Alan Shepard and his leadership throughout the space race. It actually turned out to be better than she had expected, so she signed her name and sent it off to *TSN*.

By Monday night, Baker called to tell her it was a good piece, but not something he could use in the July issue. "Alan seems like a nice guy but he's old news, Dani. Neil Armstrong is the man everyone wants to hear from."

"But sitting with him is like sitting with the Pope. He's impossible to get to. And he's press-shy."

Baker shoveled a spoonful of clam chowder into his mouth and dripped half of it onto his tie. "Tell you what," he cleaned himself with a napkin. "This Friday Hendrix is playing the Newport Pop Fest in California. Ike and Tina will be there and so will Joe Cocker. I can set you up."

"If we're going to stick with music, why not go for Elvis?"

"Won't happen. Elvis is out of the spotlight until the 31st of July."

"What happens then?"

"Elvis returns to Vegas. Maybe you can catch him then. But by that time we're into our August issue, looking at Woodstock."

Dani sighed. "Jimi Hendrix, huh?"

"Unless you cook up something at NASA within the next couple days."

"I'll get back to you." Dani hung up and headed to the hotel bar to ponder her agenda over a Bloody Mary.

June 18th

Jack Monroe worked late. It was something he didn't mind doing, something he almost needed to do. The work could wait until tomorrow, but Jack Monroe could not. A classic Type A, he'd go crazy if he just stood around doing nothing.

He stayed in his office until darkness fell, analyzing data from the last flight readiness test. Everything looked good for the scheduled launch of Apollo 11 on July 16th. Even Elvis had passed his physical and flight competency tests with flying colors.

Now Jack went to the bar in his office and poured himself a brandy. He gazed out his window and across the space complex. It was quieter than normal; most employees had gone home for the day, but many would be working until daylight. He noticed a two-trailer semi driving across the lot. Jack wondered what was being delivered so late in the day.

Five minutes later a phone call from the warehouse answered his question. The foreman said, "They need your signature on this one, Dr. Monroe."

Jack understood. The last of the Blue Moon merchandise had arrived. He finished his drink, locked his office and headed to the warehouse.

It was the Elvis Presley lunar action figures. Children's toys Dixon had proposed they sell after the concert in the Sea of Tranquility. It was a brilliant idea. These things could generate millions of dollars in revenue for the space agency.

Tom Parker had been against the idea at first, but Elvis had insisted. As an act of patriotism, NASA would use Elvis Presley's likeness for their space toys, the coffee mugs, the T-shirts and the board game.

Monroe signed the invoice and sent the foreman on his way. No one knew what was inside these hundreds of boxes except for Monroe and Dixon (and the people at the secret government factory who had manufactured the toys). Monroe opened a box and fished inside for a Lunar Elvis action figure.

They were beautiful, and Jack Monroe grinned.

Chapter Ten

"Pete, Jack."

Dixon checked his watch. It was after 10:00 p.m. "What's up?"

"Special delivery."

Dixon moved the phone to his other ear and wrapped his free arm around Dani, who snuggled close. It was Wednesday night and they were lounging in front of the TV.

Dani could hear Monroe's voice through the receiver. He said, "I'm at the warehouse. You might want to drop by tomorrow. Those figures just arrived."

"Sure, got it." Dixon said and hung up.

"What's he mean?" Dani asked.

Dixon played dumb. "Huh?"

"What figures is he talking about?"

"Nothing, just some merchandise for the mission."

"Action figures?"

"You know," Dixon tried his best to act nonchalant. "Like those G.I. Joes for kids. Except these are astronauts. There's a Neil Armstrong action figure, and a Buzz Aldrin."

It was obvious to Dani that Dixon wasn't telling the whole truth. "Can I see these action figures?"

"It's sort of a surprise. You're not supposed to know about them until after the mission."

"More secrets," Dani said and rested her head on his shoulder. "Don't mind me."

Dixon didn't. He couldn't wait to get his hands on those figurines.

The next morning he hurried to the warehouse. He found his way to the stack of crates where the action figures were stored and tore open a box. He was horrified by what he saw. The cardstock read Lunar Elvis, but Lunar Elvis was wearing a black leather jacket and matching pants.

Ten minutes later, Dixon shoved one of these packages in front of Jack Monroe and demanded an explanation. "You don't have a problem with this?"

"No," Monroe took the toy. "I think he looks great. I wish I had my own action figure. You show it to the King yet?"

"No, and he won't see this until it's rectified."

"Rectified?"

"Jack, he's wearing a leather jacket."

"I see that."

"And not a spacesuit?"

Monroe explained. "Pete, this is all part of a bigger set. There are a whole variety of action figures in those boxes."

"How can Lunar Elvis not be wearing a spacesuit? In this leather outfit, he wouldn't last five seconds on the moon!"

"Relax, Peter. You can remove the jacket and dress him in a spacesuit. There's also a NASA jumpsuit and a prison uniform so you can play *Jailhouse Rock*. The spacesuit is just one of the accessories."

Dixon was about to lose his mind. The pain in his stomach returned with a pop, then made its way up until it was an imposing pressure against his chest. He snatched the package from Monroe and pointed at the bold letters along the bottom. "It says right here, 'Accessories Not Included!' That's rubbish! The spacesuit should be part of the package!"

Monroe remained calm. It was too early in the morning to be otherwise. "Peter, there are different sets. It's not a big deal."

"It's a travesty!"

"It's a marketing flaw."

Dixon shook his head. "It's a bad omen."

"You have stage fright again."

Dixon yelled, "Damn right I do!"

There was an awkward silence, and when Dixon realized he was infuriated over a baby's toy, he started to laugh. Monroe frowned, patted Dixon on the shoulder and invited him to sit. Once they settled, Monroe spoke quietly, in a fatherly tone. "It's natural to get butterflies before the big show. We can't blame you for having cold feet. It's how you handle it that matters. Deep down, you know everything's under control. Don't you?"

Dixon popped a pair of antacids. "This is a bit overwhelming, that's all."

"Of course it is."

"If something went wrong, we'd be burned at the stake."

"Everything is under control."

"Sure," Dixon nodded.

"If you need me to relieve you of your position, give the word and I'll cut you loose."

Dixon looked Monroe in the eye and saw he was serious. "No need to do that, Jack. It's just nerves."

Monroe smiled. "You're my main man. I'd hate to lose you."

Dixon smiled back. "You can count on me."

"I knew it," Monroe punched Dixon on the shoulder with a boyish grin. "Because landing a man on the moon is *nothing* without Elvis."

Dixon laughed, he was starting to believe nothing could be closer to the truth.

June 21st

Jack Monroe rarely had free time on a Saturday but when he did, he ran errands. Today he took a trip to the liquor store to stock up on supplies, and then went across the street to buy groceries.

After that, he stopped at a service station for gasoline and a pastry. He wandered to the magazines and newspapers as he munched on his apple strudel. There were the usual headlines: baseball, Vietnam, Apollo, The Beatles. None of those things were of any interest to him that morning. Instead he found himself reaching for *The Sensational Nation*, a publication he had never heard of. It was the magazine's name that caught his eye. He thought it amusing that the nation had no idea just how sensational it was about to become.

As he paged through, he began to admire the magazine for its quality. The level of journalism was right up there with *Time* and *Newsweek* and Monroe appreciated the content. It was LSD, free love and *Hair* on Broadway. Pete Rose, nuclear war, *Midnight Cowboy* and *Sweet Caroline*. Monroe enjoyed the short blurb on Samuel Beckett's Nobel Prize (mostly because Dr. Monroe planned to win one of those himself one day).

After a full-page advertisement for The Who's *Tommy*, Monroe came across an article on the Dalai Lama. The author's name he had not heard, but a picture of her looked very familiar. It was a girl with straight brown hair, late twenties, named Dani Mitchell. He looked closely at the photograph of the writer knowing he had definitely seen that face before.

Dani Mitchell, Jack said to himself. *Where have I seen her?*

It hit him like an asteroid. Peter Dixon—that idiot—had introduced him to this reporter. She had been inside his house, had used the name Kim, and claimed to be a liaison for CBS, but when Jack saw the picture next to the Dalai Lama interview, he was certain Peter was being used.

Nixon would hold Jack Monroe responsible for this outrage.

"Damn it!" Monroe cursed and tore Dani's article out of the magazine. How could Dixon not know he was seeing a journalist? Was he that much of a fool? Monroe stuffed the article in his jacket pocket and made for the door.

He ignored the cashier as he passed, a young man who watched Monroe tear the page out of *The Sensational Nation*. The cashier saw the half-eaten pastry in Monroe's hand, and the car sitting at the pumps whose gasoline was still unpaid for.

"Hey," he cashier called out. "You going to pay for all your stuff?"

"No," Monroe said and disappeared out the door.

He drove straight to Dixon's house, intent on ending this unfortunate relationship and praying Dixon hadn't already leaked valuable information to the crafty reporter. He had never liked Kim, or Dani, or whatever her name was. He could only hope Dixon was strong enough to keep the details of Operation Blue Moon to himself, and not let this girl coax him into talking.

Dixon was sitting on his porch when Monroe arrived. He wore shorts and running shoes, but held half a McDonald's strawberry milkshake in his hand. He was surprised to see his boss's car screeching into his driveway, and he knew something must be terribly wrong. Dixon stood to greet Jack as the NASA chief jumped out of his car and stormed to meet him.

"What are you doing?"

"Jogging," Dixon said.

Monroe looked at the milkshake. "Jogging?"

"Yeah."

"Anyway, I need you to stop seeing that girl."

"This is a little out of left field."

"Call it off."

"Why?"

Monroe reached into his pocket and handed Dixon the crumpled Dalai Lama interview. "Look familiar?"

It took a moment, but when Dixon recognized Kim's face and saw the name Dani Mitchell, the knot in his stomach nearly knocked him to the ground. It felt like someone had reached into his abdomen and poked a hole in his stomach. "I wonder what she could want," he said innocently.

"She's onto Breakfast, Pete. There's no other explanation except that she's using you. Using you to get to The Bacon."

Dixon started walking towards his porch in shock, his eyes were still on Dani Mitchell's picture. He needed to sit and consider the consequences of their relationship. Monroe walked with him.

Dixon said, "How could she know about The Bacon?"

"Somehow she knows. She was asking all about it at the party."

"She's been asking me about The Bacon too," he admitted. They sat on his front steps.

Monroe asked, "What did you tell her?"

"Nothing...Nothing useful, I don't think."

"In your house," Monroe pointed. "Is there any incriminating evidence? Anything that could clue her into Breakfast?"

Dixon thought of the Elvis coffee mug, the fingernail, and T-shirt, all of which had been safely stashed away before Dani had ever set foot in his house. There was no way she knew anything. It seemed Monroe's stroke of dumb luck in discovering this article had saved Apollo 11 from disaster.

"I think we're good, Jack. She doesn't know a thing."

"And she won't," he warned. "You call it off today. I don't want you to see her again."

Dixon knew Monroe was right, but part of him would miss Kim Clark/Dani Mitchell. Underneath what he now knew were a bunch of lies, there was something about her. "We're done, Jack," he assured his boss. "I'll never again speak to that bitch."

"Good man," Monroe patted him on the shoulder and stood. "But Peter?"

"Yeah?"

"Sometimes you're a goddamn *idiot*."

Monroe stormed back to his car and sped away. Dixon remained on the porch with the Dalai Lama article on his lap. He was supposed to meet Kim/Dani for dinner that night. She was certainly in for a surprise.

He didn't want to end things completely. Dixon wasn't a man who liked to burn bridges. Instead he figured he'd let her down easy. He'd tell her that with the crunch of Apollo 11 he wouldn't have time to see her until after the mission. Until after Elvis played his song. It would give him a chance to back off and decide if he absolutely needed to sever all ties with Dani Mitchell.

That was his plan until he arrived at her hotel that night and saw her as Dani Mitchell for the first time. Dixon knew then that he never wanted to see her again. It was the first time Dixon noticed that sneaky look in her eyes—like an angel, but she was the devil in disguise.

Oh, yes, she was.

They met in the lounge on the first floor and sat at the bar for cocktails. Dixon's stomach had been hurting since Monroe broke the news, so he unwisely downgraded to Bailey's on ice. Dani had beer.

The evening started with Dani filling him in on her week. She told him she'd been back and forth to New York, which was true. She had flown home the prior

Tuesday to tie up some loose at ends at her apartment, avoiding the *TSN* office, knowing Baker thought she was still in Houston working the NASA beat.

Halfway into his Bailey's, Dixon knew he could no longer listen to Dani Mitchell. He would never know what to believe. This stuff about her spending three days in New York was meaningless. When he looked at her, he figured that if she was talking, she was lying.

He blurted it out. "I can't see you anymore."

Dani returned a blank stare. "Just like that?"

Dixon's eyes went to his drink. "I'm sorry."

She sat back. "What did I do wrong?"

"Nothing," he said quietly. "It's crunch time at work and I just don't have the time and I know it sounds like a shitty deal, but women and I just don't mix."

"That's bullshit," Dani sneered. She knew she was about to lose this asset and she wanted to hold on as long as she could, but Dixon's unexpected rejection had struck a nerve. Nobody ruins Dani Mitchell's Elvis Presley interview and then dumps her less than a month later. She wasn't going to let Dixon get away with this.

"It has something to do with those action figures, doesn't it?"

"What?" laughed Dixon.

"You're hiding something, you have been all along. I know you've been to Graceland."

So Monroe had been right. She had been using him all along. How she knew of Dixon's Graceland visit, he had no idea but now Dixon was angry. How dare she reprove him for hiding the truth when she had lied about her entire life? This was an evil woman and he needed to stay away.

He slammed the rest of his drink and threw a five-dollar bill on the table. Then he stood and gave her one last look. "See you later, *Dani Mitchell*."

Dani sat alone in shock, wondering how long Dixon had known her real name.

The next thing Dixon did was call Jack Monroe from a pay phone down the block. He caught the NASA Administrator at home. "It's done."

"Good," Monroe acknowledged. "Did you get a read on things?"

"Yeah," Dixon said, knowing his read would surely infuriate Monroe. "She's onto the gig. She knows we met The Bacon at the Hog Shed."

Hog Shed was brand new—Monroe assumed it was code for Graceland. This was infuriating. "How the hell does she know about that?"

"I don't know, I walked away."

"Good," Monroe praised. Then, "How did you get mixed up with that girl in the first place?"

"She tricked me. Somehow she tracked me down and followed me to see Jimmy Orr."

"Who's Jimmy Orr?"

"I'll tell you later," Dixon dismissed the name, figuring Jack would know about Plan B only if it became necessary. "Anyway, she's out of our life."

"I should call J. Edgar Hoover."

"Do you really think we need that? The landing's less than a month away."

"A lot can happen in a month. I'll call the Bureau and put them on alert."

"Suit yourself," Dixon said. "I couldn't care less what happens to the bitch." This wasn't entirely true, since Dixon had genuinely enjoyed their time together. Dani Mitchell was fun when she was Kim Clark. But now that Kim Clark had been destroyed, Dani Mitchell could go to hell.

Dani remained at the bar and drank the breakup out of her mind. There was something between NASA and Elvis, but once again Peter Dixon had squashed her attempt at a story. The covert NASA visit to Graceland went all the way to the top. She was certain of that. It was a Pulitzer, if she could get there with some semblance of a theory.

But with nothing to go on and no leads to follow, Dani would have to close the books on the NASA-Elvis conspiracy. Instead, she got drunk and trashed her hotel room.

It started with her consuming enough alcohol to cover a frat party. Then she ripped her phone out of the wall at two in the morning because she didn't want Baker to call and ask about a story.

When she pulled the phone from the wall, the cord got caught around the nightstand lamp, and pulled that to the floor where the bulb popped and the ceramic cracked. In a fit of rage she threw the phone across the room, and it hit the television, smashing through the screen with a crash.

She needed to hear that sound twice, so she jerked the phone out of the television set and threw it in a second time.

Realizing what she had just done, Dani paused for a moment to collect her thoughts. With the alcohol working against her, Dani decided the best thing to do at that moment in her life was to tear the mattress apart with a ballpoint pen.

This took twenty-seven minutes, and required a series of stabs along the fabric to open a hole. Then she jabbed the pen into the hole like a dagger and ruggedly sliced herself a longer slit. She grabbed the fabric and pulled it apart, digging out the insides like she was gutting a fish.

After the mattress, Dani took the desk chair and smashed it over what was left of the television. The broken TV box crumpled under the weight of the chair, and with a thunderous clatter it broke into fifty pieces, upon which the person in the next room finally got involved and called down to the front desk. Before the hotel manager could call the police, Dani had thrown her hairdryer into the bathroom mirror, where it blasted a spider web into the glass.

She was arrested ten minutes later, and spent the next three days in jail.

Chapter Eleven

*W*ith no attorney and no friends in town to bail her out, Dani relied on the tolerance of *The Sensational Nation*. Richard Baker reluctantly advanced Dani's salary for the next month, which was enough to set her free. He wired it to a bondsman, and Dani flew back to New York the next day with the shame of the world on her shoulders.

Her first day back at *TSN*, Baker called her into his office. He was behind his desk when she arrived. "Have a seat," he pointed to the pair of chairs opposite his desk, both of which were piled high with articles and manuscripts. Dani cleared a seat and sat.

"I can't thank you enough for bailing me out, Richard. It's all I can really say."

Baker wasn't happy. "You've become a liability, Dani." He scratched his head as if he didn't know what to say next. Still Dani waited for the bombshell.

He said, "You're lucky I know media people in Houston. They agreed to keep your incident with the hotel quiet, so we hope your actions won't hurt the reputation of *TSN*. You have a court date July 21st in Houston, and I'm letting you know now that the magazine expects you to cover that expense from your own pocket."

Dani kept her head down and her hands tightly clasped throughout the reprimand. She figured she'd be lucky if she walked away with a job.

Baker continued. "You've done some great things for us, Dani, but ever since you met the Dalai Lama your performance has been a little shaky. The Alan Shepard article was okay. We decided to condense it and throw it on the *Quickies* page."

That meant she still had a job. Dani relaxed and crossed her legs comfortably. She could handle a simple warning.

"Unfortunately," Baker said. "I need to suspend your employment until this hotel vandalism works itself out. Take two weeks off and enjoy your time. Try to straighten yourself out."

Dani spent those next two weeks on the couch with a diet of potato chips and vanilla ice cream. It was a miserable roadblock to her career and Dani traced it all back to Stumpy Pete and Mr. Shiny Hair. If they had stayed away from Graceland, Dani would have landed her Elvis Presley interview and none of this would have ever happened.

Then, just when she thought she'd redeem herself with an angle on some covert scheme between NASA and Elvis Presley, Pete Dixon had to go and dump her. She took that personally and vowed to find a way to get back at them both. As she watched an Apollo update on television, Dani told herself her suspension was a mere setback. Two minutes in the penalty box. She'd be back in action in no time.

Dixon was scheduled to be at the Cape on June 30th for final launch preparations with the crew and control personnel. On the 28th he dropped by Spicer's Slop Ranch for a beer and a meeting with Jimmy Orr. After another terrific show, Dixon met Orr backstage and told him the deal was still a go and that he should drop by the space center on July 19th, the day before the landing. Orr agreed, and the two men bid farewell and went about their tasks.

Dixon and Monroe took a jet to Florida. Elvis arrived a week later—July 7th—after returning in secret to Graceland to spend the Fourth of July weekend with his family. For the next ten days, everything at the Kennedy Space Center was running full throttle. Elvis and the astronauts trained daily and perfected their ability to perform the tasks of the mission. Everything was in place for a great show, and the entire planet was anxious for the excitement of the first moon landing.

Chapter Twelve

The night before the launch, Peter Dixon barely slept. He had spent the early evening at dinner with Jack Monroe, who reminded him that Apollo 11 was their one chance in eternity for everlasting fame. "If the astronauts crash and die a horrible death on the lunar surface, they're still the first humans to land on the moon. This is the mission history will remember. It's one chance to prove Mankind is capable of defeating that old hag, Mother Nature."

They sipped their piña coladas. The two NASA heads dined beachside on the deck of a restaurant just yards from the ocean. The late-afternoon Florida sun was still blazing, so they sat at a table with an umbrella.

Jack philosophized. "Not only can we break the laws of gravity, master the science of physics, and land a man on the moon, we can also bring home The Bacon. You won't be able to find a better page in the history books."

They toasted, Jack with the proud smile of a man about to reach the pinnacle of his career, Pete with a nervous wince that told Jack he was having second thoughts.

Monroe said, "Not because it's easy, Peter. But because it is hard."

Dixon nodded, remembering the Kennedys and Monroe's fascination with what Dixon called the "the wannabe-royal family." The Elvis moon landing would surpass President Kennedy's vision of the future and grant eternal glory to Jack Monroe. But Jack's talk about death and crash landings got that stomach pain going again.

Monroe watched as Dixon's eyes aimlessly scanned the beach, then said, "Tomorrow's going to be a great day, Peter. Don't ruin it by worrying about every little detail. The Bacon is going to be fine."

Dixon watched a group of seagulls swarming around a little boy who threw little bits of bread into the wind. He mumbled, "I'm not worried about him."

Monroe signaled for two more piña coladas and told Dixon, "You did a great job getting rid of that reporter. We haven't seen her in weeks and there's nothing in the media about any surprises. Nobody has any idea what NASA has in store for this weekend."

Dixon appreciated the praise, but the whole Dani Mitchell incident was something he'd rather forget. His concern was the safety of the crew at tomorrow's launch. Because he'd have to get up at 1:00 a.m. on launch day, Dixon turned in early. Thoughts of the crew kept him tossing and turning all night. After logging less than two hours of fitful sleep, Dixon was rescued from a terrible nightmare by his one o'clock wakeup call.

A sense of impending doom engulfed him as he dressed, and was still with him when he met Jack for coffee in the lobby of their hotel. They took a limousine to the Kennedy Space Center and stopped in the cafeteria for breakfast. Dixon told him, "I had this dream last night. I'm driving my car on this roller coaster track and Elvis is in the passenger seat. We're zipping around on all the twists and turns really fast. Every time we go upside down, the car flies off the track, but right before we crash, we're suddenly *back* on the track and the sequence repeats itself. Over and over and over."

Monroe shrugged and shoveled a fork full of eggs into his mouth. "So what? It's just a dream."

Dixon had no appetite. He popped a handful of Rolaids instead.

Monroe finished chewing and announced it was time to wake the King. The mission masterminds had become Elvis Presley's servants. With the absence of the Memphis Mafia, it was now Jack Monroe and Peter Dixon who would have to wake the King, feed him breakfast, pick out his clothes and give him a ride to the show.

Those amazing control freaks would have it no other way.

Elvis slept in his private quarters inside the Kennedy Space Center operations building. Monroe knocked and opened the door a crack. He stuck his head inside the room and whispered, "King?"

Elvis stirred and rolled to face Monroe. His eyes were heavy, as it was just past one thirty in the morning. He was more asleep now than awake.

"Today's the day!" Monroe announced and suddenly Elvis snapped to attention. He was out of his bed and fumbling for clothes before Monroe and Dixon could walk into the room.

"Easy, Big E," Dixon said. "We're right on schedule."

The King gave Dixon a shy little smile. "I just want to be sure the astronauts don't leave without me."

"Don't worry," Monroe said. "You're hours ahead of everyone else."

"What time is it?" Elvis asked.

It was time for Elvis to eat breakfast. The astronauts would sleep for another two hours, which meant Elvis would eat without them. Instead Monroe and Dixon sat with the King while Elvis stuffed himself with NASA's traditional launch day breakfast of steak and eggs.

Monroe drank coffee out of a Lunar Elvis mug. Dixon drank water. They were nearly silent throughout the meal. All three pondered the planned—and unplanned—events of the next two weeks.

Elvis finally broke the silence. "Deep down, I don't think we'll make it back. I don't think any of us do, baby. But these live concerts are my favorite part of the business. And doing a show from the moon, even if it turns out to be my last, will more or less put my mind at ease. I hope it does the same to yours."

Dixon's knot tightened. It now felt like an ice pick was piercing into his gut. He hunched sideways a bit to comfort the pain but it was so bad he wanted to drink a glass of milk and lie down. Dixon was now sure that it was time to see a doctor.

Elvis continued as he cut into his steak. "But for the chance to sing from the moon, who wouldn't take the risk?"

Monroe was reassuring. "We'll bring you home in one piece, King."

Elvis noticed the design on Monroe's Lunar Elvis coffee mug. He grinned and pointed at it with his fork. "Make sure you set one of those mugs aside for when I get back."

Fifteen minutes later a group of technicians—who had been sworn to secrecy—helped squeeze Elvis into his special spacesuit. It was exactly the same as the suit the astronauts wore except for one small modification: Presley's suit was fitted with hundreds of shiny rhinestones that made him sparkle like he was onstage. It was enough to ease Dixon's pain, and for a moment he forgot all about his cramps.

Monroe jabbed him on the arm. "When we decided to put Elvis Presley on the moon, *this* is what we were talking about. What could be more sensational than a rhinestone spacesuit?"

Dixon agreed. "The spacesuit captures the essence of the mission."

"It really does, doesn't it?"

Dixon shrugged. "Well, without the rhinestone spacesuit, Elvis would just be another roadie."

"Roadie?"

Dixon corrected himself. "I meant to say astronaut."
Monroe nodded. It was an honest mistake.

The next task was perhaps the mission's most crucial moment to date. Top Secret security commandos smuggled Elvis and his guitar into a transfer van, loading them while all were safely behind closed garage doors. Then the van drove out to the Saturn V; the gigantic rocket glowed in a surrounding sea of floodlights ahead of them. Elvis kept his guitar beside him in the back seat. Dixon rode alongside for support.

The NASA man savored this quiet moment with the King. He watched from the corner of his eye and saw Elvis reverently gazing upon the rocket, humbled by his thoughts. He said to Dixon, "Image is one thing, Mr. Dixon. Being human is another. Sometimes it's hard to live up to an image."

Dixon replied, "You have nothing to worry about, Mr. Presley. You've done a better job than any of us could have expected."

Elvis took a deep breath, "I've never gotten over stage-fright. I go through it every show." He looked to Dixon. "Are you sure about this?"

Dixon nodded, unsure of how he felt. Slowly, the van crept to the launch tower. Once it arrived, Elvis hopped out and waddled to the elevator. Dixon carried his guitar.

Scouts had been spread across the space center grounds, and had signaled the all clear after searching for, and not finding, anyone with a camera or a notepad. Elvis Presley's involvement with Apollo 11 was still a secret, except to the commandos, and a small group of NASA technicians whose skills made it absolutely necessary for them to be part of NASA's inner-circle.

Now Dixon and Elvis rode the elevator to the top of the launch tower. Elvis was more excited now than nervous, but Dixon was on the verge of an anxiety attack. His heart pounded harder and harder the higher the elevator climbed, and his stomach felt the queasy flutter of a thousand butterflies.

Finally they reached the top. They stepped out and gazed up and down the expanse of coastline before them. The morning sun had yet to break the ocean horizon, and they could see dozens of headlights where cars started to line the beaches and highways. Beside them, the huge Saturn V towered like a skyscraper, ready to blast into space as fast as man had ever traveled.

Technicians surrounded the King and made final adjustments to his spacesuit. Dixon looked upon the rhinestones that twinkled in the floodlights and broke a smile.

Elvis saw him grin. He smiled behind his glass faceplate. "Not bad, huh?"

"Nice touch," Dixon said and walked Elvis to the Saturn V hatch that opened into the command module. "I wanted to tell you you've made us all very proud, Mr. Presley."

Elvis understood. "Make sure everyone knows the pleasure was all mine."

"You can still change your mind if you want."

Elvis shook his head. "No need to scrub the mission just because of me."

"You'll be in good hands." Dixon assured him. "Can I ask you a question?"

"Sure, anything."

A nervous Peter Dixon held out a 45 record jacket. "Would you mind? It's *Return to Sender*, 1962. It's pretty rare."

Elvis was amused. He took the record in his space glove, grabbed a pen from Dixon with the other glove, and scribbled his name across the record jacket. He handed them back to Dixon, who thanked him graciously.

"One more thing," Dixon said. "What song are you going to sing up there?"

Elvis smiled his unmistakable smile. He nudged Dixon and said, "I can't tell you what song I'm going to sing up there."

"Come on, King," Dixon coaxed. "Why not?"

"Because you said the world needed a surprise."

"Yes! Yes! They do!"

Elvis still smiled. "You'll be here on earth, just another human being hoping for a safe landing. I'll be up there, preparing to sing to the world. You're going to have to wait and be surprised like everybody else."

Dixon was touched. He patted the King on the shoulder and bid him the best. As he turned to leave, Elvis called to him.

"Mr. Dixon, when I get back, I'd like to talk business with you."

Dixon turned. "Business?"

"I'm getting a little tired of my manager, if you know what I mean."

"I'm not following you."

"It's over the merchandise," Elvis explained. "The Colonel wasn't too happy about NASA using my likeness for the mug, and the T-shirt and the action figures. He felt we were being exploited. I disagreed. Still do. Those Elvis mugs are a great idea and I hope you sell every single one. And since you and I seem to be on the same wavelength, Mr. Dixon, I think maybe we should sit down and discuss my future once the mission's over."

Dixon was flattered. "Of course, Mr. Presley. We will certainly chat once you return."

Elvis smiled. "See you in a week."

While Dixon made his way back to the operations building, the astronauts gathered for breakfast. They were just hours from the launch, Elvis was strapped in place and Operation Blue Moon was ready to roll.

Now Buzz Aldrin cut into his steak and nodded toward the Elvis mug Monroe was using for good luck. "When do those mugs go on sale?"

"Right after the mission." Monroe turned his mug so he could see the Apollo 11 Elvis logo.

Michael Collins took a look at the mug. "You actually made those?"

Monroe nodded. "Thousands of them."

Neil Armstrong said, "It's not just coffee mugs. They made T-shirts and a board game and a little doll."

Aldrin grinned. "I can't wait to watch him sing!"

Armstrong laughed, "Neither can I!"

Elvis was stashed in his special compartment on board the Apollo 11 command module. The diet had been a success. Elvis lay on his back below the row of astronaut couches, packed snugly where the equipment lockers had been. The astronauts' feet would dangle just above him. He was connected to life support tubes and wore a headset to monitor radio chatter. Elvis listened as launch control worked through the countdown, but he had no mouthpiece—the headset was strictly one way. NASA insisted: Elvis Presley is off the air until show time.

Later that morning, a proud but modest Neil Armstrong emerged from the operations building in his spacesuit and greeted the crowd of spectators with a friendly wave. Aldrin and Collins followed and the astronauts boarded the transfer van. The Apollo 11 crew was filmed and photographed and locked in the annals of history, and still no one besides NASA's top men had any idea a fourth passenger waited in the command module.

Dixon was among the crowd, he wished he could be aboard the Saturn V when the astronauts climbed inside and saw Elvis Presley's rhinestone suit. He had kept that secret and knew the astronauts would be surprised once they saw it.

By the time the astronauts reached the top of the launch tower, an estimated quarter-million spectators filled the beaches of Cape Canaveral. They converged on the Saturn V from every side; boats speckled the ocean well away from the shore in safe water. Cameras and binoculars were everywhere, ready to capture this once-in-a-lifetime liftoff. Even Dani Mitchell was awake and planted before the TV for this Wednesday morning launch.

When the astronauts finally climbed into the command module, Elvis had been waiting for hours. It was a relief to see Neil Armstrong climb through the hatch.

The Apollo 11 commander ginned when he saw rhinestones glittering below his seats. "Rhinestones! Alright! What do you say, Elvis?"

"Oh, my boy," Elvis said. "Good to see you."

Launch control heard this over the radio.

Monroe rushed to the Television Officer. "Can you edit that out?"

Aggie nodded. "Don't worry, I muted him before it was too late. We're running the audio on a three second delay."

Relief. Monroe said, "Make sure it doesn't happen again."

Armstrong regretted his slip the instant it happened. The excitement of the moment had prompted him to shout out in glee. And when launch control gave him the all clear, Armstrong couldn't resist reaching to his feet and exchanging a mischievous glove shake with the King.

Aggie Gallagher told Monroe, "Once they're in space we won't have to worry about pain-in-the-ass media cameras following their every move. We'll be able to delay the television broadcast up to three hours. That way we can edit and overdub whatever we need to put on TV."

Monroe patted him on the back and told him he was doing excellent work.

The countdown continued. The launch was now fifteen minutes away. Dixon sat at a computer console at the front of the launch control room. He bit his nails to the skin and tried to forget his ulcer, knowing all of this was now out of his hands.

The clock ticked below ten minutes. Dixon thought of all the people—at the beach and around the world—who prayed for the lives of the astronauts. The lives of four men were on the line, and Elvis Presley was among them. It was all Dixon's doing. To hell with stage fright, this was like facing death.

Dixon made a decision. He rose from his seat and headed briskly to the master console at the back of the control room. Monroe was there monitoring progress with the launch director. He saw Dixon coming impatiently towards them and stood to cut him off.

"Where are you going, Peter?" Monroe held his hands up, ready to push Dixon away and stop him from doing whatever he planned to do.

Dixon glanced over Monroe's shoulder to the master console and then into his boss's eyes. "Call it off, Jack."

"Don't do this."

"Abort the mission."

Dixon eyed the red abort button. If he pressed it all systems would halt and the mission would be shut down. He'd surely lose his job but at least Elvis would be safe for at least one more day.

Monroe couldn't afford to lose Dixon now. Especially with just nine minutes until ignition. As quietly as he could, he grabbed Dixon by the collar and necktie and dragged him into a private corridor where they were alone.

He pushed Dixon against the wall and glared into his eyes. "Knock it off."

Dixon glared back. "It's not going to work, Jack. It has to be the stupidest idea I've ever had."

"Be quiet and listen to me."

"Elvis Presley on the moon? What was I thinking?"

Monroe shoved Dixon again and squeezed him by the necktie. "Listen to me!"

Dixon listened.

"It's just nerves, Peter. It's all in your head. Now the show *will go on*. With or without you."

"A warning," a smug Dixon mentioned. "You can give the final Go for launch *only* if I agree. It requires my approval and I do not give it. Now let go of me or I *will go* psycho."

Monroe only tightened his grip. "Nixon is calling this the greatest week in the history of the world *since creation*. Are you some kind of Communist? First you bring that reporter-girl onto our turf and now you're trying to abort the greatest mission of all time?"

"I didn't know she was a damn reporter!"

"This Elvis moon gig was *your* idea, Peter. Now you're doing everything you can to stop it from happening."

"I won't let Elvis die!"

Monroe could see mere words no longer held any leverage. He released his grasp and glanced at his watch. Less than four minutes to go and Monroe knew he needed to take drastic measures.

He took a deep breath and jabbed a finger at his cohort. "Here's the deal, Peter Dixon," he said. "If you back out of this arrangement, and force me to cancel the first attempt to land man on the moon, I will contact every news reporter in the country. I'll tell them you concocted this whole thing, that you risked Presley's life, just so you could meet your hero. Every Elvis fan in the world will hate your guts."

"Big deal!"

"And furthermore!" Monroe took a step closer so

that they were standing nose-to-nose. "I will also contact President Nixon and J. Edgar Hoover and reveal to them that I've discovered you're a fucking Communist whose been working against us this whole time."

"You wouldn't dare!"

"They will see to it that you go to jail. I'm not putting my job on the line for you. I'm not going to forfeit the fucking *space race* because you're having second thoughts."

Dixon couldn't tell if Jack was bluffing. "You'd really report me as a Communist?"

"Without question," Jack glared. "If you undermine our chance to beat the Soviets to the moon, what does that make you?"

Dixon swallowed nervously, but he held his ground. "I guess that would make me a fucking Communist."

Jack relaxed a bit and took a step back. "Compromise. If you give the okay to launch, I'll give you a set of authentic Elvis Presley gold cufflinks, with tiger's eye stones, that I picked up back in '59."

Dixon smirked. "Do I look stupid? You don't have Elvis cufflinks from 1959."

"I do too. In the safe deposit box at the bank."

"How do I know they're real?"

Monroe gestured innocently. "Would I have kept them all these years if they weren't real?"

Dixon thought about it. "I guess you wouldn't, would you?"

"Or lock fake Elvis cufflinks in a safe?"

It seemed logical. "Deal," Dixon said. "But we go to the bank and get them the minute the launch is over."

"We'll get them when we fly back tomorrow."

"Nope. We fly home this afternoon and get to the bank before it closes."

"We'll never make it to Houston by then."

"We'll make it if we leave right after the launch. I'm holding you to these cufflinks, Jack, and I don't want you backing out after you've slept on it because that's *exactly* what I would do!"

Monroe said. "We'll fly back tonight and go first thing tomorrow morning."

"No dice," Dixon shook his head, calling Jack's bluff. "This mission is over and I guess that makes me a damn Commie, you capitalist hog. Long live Lenin. Long live Karl Marx. Long live Fidel, Jack! *Fidel!*"

Monroe was fuming. Dixon started back to launch control, determined to punch the abort.

Monroe blocked his exit, finally giving in. "Fine. We'll leave right after the launch."

Dixon wanted confirmation. "The minute the launch is over."

"Yeah," Monroe nodded. They shook on it, although both reluctantly.

Then they hustled back to the control room and gave the final Go. With two minutes until ignition, Monroe and Dixon went outside to watch it live.

All systems were stable onboard the launch vehicle. Activity peaked inside the crew compartment as the astronauts adjusted their systems in conjunction with launch interface. Elvis quietly waited in his compartment at the astronauts' feet. He was as nervous as anyone. Just seconds away from launch and he knew there was no turning back.

In her New York apartment Dani watched live coverage on TV. There was a shot of the NASA grandstand where family and friends anticipated the launch, along with half the U.S. Congress and over three thousand newsmen from fifty-six countries. Vice President Spiro Agnew was on hand for the event, and on TV Dani saw the Veep shaking hands with Jack Monroe, that miserable shiny-top swine.

He was small potatoes on a day like today. Dani couldn't help but be captivated by the excitement of the moment. Suddenly the legal problems over her hotel room incident, the subsequent suspension from *TSN* and her July 21st court date did not seem like such a big deal.

The countdown clock dropped to 3...2...1...and with a burst of smoke and fire from the base of the Saturn V, Apollo 11 rose off the launch pad and safely cleared the tower. It was 9:32 a.m. on July 16th, 1969.

Elvis thought he'd yell yee-haw during blast off, but seven million pounds of Saturn V thrust shook him with the thunder of a thousand train wrecks and he couldn't speak a syllable. He gripped the sides of his compartment with white knuckles as the rocket accelerated and pushed them higher, into outer space.

Monroe and Dixon stood among millions of spectators along the Florida coast and watched the rocket arc over the Atlantic. It left a bending column of white smoke in its wake as the rocket became a tiny yellow speck against the blue sky. It took just minutes for it to disappear completely, and by the time the exhaust trail began to dissolve, Apollo 11 was rising above Spain.

Monroe gazed at the sky and said, "Elvis has left the planet."

Dixon nudged his superior. "Jack?"

Monroe still watched the fading plume of smoke. "Yeah?"

"The cufflinks?"

Monroe, already reluctant to keep his promise, started back to the launch control building. "I'll summon the limo."

Apollo 11 blasted through the atmosphere and jettisoned its first stage. Six and a half minutes later, the second stage was spent and the astronauts were traveling well over 15,000 miles per hour. The third stage burned for eight minutes and propelled the spacecraft out of Earth orbit and onto a path for the moon.

It was time for the astronauts to undo their straps and float freely around the cramped module. There was hardly anywhere to move, but they were able to squeeze by each other and play in zero-gravity.

Buzz Aldrin tried to do an Elvis hip gyration but it there was not enough room to shake.

Elvis said, "No, baby, it's like this!" He tried his own gyration but he pushed out of his compartment so hard, he couldn't stop himself from slamming into Buzz and sending the astronaut's head into an instrument panel up above.

Alarms started blaring everywhere and the jovial mood became suddenly frantic.

Flight Control in Houston went berserk. The CAP-COM called into his radio, "*Columbia*, Houston, we read a possible depressurization in mode–"

Armstrong cut them off. "No problem here, Houston," he said after he solved the problem onboard. "The situation is under control."

NASA Flight Director Gene Kranz shook his head and muttered, "Elvis is going to get them killed."

Onboard the spacecraft the astronauts were giggling to themselves, making sure they were off the air. Elvis asked what happened.

Armstrong snickered and said, "Nothing, Elvis. But you almost got us killed."

Chapter Thirteen

July 17th

After the astronauts' live broadcast was off the air, Buzz Aldrin filmed a short greeting from Elvis, which was taped and archived by the crew for later review and release. As Buzz put the camera away, Collins saw Elvis fiddling with his spacesuit.

"What's wrong, King?"

Elvis concentrated on his spacesuit. "NASA's good with all the science and technology stuff, but their tailoring skills leave something to be desired. One of my rhinestones fell off!"

Elvis held up a shiny rhinestone for the astronauts to see.

"I wouldn't worry about it, Big E." Armstrong patted him on the shoulder. "I think the suit looks great."

Elvis smiled. "I wish they'd have let me bring the cape."

Jimmy Orr had perfected his look. Since his meeting with Peter Dixon, he had studied hundreds of pictures of Elvis and hours and hours of TV footage. Orr made sure his hair and sideburns were perfect, and that he was roughly the same weight.

When it came to autographs, he had the King's signature down pat, but writing Presley's shorthand was Jimmy's weakness. It was something he'd need to adapt to. Apparently, this was no longer about being an Elvis lookalike. Apparently, he needed to be perfect one hundred percent of the time. Not just in lyrics and looks but in lifestyle.

He'd have to sing *Love Me Tender*, but he didn't have to like it.

Orr read everything he could find about the King's life. He studied the character harder than any professional actor would, from Presley's early years to his least-favorite foods. Orr made sure he knew everything there was to know about the EP Enterprise. He could be the King in any situation, reacting exactly the way Elvis would.

He was certain he could be Elvis on stage, under a spotlight with a backup band. But the casual everyday Elvis was a different animal. The public would need to recognize the habits and mannerisms as well as the wardrobe and flair. He needed to take casual Elvis onto the streets, to try him out in public.

Blue jeans and a flannel shirt made him look somewhat inconspicuous. Then Jimmy drove to a service station on the edge of town. He stepped out of his Chrysler and took the pump to fill the tank. A twenty-something girl on the opposite side of the pumps immediately noticed his sideburns. When she finished filling her tank, she leaned over to whisper to someone through the passenger window. A girl in that seat turned her head Jimmy's direction and saw his hair. Before he'd topped off his tank, the two girls walked over to meet him.

"Mr. Presley?"

Orr nodded politely. He looked at one girl and said, "Ma'am." Then he smiled at the other and said, "Ma'am."

The girls stood speechless in the presence of his greatness. An uncomfortable silence crept between them as these three stared at each other. Orr finally asked, "Something I can do for you ladies?"

The girls murmured to each other and one produced a camera. Orr posed with each of them while the other took snapshots, and the group started to draw attention. A short old guy with gray hair and an oily baseball cap hobbled out of the gas station with a bag of beef jerky. Lo and behold, he spotted the King!

The old man approached Jimmy Orr and handed him a strip of dried meat. Orr happily accepted and they shook hands. When the old man smiled, Orr saw he had no teeth. Orr sneered and did his best Elvis voice. "How you supposed to gnaw that beef jerky with no teeth there, fella?"

The old man didn't seem to hear him. Instead he patted Orr on the back and said, "I been a fan for years."

Orr said, "Well, it's a pleasure to meet you too, baby."

And the hoax lived on. The crowd soon grew into the dozens, and Jimmy worked every last one of them. He signed autographs for old folks, greeted mothers and kissed their babies.

None of these people had ever seen Elvis this close so they didn't know to look for the little things Orr was unable to copy. An extra eyebrow hair, or a tiny misplaced freckle went unnoticed to an audience of strangers. He wondered how well it would work on the Memphis Mafia. Surely none of them could be fooled.

Jimmy moved on, determined to try his regular-guy Elvis on an all-new crowd. He found a playground, sat quietly on a park bench and waited for people to notice. Most of the children had no idea who he was supposed to be, but the mothers did, and soon Orr had more babies to kiss.

He enjoyed the people and how they thought they'd experienced a brush with fame. They probably told friends and family about the day they met the King and shook his hand. Years later, some would even tell how they were kissed as a baby by Elvis Presley, in the summer of 1969.

Sadly the joke was on them. Did anyone not wonder what the heck Elvis Presley was doing on a playground in Houston? They didn't, because Jimmy Orr was nearly perfect. And in three days he would know if he was a gimmick or a go. Peter Dixon had invited him to visit the space center on July 19th, the day before the landing, but Jimmy didn't want to wait until then. He was so excited he figured NASA wouldn't mind if he dropped by a little early.

Monroe and Dixon were sipping coffee in mission control. Dixon used more cream than he normally did, and he still hadn't mentioned his visit to the doctor. He didn't want Monroe to know about his ulcer. He went about the mission, happy that it would be over soon. This one had been a doozey, but Elvis and the astronauts would return in exactly one week. Then maybe Dixon could retire from NASA, because nothing could top meeting Elvis Presley and putting him on the moon.

Perhaps Elvis would fulfill his promise to talk business with Dixon once he returned. A job as the King's manager didn't sound like a bad life. He could leave NASA and go right into the Presley business.

Monroe caught Dixon smiling and elbowed him in the gut. "What's so funny?"

"Nothing," Dixon sobered and watched the readouts. There wasn't a hitch in Apollo's progress. The landing and the concert were still scheduled as planned. In less than three days, man would be walking on the moon.

Everything changed when the Television Officer suddenly cried out, staring wide-eyed into his monitor. "We have a problem!"

Monroe and Dixon rushed to Aggie's console. One of his screens was a feed from a NASA news cam. It was a live shot taken right outside the space complex: Elvis Presley walking through a crowd of hungry reporters and TV cameras.

"He's right outside," Monroe gawked. "How'd he do that?"

"Shit" said Dixon. "He's early."

"Impossible," said Monroe. "Who the hell is this guy and why is he here?"

Dixon already felt guilty for not telling Monroe about Plan B. Jimmy Orr was to be his ace in the hole, but now the cat had clawed itself out of the bag.

Monroe's temper stared to flare. "He's ruining the surprise, Peter. Who the hell is he?"

"I'll handle it," he said and rushed away.

Monroe and Gallagher kept their eyes on the monitor. Elvis was walking through the crowd as reporters shouted questions and shoved microphones in his face.

"What are we going to do about this, Jack?"

Monroe was still mulling it over, watching Elvis on TV. "I don't know. But this guy's a dead ringer."

"He's not too bad."

Monroe agreed. "Not bad at all."

In a minute, Dixon appeared on TV at Elvis's side and escorted the King toward a building. The reporters followed, but soon Elvis and Dixon disappeared into the building's side door. The reporters then turned back to their cameras to update millions of people on what had just happened.

Monroe left mission control and hurried to find Dixon.

"I told you the 19th!" Dixon shouted. They stood toe to toe in a broom closet, the first private room Dixon could find.

Jimmy smiled innocently. "Did you see how well I did with the press? I fooled every last one of em."

"You ruined the mission!"

"How did I do that?"

Monroe burst in, hitting Dixon with the door and knocking him down. "What the hell is going on? Peter, tell me you didn't leak Operation Blue Moon to an outsider!"

"It's okay, Jack," Dixon sulked and picked himself up.

Monroe demanded an explanation. "What's the story?"

Jimmy Orr smiled at him. "I'm Elvis Presley."

"You're nobody," Monroe said and looked at Dixon. "Who is he?"

Dixon brushed himself off. "His name's Jimmy Orr. He's a lookalike."

"No shit, he's a lookalike," Jack raised his voice and made Dixon fear the worst. "Now half the planet will think The Bacon was in Houston on July 17th. And if half the world thinks The Bacon was in Houston the day after we launched, how the hell can it be where we need it to be on the 20th?"

Dixon thought about this.

Then Monroe asked, "What is the purpose of this?"

"He's my backup plan, Jack. Jimmy can stand in for The Bacon if anything happens to him before he returns."

"Happens to him? What could you possibly mean by that?"

"If the mission were to fail. If something were to *happen* to The Bacon, we insert Jimmy. Unless you want to take the blame for killing Elvis in an Apollo 11 accident, I say we keep Jimmy around just in case. All great leaders have a backup plan, Jack. You said that yourself about JFK, I've heard you."

Dixon was right, but his idea for a replacement Elvis was useless. "Send him home, Peter. I don't want to see him again. Make sure he keeps his mouth shut." They glared at each other. "And you're on thin ice, kiddo."

Monroe stormed out and left Jimmy Orr wondering if he'd just destroyed his only chance to be the King. "Sorry about this," he said, falling out of character.

Dixon took some deep breaths, which was difficult with the pain in his chest. The doctor had said he needed at least a couple days off and that he should check into the hospital for treatment. Dixon had insisted that he had to supervise the entire mission before he took time off. Now he was paying for it with a terrible cramp and a botched mission.

"Did I really ruin the surprise?"

"We'll see, Jimmy." Dixon felt bad about squashing Jimmy's dreams. "Looks like you're not going to work out. You'd better head on home."

Monroe stomped back into mission control and headed to the Television Officer's console for an update. "Dr. Monroe, it's already out on the major news channels," Aggie reported.

Monroe already had it worked out. "We'll reveal him as a fake. I'll issue a statement. He was here to entertain the nervous NASA workers. End of story. Then *bang*! On July 20th we sock it to em!"

A thousand miles away, Dani Mitchell sat on the edge of her seat in wide-eyed shock. She had just watched a news update on her local TV station where she saw that Elvis Presley was in Houston. There it was on live television. Elvis Presley and Peter Dixon, walking into the space center side by side.

Dixon had been lying to her all along and the proof was right before her eyes.

It was a chance to redeem her career. If she could uncover the Elvis-Moon conspiracy before anyone else, she'd be back on top, and a messy little court date wouldn't matter. By the time Jack Monroe issued his statement to the press, Dani was on a plane to Houston. She had no idea NASA's visitor was a fake.

Chapter Fourteen

July 18th

Dani got off to an early start. After landing in Houston the night before, she had checked into a new hotel where they knew nothing of her previous outburst. Today was Friday, and her court date was Monday morning. She planned to fly back to New York that afternoon unless the judge gave her prison time for trashing a hotel room.

Now Dani had three days to get to the bottom of Pete Dixon's secret; the landing was scheduled for Sunday.

She went right to the source and arrived at Dixon's house before he left for work. She parked on the street down the block and walked to the house. The front curtains were open and Dani could see Dixon moving about the kitchen. She knocked on the front door.

Moments later Dixon answered with a look of stupid surprise. "What are you doing here?"

"I just want to talk to you and it will only take a second."

Dixon considered slamming the door in the sneaky reporter's face, but there was something about the way she pouted that attracted him. He thought of their good times together, though they had been brief, and he couldn't make himself ignore Dani's return.

"What do you want?"

"What's going on with Elvis?"

"After all you've done you think I'm going to help you?"

"I saw you with Elvis Presley."

Dixon waved it off. "You saw me with an imperson-ator. Jimmy Orr, remember? It was for employee enter-tainment, don't you pay attention to the news?"

Dani took a step closer. "Prove it."

"Don't have to." He tried to close the door but Dani wedged her foot in the doorway.

"I saw you meet Elvis at Graceland with Jack Monroe. You almost hit me with your limo."

Dixon was stunned. Now it all made sense. This reporter had been onto him since the day he pitched Operation Blue Moon to Elvis. She had tracked him all the way from Memphis and wormed her way into his bed. Though Dixon knew their relationship was over, he suspected Dani Mitchell would never give up on her journalistic mission, which meant he needed to hold her off for two more days. "I've never met Elvis Presley. That wasn't me you saw at Graceland. Now be on your way before Jack gets the FBI involved in this."

"Is that a threat?"

"It most certainly is. This pursuit of your empty the-ory about Elvis, whatever it is, may be seen by some as a threat to the nation's security."

She laughed. "Don't give me that bullshit! I saw you with him! Twice!"

Dixon's blood boiled. "What are you, some kind of Communist? I told you we've never met!"

Beep! Beep!

They both looked to the driveway, where a mail truck parked and honked a morning greeting. An old man in a blue uniform stepped out and pulled a rectan-gular package from the back. "Morning!" He called as he approached the front door.

Dixon and Dani both wondered what was inside the box. It was roughly two feet long and a foot wide, and judging by the way it made the carrier hunch over, it was somewhat heavy as well. The carrier handed Dixon the package along with a few envelopes containing bills, tipped his hat to Dani and was on his way with a friendly whistle.

Dani looked at the box and saw the postmark was from Memphis, Tennessee. Dixon was looking at her, ready to react to anything. There was a tense moment when neither could decide what to do next.

Dani smirked. "Memphis, eh?"

Dixon was still looking at her. They both knew the contents of the package could be the clue Dani needed to shatter Dixon's credibility and formulate a theory. Whatever was in that box could be the key to everything.

He tried to slam the door, but Dani blocked it with a forearm and pushed it back open. "What's in the box, Petie?" She lunged for the package and was able to hook two fingers under a strip of loose tape, but Dixon yanked it away and the tape ripped off the side. He took a step backwards into his house but Dani followed, still focusing on the package from Memphis.

"What's inside?!" She lunged again as Dixon backed away and tripped over a pair of shoes he had left in the foyer. He fell and the box slid across the floor towards the living room. Dani was still on her feet. She tried to jump over Dixon and dive for the box, but Dixon grabbed her ankle and pulled. Dani toppled over, rolling past the box and into the living room.

Dixon got to his knees as Dani reached out and tore half the bottom panel from the box. Lunging, he yanked it away again, but this time Dani was holding on and they nearly tore the box in half. Now that the box was ripped open, they both reached for what was inside. Dixon turned so his body blocked Dani, but she wiggled her way around and soon both of them were wrestling on the floor and tearing through the packaging like wild hyenas.

They both reached in and felt something cold and hard and smooth and contoured. Dixon's tearing exposed a small sculpted hand and a tiny microphone. He ripped the rest of the paper away and the original Ivory Elvis stood on the floor between them, gleaming in all its glory. They knelt on either side of the statue—much as the villagers had when worshipping this idol in Tanzania.

It was the biggest surprise of Dixon's life. "Holy shit" was all he could really say.

"Holy shit what?"

"Nothing."

Dani pointed to the living room, where the same figure stood atop Dixon's symphonizer. "You already have one of these."

"I have nothing like this." Dixon said and looked over the Ivory Elvis, wondering why it had been mailed to his house.

"You told me the legend, Peter. You have one of these, and yours is a fake. A replica. Is this supposed to be the real thing?"

"No." There was a note. Dixon snatched it before Dani could.

"Why would you need two fakes?"

Dixon didn't know what else to say, so he pretended to ignore the question. He looked at the note. Words were scribbled in blank ink.

> Mr. Dixon, since I may not return, I thought you'd like to have this.
>
> Thanks for everything... Big E.

Dani took the note from his hand. Dixon felt defenseless, like he could not stop Dani from figuring it all out. He let her read the note and figured he'd make it up as he went along and hope everything worked out in the end.

When Dani finished reading she grinned at Dixon with a gleam of triumph in her eyes. "This is from Elvis."

"No, it's not."

"You told me yourself the real Kilimanjaro King ended up in Presley's Jungle Room. I've been to the Graceland Jungle Room, Peter. I've *seen* the Ivory Elvis. Did you go to Graceland because you wanted to buy this or something?"

Dixon had been busted and they both knew it. Monroe had told him more than once, when in doubt: deny, deny, deny. "I told you, Dani, I do not know Elvis Presley."

"Then why is it signed Big E?"

"That's my fat Uncle Ernie."

"Uncle Ernie calls you Mr. Dixon? Why is this post-marked from Memphis?"

"Because that's where Uncle Ernie lives!" Dixon was overwhelmed. It felt like his stomach would explode any minute.

"You're full of shit!" She consulted the note. "Why does it say 'since I may not return?' May not return from what?"

"May not return from nothing. I don't know what you're talking about!"

"I'm talking about the note."

His chest burned, begging him for a hospital. "How should I know what the note means? I *don't know* what it means"

"How does Jimmy Orr fit into this?"

"We hired him to entertain the employees."

"I don't believe you. Now tell me, Mr. Dixon, what did you do with Elvis?"

Dixon lost his temper and yelled, "Leave me alone!!" And then he hunched over clutching his gut. He shuddered for a moment, inadvertently hoping the ache in his abdomen would make him vomit.

"Are you okay?" Dani watched Dixon convulse. He looked bad, like he needed medical assistance. "Should I call a doctor, or a…?"

"No," he waved an arm. "I'm fine." He crawled to the couch and pulled himself up to sit. Dani stood and placed a hand on his back, looking down as Dixon leaned forward hugging himself.

"Do you need anything?"

He shook his head and said, "Antacids. Milk."

"Okay," Dani went to the kitchen and returned with a milk bottle and a handful of Rolaids. Dixon took them and washed down the pills with a gigantic gulp of milk. He took a few deep breaths, and sat back when it hit his stomach and eased the pain.

He chuckled softly. "My doctor told me I need to relax."

"He was probably right."

"I need to quit boozing." He took another gulp of milk. Without looking at her he said, "You better be on your way, Dani. Go home and watch TV. Everything will make sense in a few days."

Dani saw another chance for information. "What do you mean by that?"

Dixon closed his eyes and shook his head. He touched the cold milk carton to his brow and kept it there until Dani quietly left.

She returned to her car feeling sorry for that lonely man with an Elvis obsession and a terrible ulcer. Dixon was hiding something so nerve-racking it was killing him. But whatever it was, he had said it would all make sense in a few days.

She stuck to her mission. There was no time to spare, and her next task was obvious. She needed to track down Jimmy Orr and verify that bit about him visiting the space center and singing for a NASA crowd. Something told her the Elvis impersonator would provide the missing link in her chain.

Dixon decided he would not tell Monroe about this encounter. The girl was out of his hair, and it was too late for her to break any worthwhile story before the big show. Dixon stayed on the couch for another ten minutes, and then, with his stomach feeling only slightly better, he went to the phone and called Jimmy Orr.

The novelty rock singer was still in bed, hung over from last night's bender. His voice was groggy and hoarse.

"Listen," Dixon said. "This girl, going either by Dani or by Kim, might show up today or tomorrow asking questions about NASA. You tell her you don't know a thing, understand? I'll do what I can for compensation."

"Does this mean I have the job?"

Dixon sighed. "Stick with me, Jimmy. You might."

Jimmy grunted and hung up. Dixon stood and clutched his stomach. The pain had subsided, but he knew it would return with a vengeance the instant he felt any more stress. He knew he should see his doctor again, and he planned to go on hiatus after the mission, but he wasn't going to leave the Apollo 11 crew hanging at the moment of truth.

This had been the most challenging mission he could remember, with more conflicts of interest than Dixon cared to handle. He couldn't wait to quit the space agency and work full time for Elvis. Until then he had a job to do. His aches and pains told him to drive to a hospital. Instead, Dixon got dressed and headed in to work.

Orr was not happy with Peter Dixon. First he had offered the Elvis lookalike a chance to stand in as the real thing. Then only weeks later, the offer had been offensively revoked by Dixon's boss, some jerk with perfect hair. Orr didn't appreciate how they made him jump from one foot to the other. Especially when one foot meant sold-out concert arenas and multi-million dollar paychecks, and the other foot meant dive bars and high school reunions.

He shouldn't have set his hopes so high. Dixon had said the Elvis gig was a one-in-a-million shot and Orr had made the mistake of thinking he'd assume the throne of the King. Now he felt so cheated he'd spent last night drowning his sorrows in whiskey.

As he stumbled out of bed, the pain of last night's binge hit him hard. His head ached and his stomach hurt. There was no deal at NASA, which meant Jimmy was back to singing covers with Small Potatoes. It could be worse, he figured. The members of Small Potatoes were the best folks he could be stuck with. They were talented musicians and lifelong friends and tonight they had another gig at the Slop Ranch.

If he was destined only to be the best Elvis imper-sonator in the land, then he could accept his fate. It was the music that kept him from going crazy. The chance to sing his favorite songs the way his favorite singer would. Jimmy headed for the bathroom. His sideburns needed a re-dye.

When Dixon strolled into Mission Control, Monroe was already there. "Pete," he said when Dixon found him at Flight Director Gene Kranz's console. "You feel-ing okay?"

"I'm fine," Dixon lied. "Can we see Elvis?" He nod-ded toward the screens up front.

Monroe followed his gaze and sensed something with Dixon was amiss. "Hey, Peter maybe you should go home and get some rest."

Dixon would have none of this. "When can we see him?"

"Soon, Peter, soon." Monroe invited him to sit. Then he said, "I swear, Peter, you're working yourself stupid. Maybe you should take tomorrow off. Get some sleep before the big day."

Dixon hunched over slightly and rocked back and forth. It helped ease the pain. Monroe watched him carefully. It was pathetic. Dixon was in serious need of a vacation. Monroe decided he'd insist that Pete take tomorrow off and return for the landing the day after.

The astronauts sent back another TV transmission. The NASA workers watched the view screens as Armstrong opened a hatch and looked down a dark tunnel into the *Eagle* lander.

He squeezed through the thirty-inch hole and floated into the LEM. Aldrin followed, and moments later the lights and power were up in the *Eagle* spacecraft for the first time.

Dixon watched, knowing the astronauts were under strict orders to keep Elvis off the air. But the instant the coast was clear Dixon expected to see a token shot of the King.

Monroe consulted with the Television Officer, who told him they had finished recording and all cameras were on standby. If Pete Dixon wanted to see Elvis, he was free to do so. He gave the word and that unmistakable smile was suddenly gracing the giant TV screen.

Everyone in the room applauded when they saw him, and Elvis waved into the camera. He was holding a notepad and a pencil. In zero-gravity, his hair was inflated with a shaggy poof. Monroe asked what he was working on and Elvis said he was scribbling lyrics to a new song about his astronaut buddies.

When Dixon was satisfied, he nodded to Monroe, who gave the okay to end the transmission. Then Monroe gave Dixon a dirty look and told his second-in-command to head home for the day.

"Get some rest. You need it."

Dixon agreed and went home. He was asleep the instant his head touched the pillow.

Orr led Small Potatoes through *Blue Suede Shoes* and closed the band's second set at the Slop Ranch. Then they migrated to the bar for drinks. Drummer Tom Washburn and bassist Petie Podobinski met their girlfriends at the far end, while the single guys, Jimmy Orr and Johnny Wichita, took a seat in the middle.

"How often do you guys play?" A female voice inquired. Orr looked to see who it belonged to and saw a pretty brunette sliding a stool in place beside him.

"Three, four times a week," he replied.

Dani acted nonchalant, like she didn't give a rat's ass about Jimmy Orr. "Sounded good up there."

He nodded and was mobbed by a group of giggling sorority girls, who gathered around Jimmy and posed for photographs. Dani waited for them to leave and then casually said to Orr, "I saw you on TV the other day."

He smirked. "You can't believe everything you see on TV."

She smiled. "It was you. I'm positive."

Orr had no idea where this was going. "It's just a job."

"Entertaining the troops at NASA?"

"Something like that."

They sipped their beers quietly. Orr shared a few words with Wichita as Dani watched from the corner of her eye. She didn't know how many drinks Orr had consumed that night, but every drop would help her cause. He looked back to her, noticing she was staring into nothing, yet watching him at the same time.

"You here with anybody?"

Dani shook her head. "I came to see you."

This caught him off guard, but Orr maintained his composure. "I hope you enjoyed the show."

"I don't give a damn about the show."

Now he gave her his full attention. "Why don't you tell me what's going on."

Dani fired from the hip. "Did you really go to NASA to sing for the workers or did somebody put you up to something?"

Orr suspected this girl was the one Dixon mentioned. "You're a reporter, aren't you?"

"I'm with *The Sensational Nation*."

"I've been expecting you. What do you want?"

She was surprised to learn she was expected. Dixon had beaten her to the singer. She tried not to let that information throw her off. She said. "I want to know about Peter Dixon, your relationship, what he told you, what you agreed to do for him, and for NASA."

Orr glanced around the bar and wondered if this was a test—if Dixon had sent her to the bar, and if the FBI was watching to see if he'd talk. "Maybe we should go backstage."

They did; backstage turned out to be nothing more than an open storage area at the rear of the establishment. In the middle of the room were some folding chairs and a table covered with empty beer cans and ashtrays full of cigarette butts. Here Dani and Jimmy were alone.

She set a notepad on the table and sat ready to write as Jimmy Orr lit a cigarette.

"I've been instructed not to talk to you," Jimmy said. "No matter what."

Dani was about to protest and convince him otherwise when Jimmy said, "But he lied to me."

"He lied to me too," she said quickly.

Jimmy nodded, visibly irritated that Dixon had retracted the offer. He sat back and recounted his encounter with Peter Dixon. "A few weeks ago this guy comes to talk to me. Says that he's a scientist and has a proposition. A business opportunity. So I'm all ears. I'm sworn to secrecy but I don't know why, because Dixon hardly tells me a thing. The pitch goes like this: Dixon tells me I may need to stand in for Elvis Presley on July 20th. He won't tell me why, only that this may or may not happen. He said the job could last anywhere from a week to a decade and that I needed to report to the space center on July 19th. I showed up yesterday and they sent me home."

Dani was scribbling everything on her notepad. "What do you mean by 'they?'"

"Two guys. Dixon and some other guy, acted like his boss."

"Did his boss have slicked back hair, relatively shiny?"

"Well," Orr took a drag. "Not shiny, but polished. He sent me home, said that I wouldn't be needed."

"Did they tell you why Elvis needed a stand-in?"

He shook his head. "I assume he was in some kind of danger."

"Danger?"

"They said something might happen to Elvis, that he may be involved in some kind of an Apollo 11 accident. You know, they kept referring to him as The Bacon."

Dani remembered the notepad she found in Dixon's study, and the breakfast lingo he had used when she first saw him at the space center. Suddenly everything made sense. As crazy as it was, everything clicked and Dani knew exactly what NASA had up its sleeve. "Impossible," she muttered incredulously. "Impossible!"

"What?"

She shook her head. "It's just not possible."

"What's not possible?"

Dani looked him in the eye. "They mentioned an Apollo 11 accident involving Elvis Presley—are you absolutely sure?"

"Yes!" Orr insisted. "That was the whole reason they wanted me around. They said I would stand in for Elvis if anything happened."

Dani shook her head. "It just can't be."

Orr was missing it. "What are you talking about, miss?"

She thought her way through and stated facts. "According to NASA, Elvis Presley's life is in danger."

"That's what they said."

"His life is in danger on July 20th, right?"

"Right."

"July 20th, the day we land on the moon."

"Yeah."

"NASA is putting Elvis Presley in danger that day."

"I suppose."

"Okay," she paused to look over her notes. "They need you, an Elvis lookalike—and a very good one might I add—to stand in for the King."

"Yes. To be inserted into his life, yes."

"On July 20th. *Maybe* on July 20th."

"According to Dixon, that's correct." Orr watched her intently and waited for her point.

"Terrific." Dani took a deep breath. "It would be fair to say that, on July 20th, NASA is attempting to land Elvis Presley on the moon."

He laughed. "Come on. You think that's what they're talking about?"

She nodded yes.

"How could that be? There are only three astronauts on the spaceship. Neil Armstrong's going to be the first man on the moon and then there's Buzz and that other guy. NASA never said anything about Elvis."

"Never said anything *publicly*," Dani corrected him. "I saw those guys at Graceland. I saw them meet the King. They won't talk about Elvis and for the last six weeks, the King can't be found anywhere. If you ask

Dixon about Elvis, he'll play dumb, even though he's been hanging out with the guy for over a month. Elvis even sent Dixon this ivory statue thing in the mail. Some relic from the jungles of Tanzania."

Orr squinted. "Huh?"

"Nothing," she shook her head and continued. "The NASA guys mentioned these action figures. I think I have a good idea about those."

"They mentioned Operation Blue Moon."

"Ha!" She threw her head back and cackled. "What a great name! What shysters!"

Orr smirked, amused at Dani's joy over this awkward, impossible moon landing theory.

"And you said they needed you for anywhere from a week to a decade?"

"Uh-huh."

She snapped her fingers and pointed his way. "My friend, we're on our way to a Pulitzer."

Orr nodded, although he did not understand. "Okay."

"Yep," Dani grinned. "We got em."

Chapter Fifteen

July 19th

The astronauts strapped themselves in place and began to make final preparations for lunar orbit. They were about to burn a course correction, a maneuver that would place the moon in the spacecraft's field of view for the first time.

Armstrong fired the engines, and a giant half-moon swung magnificently into place outside their windows. Before them were silver craters and hills of every size. They spotted gigantic boulders—some of which rivaled the mountains of earth—and sand dunes nearly as deep as our oceans. It glowed before them, ready to host their arrival and the glory of the King.

The sight of the moon so close stunned the astronauts into temporary silence. Aldrin muttered, "Unbelievable."

Collins said, "That's a moving target a quarter of a million miles from Earth. When we launched, it was nowhere near where it is now, but here we are in a spaceship, without so much as a whimper."

Armstrong murmured his agreement and went back to work. Elvis sat quietly in the spaceship, a tiny speck against the great face of the moon, less than twenty-four hours from performing the greatest concert of all time.

While Monroe stood at the back of Mission Control like a general watching over his troops, Dixon was home in bed. He slept past noon, and stayed another hour, before dragging himself to the bathroom for a shower.

His stomach was better and Dixon felt fit to go into work, but he knew his body needed the rest. The mission was in good hands and Dixon would return for the landing tomorrow.

After his shower Dixon put on a robe and shuffled to the kitchen for an apple. Then he sat on the living room floor and gazed at his pair of ivory statues on the piano. Once his idol, Elvis was now a friend and a future business associate. Once they pulled off this moon landing, Dixon would quit his job.

Dixon looked to his Elvis shrine on the mantle and marveled at his most recent additions. There was the freshly autographed, rare *Return to Sender* 45 from 1962. There was a pair of cufflinks with tiger's eye stones from 1959. An Elvis Presley fingernail clipping sat in a jar, and a placard beside it marked the spot he'd reserved for the official Elvis moon rock.

With Dani out of his life, it was safe to bring the moon rock placard out of seclusion. He was lucky that she had never learned the truth. And even if she did, she was too late to do anything about it with the landing tomorrow and morning newspapers going to print in just a few hours.

Dixon lay back on the carpet and chomped on his apple. He stared at the ceiling and chuckled, knowing Dani Mitchell wasn't the only person who'd be surprised tomorrow afternoon.

With everything on schedule for Apollo 11 and no loose ends in Operation Blue Moon, Dixon finished his meager breakfast and enjoyed the rest of his day off.

NASA had ruined Dani Mitchell's Elvis gig, now she was going to ruin theirs. Granted, landing Elvis Presley on the moon was a more ambitious achievement than publishing a King interview in *The Sensational Nation*, but Monroe and Dixon didn't need the recognition.

She could do nothing to stop the moon landing, and Dani had no intentions of standing in the way. But this

Elvis landing was obviously planned as a surprise. A surprise Dani hoped to spoil. Elvis would walk on the moon, but the rest of the world would be ready.

She woke with the dawn, ordered room service and planted herself at her small hotel-room table. She remained there for hours with her pad and pencil, furiously scribbling notes and organizing what she knew about Operation Blue Moon.

There was still a court appearance for Dani on Monday, but preparing for that could wait. Time was precious, and there was a crunch to finish the article and get it to Baker before tomorrow's news went to print. *TSN's* next issue wasn't due on the press for another week, but Baker had connections at the *Times* and *Newsday*. He'd surely do all he could to get a story this good into the paper.

She finished just after three that afternoon and called Baker at the office. "I'm sending a story over the wire."

He immediately reminded her, "You're on suspension."

"I know that, but this story needs to go to print tonight."

He laughed. "Who do you think you are, Cronkite? I had to reach into my pocket, thirteen hundred dollars, to cover hotel damages, Dani."

"I thought that was coming out of my paycheck."

"What about your little story?"

There was a lonely silence. Then Dani said, "It's a conspiracy...between Elvis and NASA. I've been on this one for six weeks and last night something finally broke."

Baker was somewhat interested. He gave Dani thirty seconds to capture his attention. She told him everything she knew about Operation Blue Moon: her relationship with Dixon, the conversation with Jimmy Orr and the secret NASA mission to land Elvis on the moon.

Dani's total lack of credibility made Baker laugh. "Why are you wasting my time with this crap?"

"Are you kidding?"

"Elvis Presley on the moon? I wouldn't say that's fit for the *New York Times* and you're certainly not going to find that rubbish in *The Sensational Nation*. Your Elvis goes to space tale wouldn't even be a good comic book."

She pleaded. "This is a great opportunity for the magazine."

"So was Led Zeppelin."

Dani was enraged that he brought up her unwillingness to interview the British rock band, a reclusive bunch that would supposedly be the next music sensation. It wasn't fair to use them against her when she was after matters so much larger than life. "Led Zeppelin is a bunch of no-talent long hairs!"

"Yeah," Baker muttered. "Well, it's been nice knowing you."

Click!

Chapter Sixteen

July 20th

Apollo 11 was just moments from separating into two spacecraft. Armstrong, Aldrin and Presley squeezed into the *Eagle*, which would break away and descend to the surface for landing. Collins would stay behind in the orbiting *Columbia* and await a rendezvous with *Eagle* after it had completed its mission.

Elvis Presley's guitar was attached under an instrument panel in the *Eagle* and he kept his notebook in hand. He had not yet finished the lyrics to his latest song about his moon journey, and he hoped to add a few phrases on the ride down.

"Still three hours until we separate from *Columbia*," Armstrong said after he took his place in the *Eagle* commander's chair. "And then another two hours until we land."

Buzz Aldrin turned to Elvis, who was hunched in place behind them. "Like I was saying, King. The thing about the rhinestone spacesuit is that the moon has no atmosphere to block the sun. Imagine the sparkle from *pure* sunlight hitting those rhinestones."

Three hours later, Apollo 11 broke in two and the *Eagle* began its descent. Collins pressed his face against the window of the mother ship *Columbia* and aimed his camera at the LEM. *Eagle* appeared to be flying upside down as it drifted away from the command module.

Collins spoke into his radio. "I think you've got a fine looking flying machine there, *Eagle*, despite the fact you're upside down."

Armstrong's voice returned, "Somebody's upside down."

Collins watched *Eagle* drift further and further away until it became a speck against the backdrop of the moon. He radioed back to Mission Control.

"Houston, *Columbia*."

"*Columbia*, Houston," capsule communicator Jim Lovell replied as he watched the giant TV screens in Mission Control.

"The landing craft is on its way to the lunar surface. Everything's going just swimmingly. Beautiful!"

Monroe was at the NASA doctor's console. They monitored the health of Elvis and the doctor gave Monroe a safe thumbs-up. Then Monroe headed to the back, where Dixon was lurking at the Flight Director's console.

Monroe said, "You look refreshed."

Dixon shrugged. "Slightly." The truth was, the anxiety was already starting to make him sick. It was just a matter of time until the ulcer kicked in again.

Dani decided she didn't need a job anyway. The Pulitzer was farther away than it had ever been, so what did it matter? She had exhausted her efforts with Dixon, and knew of no better solution than to head to the bar and stay there for as long as possible.

After Baker's cold-shoulder hang-up the night before, Dani had called the *New York Times*, the *Chicago Tribune*, the *LA Times*, and the *Washington Post*, but none of the big papers were interested in her story about Elvis and the moon landing. She had also tried the local papers, but by that time, most of them had already gone to print. It was too late and Dani had no one to turn to. The only publication that seemed even remotely interested was the *Weekly World Update*, a tabloid rag where most of the ridiculous stories were made-up, with the intention of generating laughs at the supermarket checkout line.

As her Elvis theory slowly fizzled into nothing, Monday's court appearance loomed larger and larger. She still had no attorney and planned to rely on the public defender. *TSN* had refused to pay for any legal or travel expenses related to hotel vandalism, which meant Dani was down to her last dollars.

Having consumed an impressive quantity of alcohol, and unable to stop thinking about past (and probably future) career and legal disasters, she slept fitfully through the night and awoke late Sunday morning feeling groggy and hung over. Then, remembering *why* she had gotten drunk, she showered, dressed, and decided to catch the afternoon moon landing at a bar. She chose Spicer's Slop Ranch, as it had become a familiar location for Dani. Briefly she considered ransacking Dixon's house in a last-ditch attempt to recover proof of Operation Blue Moon, but it was too late to bother with any of that nonsense. Instead, she would fill herself with beer and lots of greasy food.

After the landing, Richard Baker would see how wrong he had been.

When she arrived at the Slop Ranch, she was happy to see Jimmy Orr was already there—among others. The house was packed with people who had come out to be together for the moon landing. It was an achievement everyone wanted to share. With television, nobody was isolated.

Dani found a spot next to Orr, who was filling beer mugs from a pitcher and passing them out to the members of Small Potatoes. The bar was filled with excitement. Even Jimmy Orr couldn't help but feel the patriotic pride of this day. He handed a mug to Dani and invited her to join them at their table.

"Apollo 11!" Petie Podo announced as she sat.

She clanked her mug to his and then clanked Orr's mug. "I'll drink to that!"

They ordered food, drank, and settled in their places awaiting the big show. Apollo 11 was a television event as well as a voyage of exploration. In a few hours millions of eyes in dozens of countries would be glued to their TV sets. The astronauts' ratings would surpass those of any Super Bowl or televised presidential debate.

Only Dani and Jimmy anticipated the surprise appearance from Elvis. They had agreed to keep their mouths shut. Jimmy was under orders from NASA, and anyone Dani told thought she was crazy to think Elvis Presley would be walking on the moon in a few hours. Despite what she knew, even Dani had her doubts.

Apollo 11 would be broadcast to forty-seven countries worldwide. Over seven hundred million people, one fifth of the world, would be tuned all day to NASA television coverage.

European businesses shut down any operations that functioned on Sunday and allowed workers to watch the landing on TV. Jet setters in Paris held moon parties while the Swedes anticipated Nixon's plan to phone the moon. Bars in Czechoslovakia held contests and awarded prizes for the best moon rock name.

Most Americans gathered around their living room television sets. Some turned off the lights and made their room as dark as a cinema to accommodate their grandstand seats at this historic event. Those who watched Apollo 11 on TV had a better view of history than those involved in (and overwhelmed with) the actual events.

NASA satellites would bring the historic landing to the most remote parts of the world. Places well outside the range of ground transmitters would now witness history in the making, directly connected to an event that was happening right before their eyes.

On that day, nothing about the moon landing came from any source except NASA television. The world thought live TV meant it was impossible to lie. But on July 20th, 1969, seven hundred million people saw only what Jack Monroe and his loyal Television Officer wanted them to see.

The cameras on board the *Eagle* recorded the descent inch by inch. The signal was encrypted so that only the NASA satellites could pick up the transmission. At Mission Control, Aggie Gallagher held the broadcast in delay for two hours. This gave NASA plenty of time to edit for content before sending the "live" broadcast to television stations around the world.

At the point when everyone expected the astronauts to be landing in two hours, the truth was that *Eagle* was just minutes from touching the lunar surface. Armstrong flew the spaceship carefully, controlling it with the calmest movements his anxious nerves would allow. Aldrin announced their altitude had dropped below one mile as Elvis watched in awe.

The mountains and craters down below left him speechless as they whisked by the windows of the LEM. Man had never been this close to the moon before, and in a matter of hours, Elvis would be the first person to ever set foot here. He thought about his family and all of his friends, including Peter Dixon, the astronauts and all his new NASA buddies. The pressure was great, but Elvis wasn't going to let anyone down.

Armstrong's heart rate had slowly risen from a steady 77 to an eager 156 beats per minute. Now, less than a thousand feet from the surface, the moon's features became more distinct. They could make out shadows and contours, ridges and valleys. Sand dunes and boulders now spanned every window of the spacecraft, but Armstrong kept his concentration on the complicated landing, a maneuver that had never before been attempted.

Mission Control was silent, and Dixon had chewed his fingernails to the quick. The workers listened helplessly as Aldrin narrated Apollo 11's final approach. "Seven hundred and fifty feet," he announced. "Coming down at twenty-three degrees…Seven hundred feet, down twenty-one…"

At the Slop Ranch, Dani and Orr's crew were on their third pitcher of beer. The live Apollo update informed them the *Eagle* had just broken away from the *Columbia* command module and was starting its descent to the surface.

While *Eagle* was just about to land a quarter-million miles away, viewers on Earth were just now hearing Michael Collins' delayed announcement that "The landing craft is on its way to the lunar surface. Everything's going just swimmingly."

Dani concentrated on the beer and the company and for a few short hours would completely forget about her court date and her troubles with *TSN*. When the astronauts landed and Elvis hopped out, Richard Baker would come crawling back to her like a little lost puppy. Dani smiled and poured herself another beer.

Armstrong guided the *Eagle* to hover just above the surface. They moved less than five feet per second as the Apollo 11 commander delicately directed the final moments of the landing.

"Seventy-five feet," Aldrin monitored the altitude. "Things looking good...lights on..."

Elvis wasn't even aware of having a white-knuckle grip on the sides of his seat. It felt like they were moving too fast and that they would land too hard and topple over. If they did there would be no way to pull the *Eagle* upright for launch, and they would be stranded.

"Four forward," Aldrin said. "Drifting to the right a little bit...contact light. Okay, engine stop."

The vehicle stopped moving. The surface of the moon waited safely outside the windows. They were down. The astronauts took a moment to realize they had made it and then breathed sighs of relief.

Houston chimed in. "We copy you down, *Eagle*."

Then Buzz Aldrin's cheerful voice echoed throughout Mission Control. "Houston, Tranquility Base here. The *Eagle* has landed!"

There was a nervous applause and a lot of handshaking at Mission Control, but Aldrin's announcement barely did anything to break the tension.

Jim Lovell replied to the first lunar base, "Roger, Tranquility. We copy you on the ground. You've got a bunch of guys about to turn blue. We're breathing again. Thanks a lot."

Armstrong, Aldrin and Elvis curiously surveyed their surroundings. Aldrin gave NASA a brief description. "We'll get to the details of what's around here, but it looks like a collection of just about every variety of shape, angularity and type of rock imagined, blah, blah, blah…" He let his report trail off as he turned to Elvis and asked, "Are you tuned up?"

The King nodded as he adjusted the tuning pins on his guitar.

Monroe and Dixon were at the Television Officer's console. "Okay," Monroe played director. "They're down safe. We can run the rest of the descent footage and the landing."

Gallagher hit a few buttons and switches on his terminal. "We'll air the landing exactly the way it happened. Elvis never showed his face, so we can hide his presence for one last moment."

"Alright," Monroe said. "Put us on the air."

And NASA began to broadcast the last leg of the descent. It would be another two hours before the rest of the world learned that man had finally landed on the moon.

Monroe patted Dixon on the chest. "Prepare for sound check, Peter."

Dixon nodded and called across Mission Control, "Give me sound check!"

And just like that, NASA was back to work.

Chapter Seventeen

"*I*t's not the greatest."

"But it is!" Petie Podo insisted.

Tom Washburn shook his head. "It's not the *greatest* day in the history of the human race."

"It's man on the moon, Tom. I challenge you to name a better day."

Dani, Jimmy, Podo and Small Potatoes guitarist Johnny Wichita leaned in as Washburn considered what day was of greater historical significance than today. When he had it, he announced it proudly. "The birth of Christ."

"Ha!" Podo laughed. "That's great to a religion but not an entire species! If you're not Christian, the birth of Christ means nothing! You can't prove that it even happened."

Washburn shot back, "You can't prove the moon landings are even happening."

Podo pointed to the TV above the bar. "Are you implying that NASA is about to *fake* the moon landing?"

Washburn shrugged.

Then Johnny Wichita said, "The Beatles on Sullivan. *That* was a great day."

"Elvis on Sullivan," Jimmy Orr said. "Was even greater."

Everyone at the table laughed, including Dani, and then Podo said, "But concerts and virgin births do not represent the collective talents of the human race. What I'm saying is that today's moon landing is the ultimate showcase of mankind. It tells me that nothing is impossible."

"Great," Orr said. "Now show me another pitcher of beer."

More drunken laughter and Podo made his way to the bar for another round.

On television, the first moon landing was less than thirty minutes away.

To compensate for the added weight of Elvis Presley, his guitar, his spacesuit and his amplifier, all lunar experiments had been left behind. The Apollo 11 astronauts would only gather moon rocks and photograph the landscape—there would be plenty of other moon missions that would focus on science. Apollo 11's top priority was the Elvis moon show.

Now they sat on the lunar surface, safe and sound, and unpacked their spacesuits for lunar excursion. "We all know the drill," Armstrong said. "Elvis goes first, then me, then Buzz."

Aldrin and Elvis nodded concurrence. The King took a moment to gaze over the landscape outside. He was always a little nervous before a show, but this unusual venue made him especially tense.

"Relax, King," Aldrin patted him on the back. "We know you're going to sound great out there. Just remember to sing your heart out."

"Ain't gonna be any other way, baby," said Elvis.

Armstrong asked, "You ready to tell us what song you're going to sing? See, all of us at NASA who know about this little gig—Buzz, Mike and me, and everyone down at Mission Control—we have sort of this office pool going. We've all placed bets on what song you've chosen to sing."

Elvis smiled and shook his head. "Sorry. Can't tell."

"You can tell Buzz and me," Armstrong grinned.

"We're off the air!" Aldrin said.

"Sorry, guys," Elvis insisted. "It's supposed to be a surprise. Even Monroe and Dixon don't know."

The two astronauts begged and pleaded unsuccessfully with Elvis until Monroe's voice squawked over the radio.

"Knock it off up there! We're on a tight schedule."

The astronauts went back to work. Armstrong and Aldrin readied their spacesuits while Elvis rummaged through a storage locker. Suddenly the King panicked and his search became frantic.

"Problem, King?"

Elvis grunted. "I think so."

Armstrong and Aldrin stopped what they were doing and hunched over Presley's shoulder. "What's wrong?" Aldrin asked.

"Well," Elvis muttered sheepishly. "I seemed to have left my pressure suit in the command module with Collins."

A horrified Aldrin shouted, "You forgot the rhinestone pressure suit?!?"

"You left it behind?" An angry Neil Armstrong scowled.

Monroe's voice buzzed over the radio. "What's going on up there?"

"*Columbia, Tranquility!*" Armstrong shouted into his microphone.

"*Columbia,* copy," Collins replied from lunar orbit.

"Equipment check," Armstrong said. "Do you see a rhinestone pressure suit?"

"Come again?" Collins said. The moon was blocking the transmission and turning Armstrong's voice to near static.

The Apollo 11 commander shouted again, "Do you see a rhinestone pressure suit?!!"

Monroe turned to Gallagher and shouted, "Edit all of this out of the broadcast!" Aggie complied, punching buttons and turning dials. Monroe swiveled to face Dixon. "Find out what's going on!"

Dixon took the radio. "*Tranquility*, Houston. Can you find the pressure suit?"

"We're checking on it now," Armstrong replied.

Panic had broken out in mission control. An abort simply could not be discussed. That spacesuit had to be up there somewhere.

Monroe nudged Dixon. "He can always sing from inside the *Eagle*."

And Dixon's scowl told Monroe that idea was a bad joke.

"*Columbia, Tranquility!*" Armstrong barked into the microphone.

"Negative, *Tranquility*," Collins replied sadly from the orbiting mother ship. "There is no rhinestone pressure suit onboard *Columbia*."

Armstrong gave Aldrin a desperate look. Both astronauts caught themselves eying the mission abort button. If they pressed it, the *Eagle* would blast off and head back to lunar orbit, leaving the moon for Apollo 12.

"What's the story, *Tranquility*?" Dixon called from Earth. They could hear the desperation in his voice.

Then Elvis turned and smiled that unmistakable smile. His teeth sparkled in the moonlight. He reached into the storage locker and held up the sleeve of a shiny spacesuit covered with dozens of dazzling rhinestones.

"I was just kidding," Elvis smiled.

"Aw, hell," Buzz Aldrin slapped him on the back. "You've just been too much fun, King!"

The Slop Ranch had been overcome by an awe-struck silence. All eyes in the packed bar were on the TV, where a mess of craters and shadows zoomed across the screen. Buzz Aldrin's fuzzy voice narrated the landing.

"Seven hundred and fifty feet, coming down at twenty-three degrees…Seven hundred feet, down twenty-one."

They would land in a matter of seconds. Dani tried not to care, but suddenly NASA was no longer just a company of arrogant, dishonest cover-up artists. As much as she'd thought that she hated everything NASA stood for, she knew deep-down that they were pioneers who were on the brink of accomplishing the most fascinating task in the history of the world. And according to what she and Orr had decided, Monroe and Dixon were planning a little surprise as well.

Dani was tempted to mention the Elvis appearance, and the three beers she'd consumed urged her to do so, but Orr was onto her and he warned her with a stern headshake. She agreed to keep quite. Discussing Elvis on the moon had already cost her a job; she didn't want to cause any problems for Orr too.

She turned her attention back to the TV, where the moon's surface was just yards below the *Eagle's* television camera.

"Seventy-five feet," Aldrin said. "Things looking good…lights on…"

Dani's vendetta against Peter Dixon and Jack Monroe became meaningless. She was locked in the moment, her attention on nothing but the moon landing. The patrons of the crowded bar held their breath and millions of TV viewers clenched their fists and waited in proud, edgy anticipation.

"Four forward," Aldrin said. "Drifting to the right a little bit...contact light. Okay, engine stop."

"We copy you down, *Eagle*." The TV picture rested above a blurry square of gray sand. Apollo 11 had landed safely.

Buzz Aldrin announced, "Houston, Tranquility Base here. The *Eagle* has landed!"

Cheering erupted in the bar. Most of the customers broke into applause, while others hugged and raised their glasses in a toast to the historic accomplishment. Dani was as much a part of the excitement as anyone else who'd witnessed this moment. She was almost able to forgive Monroe and Dixon for her troubles.

Walter Cronkite shouted, "Man on the moon! Oh man!"

Contrary to what was on TV, the moon story was far ahead of its time. Elvis squeezed into his rhinestone spacesuit as Armstrong and Aldrin helped him pull it over his shoulders. They hoisted the helmet over his head and fixed it in place. Elvis eyed the songbook he'd left on the floor of the *Eagle*. Lyrics were scribbled on the page but the second verse was incomplete, a struggle for words, which had been finally scratched away in a bout of frustrated writer's block.

"I can't seem to get the chorus to work."

"It'll come together," Armstrong said as he tightened a few nozzles on Elvis's spacesuit. He explained, "You've got a portable life support and communications system on your back."

Elvis nodded. "Sure, with provisions for pressurization, oxygen and carbon dioxide removal."

Armstrong was proud. "You're going to do fine."

When Elvis was suited up, Armstrong and Aldrin stepped into their own spacesuits. When their suits and helmets were sealed airtight, Elvis opened the hatch and man was exposed to the lunar surface for the first time.

Elvis flipped so he could back out and step down to the ladder that descended to the moon. He gripped the railing on either side as Armstrong helped him navigate. The bulky pressure suit prevented Elvis from seeing behind himself, so he relied on Armstrong's guidance.

Now Elvis dangled halfway out of the hatch and let his right foot swing for the top rung of the ladder. He found it, adjusted his grip on the railing, and under the eager watch of Neil Armstrong and Buzz Aldrin, Elvis descended to the lunar surface.

Before he stepped off the ladder, Elvis reached to the outer wall of the *Eagle* and pulled a metal ring that deployed a television camera. It slid down a cable and rested outside the spacecraft. The lens was aimed at the base of the ladder, where the King of Rock and Roll waited to take the first step.

Mission Control watched in silence as Elvis Presley appeared on the giant screen before them as a distorted black and white image, encrypted only for NASA eyes.

"I'm at the foot of the ladder," Elvis announced.

In the *Eagle*, Buzz handed Presley's guitar to Armstrong. The spiral notebook Elvis used to write his songs was entwined in the tuning pins. Armstrong took the guitar, untangled the notebook and gave the instrument back to Aldrin. The notebook was opened to the song Elvis had been working on for the last four days, a few lines of lyrics and a chorus that had been scratched out.

Just below him, Elvis stepped back and planted his left foot on the moon. He felt a solitude man had never known.

Armstrong was busy reading from the songbook. He read the first line of lyrics out loud, "That's one small step for man/ One giant leap for Mankind..."

The messy, unfinished song page looked like this:

Lunar Rock
E. Presley

That's one small step for man
One giant leap for mankind

Got no room for the band
But I don't think they'll mind

I got Neil, Buzz, Mike and me
Let's rock

The rest of the lyrics were illegible, scratched away and covered with X's. Armstrong waved the songbook at Aldrin. "Hey, Buzz, this tune has quite the jingle-jangle."

Buzz pointed over Armstrong's shoulder. "Neil, he did it."

Mission Control had been silenced. Only Monroe could lean over and whisper, "Excellent work, Mr. Dixon."

All of Dixon's worries, the trouble with Dani, the pain in his stomach, it was all suddenly worth the effort. For those few short moments, Dixon enjoyed total peace of mind.

He said to Jack, "Why can't I feel this good all the time?"

Monroe shrugged. "Who says you can't?"

Elvis stood with both feet on the lunar surface. The bulky spacesuit and life support pack did not feel as heavy as they had on earth. Elvis had been there a matter of seconds when he noticed the earth floating over the horizon. Its blue oceans and greenish landscapes were the only color in this world of gray sand dunes and black sky. Elvis was overwhelmed with where he was and lost his center of gravity.

"Oops," he said, and fell backwards in shock. He toppled softly to the moon's surface and a tiny cloud of dust settled around him. He lay there for a moment and gazed at the earth.

Armstrong called through the hatch. "You okay, Elvis?"

"Oh, my boy. This sure beats stargazing from my front lawn, baby."

"Boy, you said it!" Armstrong bounded down the ladder and jumped to the surface with both feet. He leaned over as best he could, grabbed Elvis's space gloves, and pulled Elvis to his feet.

"Be careful." Armstrong said as he cleaned the dust off the rhinestones. "Monroe will kill us if he finds out we got your suit dirty."

Monroe suddenly chimed in through their headsets. "Keep that spacesuit clean! And hurry this up, we're short on time!"

Elvis looked up the ladder and into the belly of the *Eagle*. "Where's my guitar?"

Aldrin appeared in the doorway with Elvis's guitar. "Coming down!" He hopped down the ladder and presented the guitar to Elvis.

Buzz said, "I love that *Lunar Rock* song you're working on."

Elvis shrugged modestly. "It's okay."

"I might have some ideas for the second verse," Aldrin said.

"Me too," Armstrong said and started snapping pictures.

Aldrin continued. "Maybe we can help you work it out on the way back to Earth."

Elvis was pleased Buzz wanted to help. He smiled. "That's a deal."

Armstrong pointed the camera at one of the landing craft's legs, where a plaque was attached. He read the words as he filmed. "Here men from the planet Earth first set foot on the Moon. July 1969, AD. We came in peace for all mankind."

Under the inscription were the faces of Armstrong, Aldrin, Collins, Presley and Nixon. It was quite the crew. The varsity lineup of the Blue Moon Conspiracy.

He swung the camera around to find Elvis standing behind him, leaning against his guitar, which stood upright on the ground. Armstrong could see his own reflection in the faceplate of Elvis Presley's space helmet. He snapped a picture.

Then Elvis handed his guitar back to Aldrin. Aldrin handed him the U.S. flag, which Elvis planted in the lunar soil. Once it was in place Elvis stood at attention and saluted, an honor that certainly topped any from his days as a U.S. Army soldier.

Armstrong snapped another picture.

Meanwhile Aldrin helped Elvis prepare for the performance. The staging was different than dress rehearsal; instead of sitting on a metal stool, Elvis stood. Aldrin helped Elvis hoist his guitar over his head, and place the strap over his shoulders. It was time. Armstrong notified Houston and the lights went down.

"Jack!" Dixon cupped his hand over the phone. "I've got the President here."

Monroe snatched the phone and listened. "Yes, sir," he said after a moment. Determination was frozen on his face. He held the telephone in one hand and took the radio with the other.

"*Tranquility*, Houston," he called.

Armstrong answered. "*Tranquility*, copy."

Monroe said, "The President of the United States is in his office now and would like to say a few words."

"That would be an honor."

Dixon checked with the audio technicians, who assured him they were ready to record the crisp transmission from Washington. It would be broadcast hours later as a "live" phone call.

Nixon was patched through to the *Eagle*. His words had been scripted several days earlier by a team of NASA writers, under the close supervision of Jack Monroe.

President Nixon said, "Neil, Buzz, I am talking to you from the Oval Room at the White House, and this certainly has to be the most historic telephone call ever made. And for people all over the world, I am sure they too join with Americans in recognizing what a feat this is.

"Because of what you have done, the heavens have become part of man's world. As you talk to us from the Sea of Tranquility, it inspires us to redouble our efforts to bring peace and tranquility to Earth. For one priceless moment, in the whole history of man, all the people on this Earth are truly one."

Armstrong replied, "Thank you, Mr. President. It's a great honor and privilege for us to be here representing not only the United States, but men of all peace and nations. With the interest and a curiosity and a vision for the future, it's an honor for us to be able to partici-pate here today. Especially for this moment."

After a short silence, Armstrong asked, "Mr. President? Would you care to do the honors?"

Nixon replied from the White House, "Thank you, Neil, it would be my pleasure."

Spiro Agnew, Henry Kissinger and J. Edgar Hoover leaned in to listen as President Nixon read the intro-duction off his desk. "And now, it's time for a special surprise. Brought to you by the United States of America. For one night only. Planet Earth, say hello to the King of Rock and Roll. Here he is, live from the sur-face of the Moon, ladies and gentlemen, Elvis Presley!!"

Mission Control applauded and cheered when Elvis appeared on their screens with his guitar. The moon glowed around him in the sunlight and made his space-suit sparkle.

Elvis let his eyes rise to the Earth, which hung silently over the horizon. He said softly into his radio, "This is dedicated to that tiny blue rock in the sky."

The music started, and Elvis started to jiggle inside his spacesuit as best he could. It was a big band showpiece, with lots of horns and percussion, and a happy, vague rhythm that could prelude almost any show tune.

The music blared throughout Mission Control so suddenly that it startled every person in the room. With the horns and the drums pounding his eardrums, Monroe angrily looked around for an explanation. "Now what the hell is this shit?"

Even he wasn't anticipating what, or how, Elvis would perform.

"There's no air on the moon," Dixon reminded him with a happy smile. "We had to use our own soundtrack."

"Why is it so gaudy?"

Dixon only nodded and watched the King shake. "Very colorful!"

On the moon, Elvis was still shaking as the horns finished the song's intro and fell silent as the percussion took over with a steady beat. Now it was time for Elvis to speak.

"Never ceases to amaze me, baby! Before we get going, I'd like to introduce everybody to the crew of Apollo 11. You know them already, but here they are in the flesh. Immediately to my left, standing with the television camera, is the mission commander, Neil Armstrong."

Elvis took a step back, tapping his boot with the beat of the drums that echoed inside his headset. "Beside him is Edwin Aldrin, but everyone calls him Buzz."

He paused again, as if he could hear a crowd applauding. "Finally, up above, circling us in the *Columbia*, is Michael Collins. Michael Collins, ladies and gentlemen."

Another pause, while the imaginary crowd cheered. Then the horns kicked in again, and Elvis broke into *Hound Dog*.

The Television Officer jumped up from his console and shouted "Smackaroo!" *Hound Dog* had been his pick in NASA's Elvis pool. Aggie Gallagher was now five hundred dollars richer.

Dixon and Monroe stood in the back of Mission Control and watched the show. The space helmet gave his lyrics a hollow sound, but Elvis was perfectly in-tune with the background music. Dixon went to the audio crew to see about enhancing his voice before they put it on the air.

They assured him. "We'll have plenty of time to clean up the track before it's broadcast. It'll sound like Elvis is standing in your living room."

Dixon was satisfied. He watched Elvis on the big screen and started contemplating the Apollo 11 sound-track. It could be released with the Elvis coffee mugs and T-shirts the day the astronauts returned.

Now Neil Armstrong snapped pictures of the King while Elvis went into the second verse. He shook as much as he could as he sang, and had to concentrate on keeping his balance but nailed every note. Buzz Aldrin stood off-camera smiling at Elvis. The rhinestones on his bulky spacesuit glistened, and his voice was terrific.

As he came around to the end of the song, Elvis performed a series of karate chops and kicks and went right into *All Shook Up*. It was a medley, and down below, all of Mission Control clapped and bounced with the beat. Planning to go into *Heartbreak Hotel*, then *Don't Be Cruel*, and finally *Jailhouse Rock*, the show was cut short when something terrible happened.

As Elvis karate kicked and chopped his way through *All Shook Up*, the sleeve of his left arm brushed against the guitar's tuning pins. The end of the lowest string—where it's wrapped around the tuning pin and snipped like a bud—had a very sharp point. Sharp enough to puncture skin, and certainly sharp enough to snag the edge of a rhinestone from the sleeve of Elvis Presley's spacesuit. When he reached out and karate-chopped, that is exactly what happened.

The sharp tip of the string cut the material behind the rhinestone and ripped the jewel right off Elvis's spacesuit. A square inch of protective material was ripped away and left Elvis at the mercy of God.

Air leaked and the suit deflated like an untied balloon. Elvis toppled backwards and fell motionless before Aldrin or Armstrong could figure out what had happened.

Alarms were blaring throughout every corner of Mission Control. The doctor saw the King's heart rate had suddenly flattened. Across the room, a technician shouted, "We have a depressurization in the King's suit!"

The doctor panicked, "We're losing him!"

"Cut the music!" Monroe yelled and ran with Dixon to the doctor's console.

Beads of sweat dripped from Dixon's brow. "Tell me this is a glitch."

The doctor punched a few buttons and turned a couple dials. "Negative, sir, no glitch. The King is on his way out."

Elvis had one last gulp of oxygen in his lungs. Armstrong and Aldrin knelt beside him, powerless and uncertain of what to do. It had been so quick.

"Stay with us," Armstrong pleaded as a calm glaze appeared in Elvis's eyes.

"You sounded terrific." Aldrin said and grabbed Elvis's glove for the goodbye.

With his final breath, Elvis Presley whispered his dying words, "Thank you…thank you very much."

Chapter Eighteen

*M*ission Control was overcome by a silence more powerful than the Saturn V rocket, more powerful than a thousand rockets. No one could believe what happened, but the NASA doctor confirmed the King was dead.

Dixon felt like he'd been shot in the gut. His ulcer throbbed so hard it brought him down to one knee. He had to hold the back of a chair to steady himself and keep from falling over completely.

"Lock the doors," Monroe said. The NASA Administrator knew the historical significance of the mission would be determined by what he did right now. He went into crisis mode, and thought back to his days with JFK. Kennedy kept him around because Monroe had a knack for staying one step ahead of the rest of the world. He had handled Khrushchev and he had handled Castro with meticulous precision.

Now Monroe was at the ultimate crossroad, where the decision was to King, or not to King. Jack had only a moment to decide. He snapped and pointed at Dixon. "Get that guy back!"

Dixon was drained and utterly defeated, in dull contrast to Monroe's command. "Which guy?"

Monroe was firm. "That guy who was here!"

Dixon could think of hundreds of guys. "Who are you talking about?"

"That fucking Elvis lookalike. Get him back here!"

"Him?"

"Yes, him!"

"Jimmy Orr?"

"I don't know his name but we *need* him."

Dixon pulled himself to his feet. "I thought you didn't like him."

The confusion drove Monroe crazy. "I'm going to strangle you, Peter."

"You said you never wanted to see him again."

Monroe lost his temper. "Damn it, Peter! Get that phony Elvis back here *now!*"

Dixon complied and hurried off to his office where he kept Orr's phone number. Next Monroe ordered Gallagher to edit Elvis out of the footage and prepare to broadcast only Armstrong and Aldrin. "Use that line that Neil read from Elvis's songbook, the part about one small step for man. Make those the first words spoken from the moon, instead of 'Oops.' And as far as the rest of the world will ever know, only two men landed. Elvis has been Earthbound the whole time."

The Television Officer said. "What about the rhinestones?" He rewound the tape so Monroe could see Elvis stepping onto the lunar surface for the first time. The sparkle of his spacesuit could not be doctored by the time the footage was to air. They could tamper with the still photos before they were released to the public but the video footage was another matter.

Monroe said, "Use the footage from our dress rehearsal."

"You mean the practice concert we shot on that soundstage?"

"Precisely," Monroe nodded. "It looked authentic, and the public will never know the difference. Use any shot you need from the dress rehearsal but I want you to edit together a moon mission in which two astronauts explore the surface and where Neil Armstrong is the first man on the moon."

"If we're using practice footage, why not use Presley's rehearsal song, and replace him with your backup when the astronauts return?"

"You mean, broadcast Elvis Presley singing *Twinkle Twinkle Little Star?* Are you crazy?"

Gallagher thought about it. "You're right. Bad idea." He told Monroe he needed forty-five minutes. Then

Flight Director Gene Kranz handed a telephone to Jack. "The President wants an update."

Monroe took the phone from Gene's trembling hand. It was time to take the blame for this horrible space blunder. Monroe cleared his throat and spoke. "Mr. President."

"Hi, Jack," the oblivious President Nixon said cheerfully. "How did it go? I can't wait to watch Elvis on live TV."

Monroe could hear Nixon snickering with his cronies on the other end. He said slowly, "I'm sorry, Mr. President but there's been a terrible accident."

Armstrong and Aldrin stood above the body of the fallen king. Armstrong said, "He deserves a proper burial."

"What could be a more appropriate final resting place than the moon?"

"First visitor and he stayed full time."

"How could this happen?"

"Well," Aldrin mumbled. "He did say those rhinestones were junk."

They went to work and arranged a modest grave. They carried Elvis away from the *Eagle*—on the moon he weighed about fifty pounds, spacesuit and all—and laid him on his back with his guitar at his side. Then the two astronauts went rock hunting and laid a cocoon of moon-stones around Elvis Presley's body, with a boulder rolled into place at his head.

They stood and mourned the King. Aldrin said, "Do you suppose we should say a prayer?"

"I guess so." The astronauts bowed their heads. Armstrong said, "Dear Lord, we ask that you bless the soul of our good friend and companion, and that you and he get along well in heaven, or wherever you both shall meet. We are saddened and confused by this loss, but we know you have your reasons."

Armstrong looked to Aldrin. "Anything you want to say?"

Buzz shook his head. "Let's clean up and go home."

"Agreed," Armstrong said. "You grab some rocks to bring back while I set up a few fake experiments for the cameras."

Armstrong found a metal rod, which he covered with a sheet of plastic and planted in the lunar dirt. NASA would later claim this was the "solar wind spectrometer."

Armstrong made a pile of moon rocks, covered it with aluminum foil and called it the "laser ranging retroflector."

Aldrin loaded a sack with rocks and carried it back to the *Eagle*. Armstrong followed him up the ladder and the two astronauts closed the hatch behind them. They looked to the grave outside where Elvis Presley's body would reside forever.

Businesses all over the world had come to a momentary standstill. Most of the planet's working television sets were tuned to the historic live moon landing. Dani Mitchell and the crew at Spicer's Slop Ranch were awed when Neil Armstrong backed down the ladder of the *Eagle*.

He paused above the surface; the fuzzy image of Armstrong seemed to move in slow motion. Then he stepped off the ladder, and when his foot touched the moon he said, "That's one small step for man, one giant leap for mankind."

Dani smiled. Man was on the moon, and she was alive to see it in person. It was bittersweet that she could feel happy despite the events of the last few weeks. While mankind had just reached the pinnacle of human achievement, Dani Mitchell had been thinking life couldn't get any worse. Suddenly, Neil Armstrong made her forget the mumbo-jumbo of everyday life. It was certainly a great moment to be alive.

Jimmy Orr ordered another round of drinks to celebrate the first steps on the moon. Millions watched Armstrong and Aldrin hop around gathering rocks and taking pictures. They set some experiments in place and even took a phone call from President Nixon, but there wasn't a single mention of Elvis Presley.

Dani watched as the astronauts spent over two hours exploring the lunar surface, but never once was Elvis connected to the mission. It was as if she had been chasing a shadow this whole time. The conspiracy had been nothing more than a Dani Mitchell delusion.

"This is it?" She muttered. No Elvis meant Baker thought she was a fool and would never consider another chance for Dani Mitchell at *The Sensational Nation.*

"Huh?" Orr grunted. His eyes never left the television above the bar.

"This is just two nimrods hopping around a giant sandbox with glass bubbles on their heads."

"How many beers did you drink? This is amazing. Maybe you should slow down."

"Don't you see, Jimmy?" She lowered her voice. "Landing a man on the moon is great, yeah. But it's *nothing* without Elvis."

He nodded, although he was sure Peter Dixon's unusual plans hadn't actually involved landing Elvis Presley on the moon. Maybe he had been after something else when the NASA man first enlisted Orr's services.

He said to Dani, "Neil Armstrong and Buzz Aldrin walking on the moon is certainly *something.*"

She sulked and pouted. "I know. But it could have been so much better."

Orr didn't know what else to say, so he grabbed the pitcher and topped off her beer. Dani eagerly accepted and quickly downed another mug. She burped twice and nudged Orr. "I'm going to take a leak."

He nodded and she was on her way. Orr turned his attention to the TV, which showed the astronauts still hopping around in spacesuits. As he watched and helped Podo with a basket of French Fries, he noticed a man standing below the television, waving in his direction. It was that NASA suit Peter Dixon. And he seemed frantic.

Jimmy excused himself and went to meet him at the bar.

Dixon lowered his voice. "Need to talk to you outside."

"Now?"

From Dixon's shaky nod, Orr knew the situation was urgent. He threw a twenty on his table, told his band mates he'd be back shortly and headed to the front door with Dixon.

Dani returned from the bathroom just as Orr and Dixon left the bar. She hunched down when she saw the back of Dixon's head, but he was on his way out and didn't notice her. Carefully she made her way to the front and hid behind the cigarette machine at the door. She could see out the window where Dixon and Orr were talking in the parking lot. Quickly, Dixon pushed Orr into a limousine, and followed before they were whisked away.

Dani crept out the door of the Slop Ranch and hurried to her car. She fumbled for the keys and realized she was probably too drunk to drive, but this was something she could not miss.

"Where are you taking me?"

"You're on."

Orr watched the Slop Ranch disappear behind them. "What do you mean?"

"I mean there was an accident."

Orr realized the burden Dixon was laying on him. "An accident?"

Dixon sighed a heavy breath. "He snagged a rhinestone, tore a hole in his suit."

"You really put him there?"

"It didn't work. He's dead."

"Dead?"

Dixon poked Orr in the chest. "*You're* Elvis."

Orr tried to swallow but his throat was sandpaper. "*I'm* Elvis?"

"Yeah," Dixon said. "And we're putting you on a plane. Tonight, Elvis Presley returns to Las Vegas."

"No way," Orr backed away. "What if I don't want to be Elvis?"

An idea like this had never occurred to Dixon. "You can't be serious."

"I don't know," Orr looked out the window. "You mean he really died up there?"

"Don't ever speak those words again. You're playing with *very* high stakes, Mr. Presley."

"Mr. Presley?"

"You'll have his house, his clothes, his music, his gigs. All your life you've wished you were Elvis, here it is on a silver platter."

"What happens if I say no?"

That was not an option. Dixon grabbed the singer's shirt with both hands and pulled him close so their faces were inches apart. "Listen to me," Dixon hissed through clenched teeth. "I hate that my job has brought me here, but I have an ulcer in my stomach the size of the Erie Canal. If I can't get you to do what we already agreed on, I might be responsible for *your* death too. Don't forget, I'm the government. I can get away with *anything*. Now focus, Elvis. You're going to Vegas."

Orr raised an eyebrow. "Viva Las Vegas?"

Dixon nodded and released his grasp. "Viva."

"Viva," Orr muttered and straightened his shirt. "Las Vegas."

"You fly in tonight and you're booked on the 31st. Plenty of time to adjust before you take the stage."

Orr was overwhelmed. He had no choice but to embrace the obligation and accept the throne. With a decisive nod he agreed.

There were two stoplights and then Highway 45, which lead south to the space center. Dani kept her distance from the limo and followed it onto the interstate. From the limo's brisk pace and impatient lane changes to pass, Dani knew the NASA situation was desperate. It wasn't difficult to guess what had happened. They really did try to put Elvis on the moon but their mission failed, and now Dixon needed Jimmy Orr to replace the King. As wild as it was, no other explanation made sense.

The limousine weaved through the traffic in a desperate attempt to return to the space center as soon as possible. Dani swerved with it as inconspicuously as she could and managed to keep up while maintaining a safe distance.

The exit for the space center was just ahead and Dani had no idea what she'd do once she got there. There was no doubt at all that she'd have to confront Dixon and she wouldn't mind a few more minutes with Jimmy Orr as well. She had a story, but she needed a way to prove it to Baker and *The Sensational Nation*. This could be her best and last opportunity to do that.

The limousine signaled for a right turn and pulled onto the off-ramp. Dani signaled to follow, but a siren was suddenly blaring and in her rearview mirror Dani saw a police cruiser speed up to her bumper with red lights flashing.

She swore and pulled onto the shoulder. The cruiser followed and parked behind her, its lights still flickering in her mirror. The limousine was gone and in a few minutes it would bring Orr to the safety of the space center. Neither Dixon nor Orr knew Dani had watched them outside Spicer's. She would get them later.

Now a state trooper tapped on her window with a pen. Dani rolled it down and looked up to a pudgy cop who wore a cowboy hat and mirrored sunglasses. Bushy gray sideburns grew on his face and in an odd way, this officer resembled an older, heavier Elvis Presley.

"Well, well, well," said Officer Dooley with a heavy Texan drawl. "I had you speeding and swerving in and out of traffic for about the last five miles here, ma'am."

Dani handed him her license and he whistled when he saw where she was from. "What you doing in Texas?"

She smiled her most pleasant smile. "I'm researching a story. I write for *The Sensational Nation*."

"Uh-huh," Dooley said. "Where were you coming from to be in such a hurry? Someone chasing you?"

"I was at a bar watching the moon landing."

"Saw it myself," Dooley said. "Quite a moment."

"If you could hurry this up..."

He snatched his sunglasses off his face and glared. "If you wanted speedy service you never should have left New York. Step out of the car."

"What did I do?"

"I can smell booze on your breath." A woman who'd been drinking all night killed Dooley's brother-in-law. "Step out of the car."

Dani complied and stood facing Officer Dooley. He was roughly six inches taller and easily a hundred pounds heavier than she was. The imposing way he looked down at her reminded Dani of the football coaches at her high school.

"You have any weapons, drugs or dead bodies in the car?"

"This is ridiculous," Dani said.

"I'll ask you again: any weapons, drugs or dead bodies in the car?"

"No, nothing. Can I have my ticket now?"

"Why're you in such a rush?"

Dani looked closely at Officer Dooley. Again she caught a flash of Elvis in his face. It was the sideburns, or maybe it was that policeman's sneer, but for some reason Dani felt she could confide in him. "I'm chasing a story," she explained. "About Elvis Presley and the moon."

"What about Elvis and the moon?"

"Well, it's hard to explain, but Elvis Presley went to the moon."

Dooley chuckled sadly. "If you could hear yourself you'd be embarrassed by how much your nonsense is slurring. How much you have to drink tonight?"

"I'm serious," she said. "NASA tried to put Elvis Presley on the moon and now they're using a lookalike to cover it up!"

Dooley shook his head. "I just watched the moon landing on TV and they didn't mentioned anything about Elvis Presley. No one ever said Elvis Presley was going to the moon, no one ever saw him on the moon, so as far as I'm concerned he never went. Now turn and place your hands on the roof of your car."

"What?"

"Turn and place your hands on the roof of your car."

"Why?"

"Public intoxication bordering on criminal recklessness. I've got to take you in."

Dani pleaded but she knew better than to resist arrest. This wouldn't look good for tomorrow's court appearance. As Officer Dooley snapped her in handcuffs, Dani Mitchell realized she didn't have a friend in this world.

hey dressed Jimmy in white bellbottom pants and a matching jacket, both of which were decorated with glitter trim. He received a red scarf and a touch-up from the NASA makeup artist before Dixon and Monroe put Jimmy on a plane for Vegas.

The singer felt more like a chess piece than a rock and roll icon. When the plane lifted off and left Texas behind, Jimmy Orr realized the sacrifice he had made by accepting this job, and he couldn't help but shed a tear. He'd miss the boys from Small Potatoes and the gang at the Slop Ranch. They'd been his friends for years, and Jimmy got no chance to say goodbye. He'd have to make up a story and get a message to them somehow.

His decision had been abrupt. Jimmy wished NASA had let him take a day to think about it, but they'd forced him beyond the point of no return. The best way to cope was to sit back and enjoy this once-in-a-lifetime opportunity. He'd mastered his Elvis onstage and now Jimmy prayed he could hack it behind the curtain.

Priscilla had been notified and Colonel Tom Parker was in on the act, but the rest of the Presley entourage was oblivious to the replacement of Elvis. Jimmy knew he wouldn't be able to fool all of them, but he had a feeling Dixon and his government lackeys would plug any leaks in the operation.

Vegas was just ahead. The crowd would go bonkers once Jimmy stepped off the plane and greeted them as Elvis. He was confident his act would fool the general public, but he didn't know for how long.

After he saw Jimmy Orr off, Dixon's only impulse was to go home and start drinking. After the tragedy he couldn't be expected to face his sorrows head-on. Instead, he opted for the same medicine he'd consumed the day he thought of this elaborate Elvis mission in the first place: scotch. Lots and lots of scotch.

He ignored the throbbing pain of his ulcer, which he expected (and subconsciously hoped) would break through at any moment, and numbed his misery with a double shot of booze—no ice.

The sun was setting outside, but Dixon kept his lights off. His house grew darker and darker with every passing minute until only the somber moonlight bathed his windows. By then Dixon was drunk and alone and surrounded by a galaxy of Elvis collectibles.

The entire collection could easily sell for ten thousand, excluding the original Ivory Elvis. Frantic fans would pay fifty, maybe even a hundred thousand dollars for the Maasai relic. It was a fortune of which Dixon was not worthy. His house, which once proudly exhibited rare mementos of the King, felt more like a memorial than a showplace.

The Elvis oil painting above the mantle appeared to watch him, standing in judgment as it waited for Dixon to explain this terrible day. The two Ivory Elvis statues likewise awaited some sort of consolation. He could no longer bear to look at the memorabilia. The burden of Elvis Presley's death was too great.

It was time to let go.

Dixon found a plastic trash bag and began to gather his Elvis collection piece by piece, like empty beer bottles after an all-night frat party. He started with the table by the front door where there were two framed King photos and a replica Elvis Presley leather-bound address book from 1956.

Then he hit the kitchen, where he trashed his Elvis Presley magazines and his framed Elvis Presley magazine covers and also the 8x10 of Elvis Presley wearing his gold suit. Dixon emptied crumbs and a pair of stale chocolate chips from his 1968 Elvis Presley Comeback cookie jar and threw that in with the rest of the junk.

It was time for the living room, his main Presley shrine. A room that had never failed to impress once people saw the Elvis show plates and the autographed McDonald's gift coupon. There was the expired health insurance card and the mounted Elvis Presley guitar pick. The Blue Hawaii poster, the pictures the postcards, all of it went into the garbage. The oil painting, as beautiful as it looked, was expired as junk.

His newest additions, the autographed *Return to Sender* 45 from 1962, Monroe's Elvis cufflinks from 1959, the Elvis Jungle Room fingernail—all of it was swept away.

Next was the Lunar Elvis paraphernalia: the coffee mug, the T-shirt, the action figure and the board game. He stuffed it all into the trash bag. Last was the Tom Parker picture and the picture of Elvis in the Army. Finally the two white statues stood alone atop Dixon's symphonizer. He left them there and went to the kitchen where he'd left his liquor bottle.

He poured his umpteenth scotch and through a shroud of drunkenness, he could feel his stomach begging him to quit. Dixon returned to the living room and sat at the bench, gazing upon the Ivory Elvis statues— one real, one fake—now the last pieces of King paraphernalia to be tossed.

Dixon wondered if the world would be at all different if Elvis had survived the mission. Elvis Presley would always be the first man to walk on the moon, but no one would ever know the truth. Would it make a difference if they did?

Elvis Presley couldn't end world hunger; he could do nothing to prevent floods and earthquakes. His voice was arguably the best in the world of rock and roll, but it was absurd to think Presley's music could halt armed conflict between nations, or guaranty clean air and healthy water.

His music made people happy, and Dixon should have left it at that. No one needed to see Elvis on the moon; the astronauts appeared to do a fine job on TV (the Television Officer had edited and aired a spectacular astronauts-only fake). The people had been happy with Apollo 11. Two astronauts had been fine. It was a successful mission that Dixon would remember as a terrible waste of a perfectly good icon.

Which brought his eyes back to the Ivory Elvi. Like a reflex his hand found the trash bag on the floor by the bench. "So much for that idea," slurred Dixon, and like the rest of his collection, the fake Ivory Elvis went into the trash. A moment later, after a deep breath and a defeated sigh, he tossed the original too.

He hauled the overstuffed bag through the kitchen and out the back door where he shoved it in an empty metal can outside. The head of the original Ivory Elvis stuck out the top. Those char marks were impossible to duplicate. When he walked back in, the house felt empty, as though he was in the process of moving out and had removed the Elvis collection first.

The couch and the symphonizer were all that remained in the living room. He considered trashing the keyboard too. The symphonizer was a close version of the one Elvis once had at his home in Palm Springs. Dixon couldn't play worth a lick. He didn't remember anything from his childhood piano lessons, and was a terrible musician. But the symphonizer was too heavy to move by himself. He'd have to get rid of it later.

The absence of Elvis could be felt in every room—even the study, which was overwhelmed with NASA-related pictures and awards, a collection that rivaled his dedication to the King. Even they brought back unbearable memories of the King.

He found a second trash bag and filled it with anything NASA. Pens, pencils and stationary bearing the NASA emblem were tossed away. A paperweight, a letter opener and stapler with the NASA logo had to go as well. It was a thorough cleaning, a complete home sanitization of any and every memory of Operation Blue Moon.

Immediately Dixon turned his sights on the space center. Those buildings were loaded with evidence that had to be destroyed: Elvis video footage, publicity shots, flight plans and spacecraft redesigns, along with boxes and boxes of Lunar Elvis merchandise. All of it had to be burned beyond recognition.

Somehow he was able to drive to the space complex. He decided to start with the documents in his office. When Dixon made it upstairs, he saw the light was on in Monroe's office down the hall.

Dixon could hear files and stacks of paper being thrown to the floor while cabinets and drawers were slammed shut. He approached quietly and listened as Monroe kicked a cardboard box and tossed what sounded like a stack of three-ring binders inside.

Now Dixon paused outside the door and Monroe became silent inside. Dixon heard a bottle clanking a glass, then the sound of liquor being poured. He entered and saw Monroe standing at his office bar in the midst of a pile of papers and folders a foot deep. He had his back to Dixon and Dixon said, "Can't live with yourself either, can you?"

Monroe set his cocktail glass on the bar. His eyes followed and he stared shamefully into his bourbon as

Dixon approached from behind. When Monroe turned and looked at his subordinate, his eyes were bloodshot and his breath reeked of booze. He wavered in place and reached for his drink but reached too far and grabbed a handful of air. He found the bourbon on his second attempt and took a hearty gulp.

"Buy you a drink?" Monroe groggily held up his glass and nodded in the direction of the bar. Dixon took a glass and poured himself what was left of Monroe's scotch bottle. Monroe shuffled to his desk and collapsed in his chair.

He watched the ceiling. "We did an amazing thing."

"We'll never get away with it."

Monroe grunted. "Sure we will. Television is indisputable. Everyone watched man walk on the moon today, and the words of Walter Cronkite were more sacred than the Holy Gospel."

Dixon kicked through the pile of papers and sat in a chair opposite Jack. "But can you live with yourself? We killed a man today, Jack. We've committed a horrific murder."

"Murder?" Monroe raised an eyebrow then shook his head. "I don't see it like that."

"I do," Dixon said.

"Condemn us if you will," Monroe said pathetically. "In history we will be absolved."

"Who do you think you are, Fidel Castro?"

Monroe shot Dixon the glare of an angry drunk. "Don't ever call me that again."

Dixon asked, "I'm not happy with what we did about the body. Don't you think Elvis Presley deserves a proper funeral?" Dixon had thought of a mission to return Presley's body to earth but suspected it would blow their cover, so he had let the idea slip away.

"Nothing we can do about it now," Monroe said. "And it's not like some wandering hunter's going to stumble across the body while he's walking through the woods."

Dixon sighed and finished his drink. He felt a warm, numb comfort throughout his body but a sickness was eating his thoughts. "I hope Jimmy Orr can hack it in the big leagues."

"He certainly had me fooled. Word from Tom Parker is that he had everyone cheering when he stepped off the plane in Vegas."

Dixon nodded. Orr was a dead ringer and NASA had reserved the right to pull the plug on him if he couldn't deliver. They could always 'stage' Elvis's death if they needed to write Orr out of the picture.

Jack asked what brought Dixon to the space center. "Housekeeping."

Monroe waved a hand at the mess on his floor. "We'll clean this shit up and then we'll do your office."

"Too bad about the merchandise," Dixon said.

Monroe shut his eyes. "Damn that Lunar Elvis merchandise!"

"We were going to make a killing on T-shirts."

Jack shook his head. "A sad day indeed."

They sat silently while Dixon finished his drink. He set his empty glass on Jack's desk and they went to work and systematically disposed of all Blue Moon evidence. They started with the paperwork on Jack's floor, then his file cabinets. They loaded it into boxes and hauled it outside to a dumpster and then they did the same for Dixon's office.

All the Elvis software was erased and they ransacked the Television Officer's stock of Elvis footage. NASA-issued clothing with the Presley name patch was also flung unceremoniously into the bin outside.

"We need gasoline," Monroe said as he contemplated the overflowing dumpster with a bottle of scotch in his hand.

"The warehouse," Dixon suggested and they were on their way. The warehouse was stacked to the ceiling with cardboard boxes. Inside was the Lunar Elvis merchandise—which until yesterday was ready to be shipped to retail outlets across the country. Sadly the T-shirts, coffee mugs, board games and action figures would never see the light of day; all were scheduled for destruction.

They walked to where the forklifts were parked and Monroe grabbed a gallon can of gasoline. He said to Dixon, "Now that we've opened the door to the moon, we're going to do things up there that will make people forget all about Apollo 11."

"Forgetting about Apollo 11 is exactly what I want to do."

They headed back to the dumpster. Monroe doused the Blue Moon evidence with gasoline and tossed a match inside. The fireball that erupted from the bin reminded them both of the fires of the Saturn V. They stood reverently watching the flames consume the Elvis documents and photos, the television evidence and the attire.

Monroe passed the scotch to Dixon, who took the last swig and tossed the spent bottle into the fire. Both men sighed and watched the evidence burn. Despite the amount of alcohol they'd both consumed, the burden of Elvis Presley's death was something neither man could escape.

They found themselves lost in a cloud of sorrow. Neither could shift the blame to anyone but themselves. Dixon came up with the idea and Monroe crammed it down Nixon's throat. But while Monroe would see the mission's final outcome as a success, Dixon would remember the Apollo 11 moon landing as the greatest failure in the history of modern science. The blood of an icon was on his hands. Pain welled in his stomach and he felt he was about to pass out when he was suddenly startled by a siren and a pair of flashing lights.

Two fire engines had turned onto the property and were speeding for the column of black smoke pouring from the dumpster in front of Dixon and Monroe. They both saw the sirens at the same time and realized that their fire had become a huge conflagration. As far as the firemen knew, it was a potential threat to the building, and to NASA's entire space program. Monroe whacked Dixon on the shoulder and they both ran inside to hide.

They ducked into a broom closet near the door that led to the dumpster out back and stood chest to chest in the cramped space. The stocky Dixon was eye level with Monroe's chin. Sirens grew louder outside and finally stopped blaring once the two fire engines were parked by the dumpster. The flames had already begun to die down by the time the fireman arrived. They sprayed the blaze with fire extinguishers and then went inside to look for people.

"Shhh," Jack warned as they heard two firemen walk along the hallway outside the closet. They heard the firemen search through the corridor finding no sign of any people. Soon they left by the same door through which they had entered.

"Look at us, Jack," Dixon whispered.

Monroe glanced down his nose to Dixon. "What about us?"

"We're hiding in a broom closet like children. We're piss-drunk, down on our luck and a disgrace to America."

"America hasn't a clue," Monroe whispered back. "They live by what they see on TV."

"What about the truth, Jack?"

Jack shook his head. "Doesn't exist."

Tears welled in Dixon's eyes and one finally fell over. "I can't believe I killed Elvis Presley!"

He started to sob. Monroe didn't know how to react. As Dixon's head hung with falling tears, Monroe could only pat his shoulder gently and console him as best he could. "There, there," Monroe said. "It's ok...you're ok..."

Dixon kept sobbing, Monroe wished he would quit. Dixon cried, "He's dead now because of me."

"There, there," Monroe repeated and Dixon kept crying. Jack never got this close to his coworkers, not even to Peter Dixon. Monroe noticed the tight space they were in and wanted out. He pushed Dixon away. "Knock it off! You're getting my tie wet."

Dixon lifted his head and wiped tears from his face with the back of his hand. "I feel like such an idiot."

"You are an idiot."

Dixon chuckled, appreciating Monroe's effort. "Go to hell, you slick bastard."

"Sometimes a guy like me is all you've got."

Dixon laughed again. "You know something, Wise One?"

"What is it, Wise One?"

"You know Elvis walked on the moon, I know Elvis walked on the moon."

"That once-in-an-eternity moment was just for us," Monroe said, and they realized they felt an odd satisfaction. Despite the utter failure of Apollo 11, Dixon still found something to be proud of.

After checking to see if the coast was clear, they slipped out of the broom closet and tiptoed back to Monroe's office. He grabbed another bottle of scotch but Dixon refused to drink any more.

"Maybe I should get you home," Dixon suggested. It was obvious Monroe had consumed several more drinks than Dixon. They helped each other to Dixon's car, stumbling arm in arm like a couple of drunken sailors. Dixon sat Monroe in the passenger seat with his bottle and they drove to Dixon's house.

Monroe passed out on the couch and never noticed what Dixon had done to his Elvis collection. Dixon remembered his stuff was in the trash and he decided the trash was where it belonged. He had enjoyed his tenure as a diehard Elvis fanatic, but the time had come to move on to something else. Dixon's last wish before passing out in his bed was that Dani Mitchell was lying beside him.

She was released from jail just after six thirty on the morning of July 21st. It was Monday morning and she was due in court at nine o'clock. Dani was scheduled to answer for that stupid vandalism incident at the hotel. She suspected she'd be liable for a hefty fine and some community service. And last night's arrest certainly wouldn't help her case.

It couldn't get much worse for the unemployed reporter. A great story—and her rise to journalistic fame and fortune—would never come about, and now she could only think about the law. Justice would be unforgiving. Dani knew the Texas judge wouldn't let a Yankee walk away from a vandalism charge lightly. It would take a long time to recover from this.

She hadn't forgotten about her conversation with Jimmy Orr and the unexpected Pete Dixon sighting. She had determined, at least to her own satisfaction, that NASA had made an attempt to land Elvis Presley on the moon, but there still had been no sign of the King. There had been no mention of him by the media or by anyone involved with the lunar landing. Word of Presley's arrival in Vegas the night before had not yet reached her, but she already expected to learn of something along those lines.

What else could explain the disappearance of Jimmy Orr?

She had a couple hours to kill before she made her way to the courthouse downtown. It was time for one last meeting with Pete Dixon. It was early enough to catch him at home before he left for work.

Dixon had passed out somewhere around two in the morning. At seven his alarm clock buzzed and brought him back to life. The headache was one of the worst he could remember. All that liquor and no water made Peter long for a steam room.

He wished he could just remain in bed, but the astronauts would be leaving the moon shortly, and Dixon wanted to be in Mission Control for the blastoff. Then he remembered the night before, when all memories of Elvis had been wiped from his life in a pathetic rage of failure.

Dixon remained in bed for awhile to wallow in the guilt of the failed lunar extravaganza—the concert in the Sea of Tranquility that the public would never see, and the death of Elvis Presley. Two of history's most significant events rolled into one. He praised himself for Jimmy Orr. Monroe would have never considered a backup plan, and now Pete Dixon was the man to thank for a brilliant cover-up.

That thought reminded Dixon that Monroe had passed out on his living room couch. He remembered nursing the inebriated NASA Administrator back here the night before. Monroe had been too drunk to notice that Dixon had cleared his house of all reminders of Elvis. Too drunk to ask if a pair of cufflinks with tiger's eye stones were sitting outside in the trash along with everything else.

"He'll kill me if he finds out," muttered Dixon as he threw the covers aside. Those Elvis cufflinks were from a show in 1959, and Monroe had locked them away all these years. Dixon would be chastised for carelessly throwing out Jack's priceless generosity. Some pretentious big-shot Elvis collector would pay top dollar for them, and Monroe would demand retribution.

The neighborhood had just broken into its Monday morning stir when Dani arrived. She slowed when she turned her car onto Dixon's block and crept to his house. She parked across the street and inspected the modest residence. The house was quiet and dark, and the morning newspaper on the front steps told Dani that Dixon was probably still asleep inside.

She stepped out of her car and approached the front door via Dixon's driveway. As she crossed the front walk she could see into the living room where a pair of hairy feet dangled off the end of the couch. She couldn't see a face, but she knew those feet didn't belong to Peter.

After a closer look Dani noticed how empty it looked in the living room. Dixon's entire Elvis shrine was gone. Other than the symphonizer and the furniture, the room was a desolate collection of empty shelves and blank walls. Dixon had taken it all down. She headed back across the driveway, and around a corner to a walkway leading to the kitchen side entrance. She peered through the door window and saw no activity. Even the coffee pot light was off. Nobody was awake. While she debated whether she should ring the doorbell or wait him out, Dixon appeared in the kitchen. He wore his bathrobe and a pair of boxers and looked terribly hung over. His hair was a mess and he could barely walk straight.

Dani slipped away from the windows and crouched behind the garbage cans next to the door. She listened but heard nothing. Moments passed and Dani considered taking another look but the kitchen doorknob rattled and forced her to dive behind a row of bushes across the walk.

Dixon stepped out and squinted to shield himself from the morning sun. He yawned and shuffled to the garbage cans. Dani watched as he lifted the lid from one and rummaged inside. He found a small, black velvet box, put it in his robe pocket and stepped back into the house.

He closed the door behind him and crossed the kitchen to make a pot of coffee. As he filled the pot with water he thought about the Ivory Elvis resting in the trash. He thought of Moja and the old ivory legend. He thought of Elvis, who had expressed his wish that the idol remain in Dixon's safe hands, as fulfillment of Moja's wish.

He may be a murderer, but Dixon was certainly no traitor. He set the coffee machine, and for religious purposes, he headed out to retrieve the Ivory Elvis from the trash. When he stepped outside, he saw Dani Mitchell standing before him holding a Lunar Elvis coffee mug. An Apollo 11 T-shirt was slung over her arm and she looked like she was ready to run.

"Stop right there," he pointed at her.

Dani took a step back and Dixon stepped forward simultaneously.

"Don't even think about it, Dani."

"Think about what?" Another step back. She set the Ivory Elvis on the pavement and held up the T-shirt. "I Witnessed the Greatest Moment of All Time? The Concert in the Sea of Tranquility? Funny, I don't remember seeing Elvis on TV moon coverage."

Dixon took a step closer, his eyes on the mug and T-shirt. "Give those back." His heart started beating rapidly. The added stress decided to go straight for his ulcer and made his chest burn.

Dani was pacing backwards, absorbing Dixon's impatient advance. "Give what back? It's just a stupid T-shirt and a mug...Right?"

"I'm warning you."

Dani increased her pace. She was now at the top of the driveway and could see her car across the street. Dixon knew she was about to make a break for it. He prayed she didn't run. In this state, with a hangover and a maddening ulcer, he'd never be able to survive a chase.

She taunted him. "What were you doing last night with Jimmy Orr? Where did you take him?"

Dixon said nothing. He only kept his eyes on that T-shirt and the coffee mug. He tried snatching the shirt, but Dani held it out of reach.

She was ready to make a break. "Why is your entire Elvis collection in the trash?"

That was the last straw for Dixon. He pounced on Dani and grabbed her arm with both hands. She yanked her arm away and the Elvis coffee mug flew into the air and shattered on the driveway. Dixon turned his attention back to the T-shirt. He grabbed for it and captured a sleeve.

"Let go!" Dani pulled it away and the shirt ripped along the seam.

"Give it to me," Dixon shoved his body against Dani and they both fell to the pavement. She scraped her knee and Dixon bruised his elbow when they landed with a thud. They fought for the T-shirt. Sweat broke out and carried the odor of stale alcohol. Their bodies and the Elvis T-shirt were entwined in a ferocious wrestling match.

Dani squirmed out from under him and pulled at the shirt, but ripped it cleanly in half. She got to her feet and backed away, looking at her half of the T-shirt, seeing she held nothing but blank material. The logo was on the other side of the shirt, and that portion was in Dixon's hand.

He noticed this too and taunted her from the pavement. "Ha!" He climbed to one knee. "You've got nothing!"

"You're right," Dani caught her breath and backed away quickly. Her instincts told her to run while she could, and seconds later she was climbing into her car. Dixon followed and stopped at the end of his driveway, out of breath. He watched as Dani started her engine. Before he could decide what to do, Dani grinned, dangled a small rhinestone-spacesuited action figure in the window, and sped away laughing.

"Shit!" Dixon ran back to the house. His stomach was getting worse. He knew he couldn't avoid a hospital much longer, but he had to take care of Dani first.

"Jack!" He yelled as he burst through the kitchen door. "Jack! Wake up! Wake up! This is an emergency!" Dixon hurried to the living room to wake his boss. The pain in his stomach was suddenly so harsh it knocked him to the floor. He fell beside the couch as Monroe started to stir.

"We there already?" Monroe opened an eye and glanced to Dixon who was on the floor clutching his stomach. Monroe sat up, completely awake. "You okay, Pete?"

"The reporter..." Dixon grunted.

Monroe wondered if Dixon had been kicked in the gut or worse. "What about her? What did she do?"

"She stole..." Dixon writhed and got on all fours. "She stole Lunar Elvis."

"The baby's toy?"

Dixon nodded. "Just drove away with it. Just now. She knows all about Jimmy Orr."

"Damn it!" Monroe jumped to his feet and grabbed Dixon by the shoulders. "Get up! This is an emergency!"

He pulled Dixon to his feet and they ran to the garage. Monroe insisted on driving while Dixon hobbled to the passenger side and collapsed in the seat. It felt like his chest was about to burst. It felt like a heart attack.

Monroe backed Dixon's car out of the garage and with the precision of a racecar driver, took off in the direction Dixon said Dani had gone. Monroe sped through the residential streets and when he reached the main road, Dixon pointed out Dani's car weaving through traffic a block away. The chase began.

"How could you put us in this position, Peter? Dating a reporter at the same time you're pulling the greatest cover-up in the history of modern-day government. Will you never learn?"

Monroe drove like a madman, crossing lanes, cutting off anyone who got in his way and making Dixon's stomach lurch and throb with exquisite pain. Dixon feared it would make him worse; he didn't need the additional stress. "Easy, Jack," he managed to utter as he held his stomach and the door handle at the same time.

They swerved this way and that and followed Dani's car onto the highway. She headed north on Highway 8, en route to the airport, but neither Dixon nor Monroe had guessed her destination. She hoped to catch a plane to New York and deliver the evidence to Baker or any other news editor who would hear her story. Perhaps she could get on television, where the masses would tune in and hear the truth.

Morning traffic was light and Dani made good time. She was due in court in less than two hours but her decision had already been made. With the nuggets she'd unearthed from Dixon's garbage, she'd rather ditch court, accept the consequences, and make a name for herself once and for all.

In her rearview mirror she saw Dixon's car approaching and weaving in pursuit. She increased her speed hoping the law of averages remembered she shouldn't be pulled over two days in a row.

Monroe caught up to her and pulled along her opened passenger side window. He yelled at her. "Give up! You'll never make it!"

Dani, not knowing what to say to Mr. Shiny Hair, said the first thing that came to her mind. "You have one testicle!"

Enraged, Monroe moved the car closer but Dani swerved out of the way and pulled ahead. Monroe followed. His erratic driving caught the attention of the highway patrol. Soon a squad car was in pursuit—his impulse was to outrun the cop and never take his sights off Dani Mitchell.

"Pull over," Dixon pleaded. He was hunched in the passenger seat with his knees curled up to his chest, obviously under tremendous pain. "I need a hospital."

"Are you sure?" Jack asked as he eased the gas and watched Dani's car widen the gap. In the rearview mirror, the cop car was catching up quickly. "We pull over and that reporter's gone."

"I don't care," Dixon said as the siren grew louder behind them. "I'm dying here, Jack."

Monroe gave up. He pulled the car to a stop on the shoulder. The police cruiser parked behind and the portly trooper hopped out. In the mirror Monroe could see this officer wore a cowboy hat and mirrored sunglasses. Sideburns grew to his jaw and the trooper wore what appeared to be a very familiar sneer.

Monroe realized he had fallen asleep wearing only boxers and a T-shirt. He hadn't bothered to dress once he learned of the Dani Mitchell emergency. Now the head of NASA had to face the Texas highway patrol wearing only his underwear. Monroe looked to Dixon and saw he wore only his underwear too.

"Perfect. Thanks, Peter," Monroe said. "We better come up with something good."

"License and registration."

"Listen," Monroe read the officer's nametag. "Officer Dooley, I'm Dr. Jack Monroe. I don't have a business card on me but I work for the National Aeronautics and

Space Administration. In fact, well, I'm the Administrator. I'm sort of the boss of the whole thing."

Officer Dooley looked at Monroe's boxers, then over to Dixon. He couldn't waver. "License and registration."

"Anyway," Monroe replied. "We're experiencing a severe NASA emergency. My friend here is in need of medical assistance, so if you could maybe provide police escort to the nearest hospital, well, we'd certainly appreciate your help."

"Pal," said Officer Dooley. "I don't care if you're the Virgin Mary, nobody drives like that on my interstate. License and registration."

Dixon groaned. Monroe said to Dooley, "Did you hear that? He's groaning miserably. This man needs a doctor! Now!"

Dooley sighed. "Do you not have your license *with you*, sir?"

Monroe smiled. "You're not letting us off the hook are you?"

Dooley shook his head. "Not two grown men driving around in their underwear."

Monroe smiled. "It's been quite a day." Then, when Dooley barely reacted, Monroe got serious. "Well then. We'll just be on our way. Thank you, officer."

Monroe acted like he was going to pull back into traffic, and if Dooley hesitated, Jack would go. And just maybe he'd be able to catch Dani Mitchell.

"Ahem," Dooley reached into the car and placed a hand on the steering wheel. "Don't even think about it, boy. Step out of the car."

Monroe tried to think of something to say, something that might outwit the officer, but Dixon was suddenly tapping him on the arm. Monroe looked over and saw the velvet case for Elvis's tiger's eye cufflinks in Dixon's hand. He looked into his colleague's eyes and saw defeat, and apathy, because those cufflinks now meant nothing to

Peter Dixon. But there was a gleam behind the sorrow. Dixon was still acting the as the strategist that he was. At the brink of death, he was still scheming.

He handed the cufflinks to Jack, "Give these to him."

Monroe took the case and looked back to Dooley. "Say, you are a fan of Elvis Presley, are you not?"

Dooley nodded. "How did you guess?"

"The sideburns," Monroe said. "It's not exactly a *new* look."

"Your point?"

Monroe tapped the ring case. "In here, I have something priceless. A set of cufflinks Elvis wore back in 1959. The real thing...with tiger's eye stones." He handed the case to Dooley.

Dooley took it and opened it. He whistled softly when he saw the cufflinks and raised an eyebrow to Monroe. "These real?"

Monroe held up his hands. "Would I have kept them all these years if they weren't real?"

Dooley thought it over. "I guess you wouldn't, would you?"

"Or keep fake Elvis cufflinks in a case?"

It made sense.

Monroe said. "Keep them. They're yours."

Dooley handed them back. "You trying to bribe an officer of the law?"

Monroe shook his head, "No, no. I just don't want the cufflinks anymore. I don't like Elvis...he tends to disappoint."

Dixon nudged Monroe in retaliation for the inappropriate comment.

Dooley took a step back and placed his hand on the butt of his revolver. "Two men dressed in underwear, trying to bribe me with cufflinks. Let's find out where the rest of your clothes went. Step out of the car, both of you."

"That's not wise," Monroe disagreed as he stepped out. "We're federal employees."

Dixon's body could take it no longer and finally reached its boiling point. The ulcer broke through and spilled stomach acid into his abdomen. It was the worst pain he'd ever felt. Worse than his visit to the dentist who gave him a filling without medication. Worse than the soccer ball he took in the nuts in the eight grade. Worse than the day his wife left him once and for all.

He collapsed on the pavement.

Neither Monroe nor Dooley doubted Dixon needed a to be rushed to the emergency room. They carried him to Dooley's car and laid him in the backseat. The Texas state trooper invited Jack Monroe to ride shotgun and the three of them headed to the nearest hospital.

Jack turned back to Dixon. "You told her."

"Told her what?"

Monroe didn't want to repeat Dani's comment in front of Officer Dooley. Instead, he glanced at Dixon's crotch, then back to Dixon.

Dixon smiled wryly. "Sorry about that one, boss."

Dani Mitchell caught the next flight to New York. She would land just before two in the afternoon, New York time. Dani hoped to be at *The Sensational Nation* by three. She started writing the minute she found her seat. Going back six weeks to her initial encounter with NASA at the Presley mansion, Dani documented her information chronologically.

She listed it all. From the information shared at meetings with Jimmy Orr to the artifacts uncovered from Dixon's garbage. Even without knowing for sure what happened to Elvis on the moon, the little Elvis action figure was enough to argue a strong case for the conspiracy of Operation Blue Moon.

She wondered about Dixon and Monroe. Surely they weren't going to let her walk away like nothing happened. They probably had already started planning ways to discredit her, but this was not the time to worry about them. She needed to concentrate and organize her facts on paper.

Dani got nabbed by literally walking into enemy hands. When her plane parked at the gate in New York, her story was only halfway finished. She planned to write more in the cab and present *TSN* with as much as she could. This one was hot, and she wanted to make sure she was the first to break the story, whether her hardcopy was complete or not.

But when she walked off the plane, three men in suits greeted her almost instantly. The one in the middle, a lanky fellow nearly a foot taller than the other two, flashed a badge and an ID and introduced himself. "Dani Mitchell, I'm Special Agent Tom Heflin, FBI. I'm sorry but I've got to take you in. You're under arrest."

Before he was finished the other two agents seized Dani's notebook and purse. She was escorted aside where she was frisked by Agent Heflin.

"You guys can't do this," Dani objected. "What's the charge?"

"Failure to appear in court," Heflin said as he cuffed Dani's hands behind her back. "Or how about stealing federal property?"

"I didn't steal a thing!"

"What do you call this?" Heflin asked and dangled the Lunar Elvis action figure in front of Dani.

"It's a baby's toy."

Agent Heflin mocked interest. "Oh, so you have kids?"

"This is baseless!"

"I'm under direct orders from J. Edgar Hoover. Now you can save yourself a lot of trouble if you just take it easy and do what we say."

Dani would resist no more. "I want an attorney."

"I was just getting to that," Heflin said and started reading her rights.

Chapter Twenty

July 26th

Dixon spent six days in the hospital. Along with his ulcer, the doctor said he had suffered a mild heart attack. Dixon cherished the care, the bed rest and the quiet. When his ulcer healed, and it became time to leave, Dixon wished he could stay. He could use one more day of sleep and peace, but he knew it was time to pack up and get on with his life.

The astronauts had returned and were hailed as heroes and showered with tickertape while the rest of NASA immediately went to work on Apollo 12. Dixon had decided to sit that one out. He thought maybe he would not go back to NASA at all. Quit while he was ahead and let Dr. Monroe worry about the moon missions.

Some guilt still lingered in Dixon, but he couldn't blame himself for a freak accident involving a guitar string and a set of faulty rhinestones. Elvis would forever rest on the moon. Dixon felt it a poetic end to an otherwise tragic mission.

He would always cherish the friendship that had developed between himself and the King. Although he'd tossed his entire Elvis collection, Dixon still held onto that one relic. He had rescued the original Ivory Elvis from the garbage and fulfilled Scott Richter's pledge of keeping it safe. As Richter had done for Moja, Dixon would do for Elvis. The legend would live on.

Dani Mitchell was in custody. When Dixon asked Monroe of the charges against the reporter, Jack said simply, "She's criminally insane, Peter."

They left it at that.

Now Jack arrived at the hospital, which meant Dixon had a ride home. He gathered his belongings and the two men headed to the elevator.

"Officer Dooley decided not to press charges," Jack mentioned while they descended to the lobby. "He decided to keep the cufflinks, and his mouth shut."

"You let him keep your cufflinks?"

Dixon saw that Jack looked good, like he had also taken a few days off, and was feeling refreshed. Monroe shrugged, "Don't worry about the Elvis cufflinks. They were fake."

Dixon was appalled. "Fake?"

"I told you they were real so you'd give the ok to launch."

"Bastard," Dixon grunted, but no longer cared. "Any news on Jimmy Orr?"

"He's got his first show as Elvis on the 31st. I sent him a bouquet."

Dixon said, "That was a nice touch."

"Thank you."

The elevator slowed and halted on the ground floor. Dixon turned to Monroe. "Now what?"

Jack raised an eyebrow. "I think I may head down to Key West to visit some old friends. Maybe look for a nice little place down there where I can retire."

"Really?"

Jack nodded, he was obviously comfortable with this idea. "I'll stick around for Apollo 12. After that, it'll be time to bid NASA farewell. Apollo 13 can be somebody else's headache."

The elevator doors opened and Jack turned to face Dixon. "You know, Peter," he felt sentimental for the first time in a long time. "It's been a pleasure working with you."

"Thank you, Jack," Dixon appreciated the gesture. They shook hands and Monroe looked away, embarrassed by the display of emotion.

"What about you?" Monroe said as they walked to his car. "What are you planning to do with the rest of your life?"

Dixon rolled his eyes. "I have no earthly idea."

"Yeah, well," Monroe said. "It could be worse."

"It certainly could."

1973

She eventually grew into the stiff, scratchy pajamas. The food was okay and it was always quiet after breakfast. She sat by the window during her free time, which was nearly all the time. There wasn't much to do at the Institute of Upstate New York, a mental hospital and Dani Mitchell's home for the last four years.

She spent her days in the sterile complex surrounded by some of the biggest maniacs the state had to offer. Everyone had their own unique encounter with insanity; Dani Mitchell's was the Blue Moon Conspiracy. She never stopped believing it had happened, even after the doctor told her she was delusional and obsessive-compulsive, that Elvis Presley was alive and well.

"Sure, he's a bit heavier," said Dr. Combs. "His singing doesn't sound quite the same as it did when he was younger, but he's alive. I was lucky enough to see him at Madison Square Garden last summer. He was fantastic!"

"You saw a phony," Dani said. "Elvis Presley died four years ago. His body is resting on the moon as we speak!"

"You've been going on and on about this Blue Moon scandal for years, Dani. Don't you remember—we read about it in the newspaper—when Elvis went to the White House and met Nixon?"

"*Dixon*," Dani corrected him. "Dixon killed Elvis."

"Nixon *hailed* Elvis! You're having paranoid delusions. And your obsessions have yet to improve. That thing about you having to hear everything twice, it's not getting any better. You have a serious disorder, Dani. You're totally...fucking...out-there."

Dr. Combs slid her file onto his clipboard and clamped it in place with a metallic *snap*. He started to leave her room, but Dani called from the bed, "You have to do that again!"

"Dani, you're never going to get any better if I keep indulging you in your obsessions."

"Please? Just one last time?"

Dr. Combs sighed. "You always say it's for the last time, but you always ask me again." He pushed down on the clamp, released it with a compliant *snap* and left her alone. Dani sulked and eventually gave up on Operation Blue Moon, deciding the world would never learn the truth about Apollo 11.

Until one day, when she was approached by a lanky fellow with messy hair and horn-rimmed glasses. She had seen this patient around the hospital but had never talked to him until now. He sat beside her at the window with a beady smile and introduced himself as Lee Alton. He offered the palm on his hand, which held several pills of various shapes and colors.

"Would you like some sedatives? I never take mine."

Dani gazed across the grounds of the institute outside. "No, thank you."

"You're afraid you'll overdose."

"I'm not afraid I'll overdose." Dani spoke with little emotion. Her eyes remained outside. With the middle finger of her left hand, she tapped the metal leg of her chair, making a dull thump.

Thump, thump. Thump, thump.

"You're afraid you'll take too many and end up like Janis or Jimi or Marilyn."

Thump, thump. "I'm not afraid I'll end up like Janis or Jimi or Marilyn."

Lee dumped the pills in his robe pocket. "You probably think she died of a drug overdose, huh?"

"You mean...she didn't?"

He shook his head.

Dani no longer gave a damn about Marilyn Monroe but she fed Alton anyway. "Then if it wasn't an overdose, how did she die, Lee?"

"She was rubbed out by RFK's and JFK's henchmen. Everybody, even children, knows about that."

Dani nodded. "Of course they do."

"Then they took her body and buried it in the end zone of Giants Stadium."

Thump..."Did they?"

"But JFK paid a price."

"Did he now?" *Thump...*

"Yep," Lee nodded. "Aliens shot down Air Force One and it crashed into Area 51. That's where the aliens are growing an army of JFK clones. And then they're going to bring these JFK clones back to their home planet to be sold as pets."

Dani agreed. "Sure."

Lee said, "It's because JFK is so cute and loveable."

"Of course he is."

Lee kept going. "Good thing for those aliens though."

Dani still stared with a blank face. "Good thing, huh?"

"If it wasn't for the aliens, Bigfoots would be running wild all over the place."

"Why Bigfoot?"

"Bigfootsssss," he hissed. "Aliens come here for Bigfoot poaching. Killed nearly every single one of them. It's why Bigfoots are so hard to find these days."

"Why Bigfoot," Dani wondered. "Why not lions or bears?"

"Because the Loch Ness Monster won't eat lions."

"Right," Dani said. "I should have guessed."

Lee lowered his voice. "You think you know the truth about all these alien UFOs and JFK Bigfoot stories? Think again!"

Dani laughed out loud. "You know something, pal?"

"What's that?"

She shook her head. "I've got a story that can top every single one of yours."

"You think?"

"Yep," she nodded. "And my story is true."

"Yeah," Lee challenged her. "I'll *bet* it is."

Memphis, Tennessee

After Scott Richter had returned to Tanzania in 1964, he assured Moja that the Ivory Elvis had been safely delivered to the hands of the King. Moja happily thanked him and eagerly joined Richter's war against elephant poaching.

Circa 1970—when Richter's work was done—he left Tanzania and brought Moja with him to the States. The villager-turned-warrior insisted that they go to Memphis and gaze upon the Presley mansion. Richter offered to introduce Moja to the King, but the humble villager refused.

"I would not burden him with my pointlessness."

Richter understood and offered to show Moja Boston and New York City. Again, Moja refused. He chose to remain in Memphis, where he fulfilled the American dream of becoming a garbage man with a territory near the kingdom of Graceland.

What better way to worship the King than to work on his garbage route?

Moja could rummage through the trash once a week and search for Presley treasures. He usually never kept anything more than old receipts and junk paperwork, but every so often, he'd find a box of the King's old T-shirts or a pair of worn-out tennis shoes. He kept all this Elvis junk, and his tiny apartment became a mess of crumpled paper and old clothes. Elvis music played constantly from Moja's scratchy record player, and he slept comfortably thinking he was finally bedding down in the same city as the Ivory Elvis.

Dixon had been housing the statue in Houston all these years. The Ivory Elvis remained on his symphonizer while Dixon redecorated his living room with the colorful pastels of the early 1970's.

His heart attack drove him to quit working at NASA after Apollo 11, and he spent the next two years writing a book about the history of manned flight. It was a textbook, something to be used in colleges and Dixon's last contribution to society. He spent the most recent years traveling, still unsure of how to spend the rest of his days.

Now he was in Memphis and the Ivory Elvis was in his hands. Dixon spent the last four years getting over the loss of Elvis, and today he would finally let go for good. For more than fifteen years Dixon had idolized the singer. He had placed him on a pedestal and formed an excessive, even obsessive, attachment to the myth and the romance of Elvis Presley.

Even in person, however, Dixon had never really gotten to know Elvis. The focus was always on the mystique and never on the man. It took years until Dixon finally realized what made his idol successful. It wasn't the charisma or Presley's inimitable talent, but rather his passion for that talent, and the music he produced as a result.

Perhaps if Dixon had never seen Elvis as an idol the King would be alive today. If he hadn't worshipped a pop star, but instead admired the talents of the NASA scientists and the astronauts, he wouldn't have spent so much time in front of the television waiting for something sensational. We needed role models, not idols. If Dixon could do it all over, he would avoid the propaganda of television altogether.

Now Dixon brought the Ivory Elvis back to Graceland because the statue made him realize he had become a man with a sad inability to stop obsessing over a dead pop singer. By returning the Ivory Elvis to Graceland, Dixon took Elvis the Entertainer off the pedestal once and for all.

Outside the gates of Graceland, hundreds of people surrounded the property, idolizing an impersonator. None of those people knew or cared that Jimmy Orr was living as the King. They were out to worship the mystique, and not the actual man.

Now Dixon walked up to the guard at the gate, a Memphis Mafia member Dixon didn't recognize. The guard stood to intercept his advance. "Help you?"

"Hi," Dixon smiled. "I'm Pete Dixon, I worked with Elvis in the sixties."

"Did you?" The guard was doubtful.

"Anyway, I wanted to return this. See that it finds its way into the Jungle Room, would you? Thanks."

The guard took the Ivory Elvis and held it before him. "Nice detail."

"It's authentic," Dixon said.

The guard glanced at Dixon and figured he was just a rabid fan bestowing the King with another tacky gift. "I'll see that it gets to him," the guard said, hoping Dixon would go away.

"I appreciate it," Dixon patted the man on the shoulder and strolled away whistling. Maybe Jimmy Orr would end up with the Ivory Elvis, maybe he wouldn't. Dixon no longer cared. It was back where it belonged and right now Dixon wanted nothing more than two scoops of strawberry ice cream with butterscotch syrup and peanuts.

The guard tossed the statue into a trashcan. Elvis Presley's ivory hair was still sticking out of the garbage when Moja's team arrived to collect the trash that afternoon.

At first he didn't believe it, but the char marks from the fires of Maasai Village were unmistakable. And the

King's sideburns had been chiseled with intricacies only Moja knew. Those waves were something even the greatest counterfeiter could not fake. Moja hadn't a doubt that he'd found the real thing in the King's trash bin.

There had to be an explanation. Why would Elvis keep the village idol in his home for over a decade just to so carelessly throw it away today? Moja yanked a rag out of his garbage-man coveralls and wiped a smudge of dirt off the sculpture.

He felt like he had been slapped in the face. Moja and his ivory statue were the only survivors of the village, a people who loved Presley's music so much they named *Jailhouse Rock* their village anthem. Richter said Elvis promised to keep the Maasai spirit alive by keeping the Ivory Elvis at Graceland. To Moja, that was an honor greater than the gift of life itself.

For some reason, Elvis threw it all away.

Now Moja glared at the mansion, demanding retribution. Sure, Elvis paid for Richter's war to avenge the Maasai, but the Ivory Elvis was sacred. Now Moja had rescued it once again, outside the gates of the very kingdom.

Elvis Presley would answer for this outrage!

Moja told his garbage team he felt sick and that they should go ahead without him. Moja had already told them the legend of the Ivory Elvis, so they didn't protest when they saw what was in his hands. He stayed outside Graceland, determined to wait because the King had to come or go eventually.

It was well past dark that night when Moja got a chance to confront Elvis. Around eleven o'clock a shiny blue Cadillac left the house and drove down to the gate. There was a new guard at the post, and he stood while the gates opened to let the car off the property.

Without a sound, Moja ran to the gates and slipped in front of the car. An older man was driving and Elvis was in the back seat wearing sunglasses and a turquoise satin shirt with frills. He appeared to be sleeping; Moja had no idea that Jimmy Orr was heavily sedated by both Tuinal and Seconal.

Orr had found it nearly impossible to adjust to the life of Elvis. He'd never suspected he'd sometimes go on stints of two shows a night, seven days a week, for weeks and weeks and weeks. Or that there would be constant pressure from the Colonel, from his audience and from himself. He toured the same cities over and over and over and essentially became an overmedicated Elvis robot.

Now this little dude was blocking the Cadillac and glaring at him through the windshield. Orr sat back; his people would take care of this.

"Out of the way, pal," yelled the guard and went to grab Moja, but the frisky villager pulled away.

"I must speak to him!"

The driver honked the horn.

Jimmy asked, "Who is it?"

The driver said, "Just another crazy fan, Mr. Presley. This one's dressed like a garbage man."

Orr's sedated eyes were only half open and his sunglasses made it even harder to focus on Moja, who was stomping his feet and pacing before the Cadillac. "Well," Orr finally said. "What does he want?"

The driver rolled down his window. "Get out of the way, little man, before we call the cops."

The guard had Moja by the elbow and was trying to pull him away, but the villager's advance was too sharp. He yanked the guard over to the driver's window and leaned in to look at Elvis in the backseat.

"I am Moja, from Maasai Village." He held up the statue. "I am the architect of this idol—which you have disgraced!"

Orr had no idea what this garbage man was talking about. "Moja *who?*"

"The legend!" Moja said. "The Ivory Elvis! This!"

"Ivory Elvis?" Orr looked at the statue Moja held at the window. "Come here for a second." Orr rolled down his own window and Moja appeared with the idol.

Orr took the Ivory Elvis and looked it over. "This is ivory?"

"What do you mean?" demanded Moja. "Has this very idol not been sitting in your home for the last fifteen years? Have you forgotten the legend? The promise you made to our friend, Scott Richer?"

Orr smirked. He was too sedated to care. "Buddy, I can't even remember last night." He handed the Ivory Elvis back to Moja. "But you can keep my statue if you want."

Orr patted his driver's shoulder and they drove off.

Moja stood in the driveway, stupefied, and watched them go. The guard looked at him and then at the ivory statue in his hands. Moja followed his gaze and regarded his ivory sculpture. A religious idol for a village that no longer existed. A society that had worshipped a singer who apparently wasn't even a nice guy.

Moja looked down the street and saw Elvis Presley's Cadillac speeding away. That jerk didn't even remember the legend and he obviously had no idea what the Ivory Elvis was doing in the trash. Moja became so enraged he threw the sculpture to the pavement, where it shattered into thousands of dusty pieces. A breeze began blowing the particles away, and the Ivory Elvis deteriorated into oblivion at the gates of Graceland.

Moja wondered why his people had ever worshipped Elvis Presley in the first place. The insignificant villager stormed off and never returned. The first thing Moja did the next day, was report back to the depot and ask to be transferred to a different garbage route.

Key West, Florida

At a small private cottage on the beach, John F. Kennedy rested on a lawn chair, reading a magazine and enjoying the sun's warmth. He sipped his piña colada and listened to the breeze whispering though the leaves of palm trees behind him.

It had been a good life. He'd been in seclusion since his early retirement from politics in 1963. His tropical beach house vastly was more desirable than Washington had ever been, and here he had Marilyn to keep him company.

She came out of the cottage wearing a yellow and white sundress and a pair of black sunglasses that were in striking contrast to her bleached blonde hair. She carried another piña colada. "Jack," she called as she went to her lawn chair. "Your friend is here."

Kennedy put down his magazine and twisted to look back at the house. His eyes lit up when he saw who'd dropped in. "Dr. Monroe!" JFK rolled off his lawn chair and stood to greet Jack with a brotherly hug.

"How you doing, sir?"

"Never better, Jack," Kennedy said and patted Monroe on the shoulder. The former NASA chief wore a golf shirt, shorts and sandals. It was the Jack Monroe Kennedy remembered from their fishing trips in the old days. JFK noticed streaks of gray in Monroe's hair. He teased his old pal when he said, "Even the gray looks good."

"I stopped dying it when I left NASA."

Both he and Kennedy laughed, and then Jack Monroe leaned over and squeezed Marilyn's shoulder. "How you doing, doll?"

She said, "We missed you, Jack."

"What brings you back to Key West?" Kennedy invited him to sit and Monroe slid a third lawn chair beside theirs and got comfortable.

Monroe became suddenly serious. "It's Nixon."

JFK shook his head in warning. "You don't want to touch Watergate."

"He's asking me to come out of retirement."

The former President sighed deeply. "It doesn't look good for him. I wouldn't get involved if I were you."

"He's asking me to step in."

Kennedy shared a troubled look with Marilyn. Then JFK said to Jack, "You were great with Castro, and even better with Khrushchev. As for my... 'assassination' in Dallas, you really had people fooled that day."

Marilyn said, "Some say even Jackie couldn't tell the difference."

Jack Monroe was flattered. "Well, it did take years to develop that mechanical JFK."

Kennedy nodded. "Very lifelike."

"Very lifelike indeed," said Jack.

Then Marilyn Monroe said, "You did a wonderful job helping stage my little disappearance too."

"You've done some excellent work in the past," Kennedy told him. "But do you really want to waste your energy on something as trivial as Watergate?"

Jack Monroe nodded politely. "Thanks. I just thought I'd run the Nixon thing by you. I wasn't too hot on it either. I had enough government headaches during that Elvis debacle to last a lifetime, and I want to enjoy my retirement."

"Here's to you," Kennedy said and raised his cocktail. Then he realized Jack didn't have one. He offered to go inside and mix another.

Jack refused. He said, "I just wanted to stop by and say hello." He stood and shook hands with Kennedy.

"Where you headed?"

Jack Monroe looked around. "I'm thinking I might move into the neighborhood. Find me a little cottage like this. Take up a hobby. Stay busy."

The former president sighed. "Retirement ain't all it's cracked up to be."

Marilyn slapped his leg. "Oh, Jack. Stop being such a humbug."

Jack wished them well. Then he decided to drive around the island and see what kind of real estate was available. Perhaps he would find someplace where he could retire for good.

He stopped at a gas station to fill his Mustang convertible. Jack chose the full service pumps, and an overweight, over-the-hill attendant whose nametag said "Speedy" topped off his tank.

Jack paid with a credit card. As Speedy swiped the ticket, he read the name. "Monroe. John Monroe."

"Yep," Jack said and reached for his card.

Speedy held it out of reach still reading the name. "John Monroe…Is that any relation to Marilyn Monroe?"

Jack hated it when people asked him this question. He snatched his credit card from Speedy and said what he always said: "Her real name was Norma Jean Baker."

"Oh," Speedy mumbled. "I wasn't aware of that."

"Well," Jack smiled. "Now you know."